C

Floradora's lips trembled in anticipation and her sex
grew moist. The rubber cloak covered her and she
breathed deeply of its warm, darkly erotic fragrance. It
clung to her buttocks, defining her bottom cleft. She
could smell Lorenzo's lust, the snake charmer's musk,
and her own sweat. She felt faint yet oddly excited, and
wanted to continue this bizarre introduction to the
ringmaster's fetishistic desires.

Circo Erotica

MERCEDES KELLY

BLACK
lace

Black Lace novels are sexual fantasies.
In real life, make sure you practise safe sex.

First published in 1998 by
Black Lace
332 Ladbroke Grove
London W10 5AH

Typeset by SetSystems Ltd, Saffron Walden, Essex
Printed and bound by Mackays of Chatham PLC

ISBN 0 352 33257 3

I would like to thank Kate Hickman, whose marvellous travel book *A Trip To The Light Fantastic*, gave me the correct Spanish terminology for the circus acts and circus folk.

Contents

1. The Lion-tamer's Daughter   1
2. Ringmaster   9
3. The Aerialists   19
4. The Great Lorenzo   28
5. Antonio Valera de Teguise   39
6. Floradora's Birthday Celebrations   48
7. The Horse Breeder   59
8. Isambard   63
9. Sibling Affection   72
10. An Invitation   79
11. True Love   88
12. A Proposal of Marriage   96
13. Lorenzo the Mesmeriser   102
14. The Triple Somersault Without a Safety Net   109
15. Señora Valera to the Rescue   118
16. The Circus Moves On   127
17. Lost Love   135
18. The Contortionist   144
19. An Accident   151
20. The Circus Disembarks   161
21. The Circus in Agadir   171
22. Antonio Searches in Vain   179
23. Nights in the Desert   187
24. Antonio and Salome   193

25. The Voyage to Agadir 202
26. Circo Erotica 211
27. The Bandit Chief 219
28. Rosalita and Rosario's Private Performance 227
29. Floradora and El Bandito 233
30. Rescue 241

Chapter One
The Lion-tamer's Daughter

*F*loradora cracked the long-tailed whip loudly, vehemently, sobbing all the while as the lions backed off from the prone, bleeding form of the man in the sawdust. The excited beasts, roaring with bloodlust, slowly moved away, tails lashing, heads thrown back, black lips dripping saliva. Floradora was shaking and trembling uncontrollably, but still she yelled at the lions and cracked the whip to make them obey her. They backed off completely, though they still defiantly lashed out with their paws, as if to catch the whip. Three clowns rushed forward and took the broken man out of the cage, dragging him gently, careful of his bloody, torn limbs.

Floradora's tears flowed freely and she swore at the lions. She loved them but they had killed her beloved father in front of her eyes. It was the new male lion, Kwasi, who had gone in for the kill. She knew he had not settled in, and her father had been worried about him before the act, but the ringmaster had insisted he be used straight away.

She sent the whip cracking at the lions' paws to encourage them into the tunnel and, as soon as the five beasts had left the cage, she pulled the strap that lowered the tunnel door so they could not return. Now they would be safely contained in their main cage.

1

Isambard, the black clown, held the cage door open for her and wrapped his huge arms around Flora's shoulders, leading her out of the circus ring and into the narrow passageway where her dead father lay, face down, his spangled clothes in shreds. She threw herself on to him, making a noise like an injured animal. She tried to turn him over so she could see his face.

'No, Floradora, do not look at him. It is better you do not see,' said Isambard, who was a dark-skinned Spanish Creole. He pulled her hands away and let her go again as she slumped over her father's back once more, sobbing quietly.

'Let her be, let her be,' said Anastasia, the dark-haired dancing girl and *bastonera*. The tall pink feathers on her headdress waved like palm-tree branches. Her pink spangled two-piece costume only just hid her nipples and sex parts. She stood watching, breathing in the black clown's sweat and the smell of the dead Horatio's blood.

The clown had to go to join the others in the ring, to try and raise the spirits of the shocked audience. Drums rolled and trumpets blared discordantly in the manner of all Spanish circus bands. The clowns whooped and threw water over each other and pulled down voluminous trousers to expose red balloons and the audience began to laugh again, the sight of the lions' attack already fading from their minds.

When Floradora at last raised herself from her father's body and allowed the circus hands – the *chamacos* – to take him away, Anastasia took the girl into her arms and cuddled her. Sweet perspiration enveloped Floradora in familiar and comforting warmth, and she allowed herself to be led to the caravan they shared.

The Mexican circus had been in Lanzarote, one of the Canary Islands, for one week only. The night sounds of howling dogs and howling wind swirled around the caravans. In the encampment on the *terreno*, the waste-ground, which had been allotted to the circus, just outside of Teguise, the circus folk were silent for once. Not tonight the gypsy guitars, the castanets clicking and

2

the dancers' feet drumming on the hard red earth around the camp fire. They huddled in quiet groups, moaning and sighing, reminiscing on other deaths the small circus had seen over the years such as the high-wire accidents, the most recent only three years before, when the Inimitable Czychosky had fallen to his death. It had been he who had taught the stars of the circus, the brother and sister trapeze artistes, Rosalita and Rosario, all they knew. They remembered the time a *chamaco* was trampled by an elephant. It was a dangerous life, all told, but an exciting one for the circus folk, most of whom could not think of existing without the travelling life: the close-knit community of fascinating people; the intensity of nightly thrills and the applause – the adoration of the crowd – which was like a life-giving drug.

'Do you remember when Horatio first came to the circus, twenty years ago?' the older *chamacos* reminisced.

'Yes, and then soon after he joined his dear wife died giving birth to Floradora. Do you remember? We were in Brazil, were we not? Ah! The horses in that country were wonderful.'

'Did he bring the lions with him?' asked Anastasia.

'No, child, the lions were already part of the circus. Horatio had to learn to tame them. He was a natural, though. Always had the touch with any animal.'

'Except that new brute, Kwasi,' said Isambard. 'He has an evil look to his eye.'

'He should be destroyed; he will kill again now he has tasted blood,' said the *chamaco*.

'I will not destroy him. He cost me too much,' pronounced the ringmaster.

The circus folk fell silent.

Later, as she slept in a sedative-induced slumber, Floradora had a visitor. She woke briefly in the dark, aware of a tall figure looming over her. But she was dragged back into her mind's recesses before she became aware of the mysterious man's presence.

Lorenzo, black-cloaked, his moustache twitching like

an animal's whiskers, stared at her naked body hidden only by the thin blanket. He pulled the edge of the blanket down, uncovering her silky shoulders, exposing the gentle rise and fall of her pert bosom and the pink peaks of her tiny nipples.

Her breath came in quiet sighs and her eyelids fluttered quickly, as if she was dreaming. He stared. His black-gloved hand strayed to her breasts. He stroked a rubbery nipple, watching as it became erect. His other hand pressed the bulge in his trousers. He squeezed her breast and she moved away from his touch. Suddenly he heard footsteps approaching. They were heavy: a man's step. He hurriedly covered her and stood back. The door opened quietly and Isambard climbed up the steps into the tiny caravan. '*Quien es?* Who is there?' he called.

'Shh!' said the ringmaster, emerging from the darkness. 'She still sleeps.'

'What are you doing here?' asked Isambard. His bulk filled the small space, his kindly, painted smile became a ferocious grimace, and the ringmaster instinctively withdrew his eyes from the powerful man's.

'All right, I'm going. Just came to give my condolences.' He twirled his black moustache and squeezed past the clown.

Behind the clown the *bastonera*, Anastasia, climbed into her caravan and sat perched on the bed she shared with the lion-trainer's daughter.

'How will she manage without her father?' she asked the clown.

'I will protect her from Lorenzo, do not fear,' he replied.

'You are a good man, Isambard, but your powerful arms are not enough to protect her from his evil. He will surely have her now.'

'Never!' said the black man, delicately touching the sleeping girl's face with the back of his huge hand.

Next morning the funeral was held. The entire circus family attended: the *chamacos* – in their best suits; the four *bastoneras*, dressed in black leotards and feathers; Hannibal, the elephant trainer; Alphonso, the sword eater; Salome, the snake charmer; and the stars of the circus – the high-wire artistes, Rosario and his sister, Rosalita. There were also clowns and bandsmen and even the ringmaster, Lorenzo, appeared, dressed in his ubiquitous black.

Floradora's long blonde hair was hidden under swathes of black veiling provided by Olympia, the wardrobe mistress, who had had a dramatically exciting time dressing the entire cast in black feathers and silk. Olympia herself was crowned in a large, brimmed hat from which fell wreaths of black net. This hid her large nose and Adam's apple. Her feet were shod in high-heeled black patent boots and her powerful buttocks and muscled calves were draped with black satin pleats.

She tripped daintily along holding Floradora's other arm. The girl moved as if in a dream, her head lowered but her slender back straight. Circus horses in black feather plumes pulled the funeral carriage. The band played slow dirges. Almost the entire local population, peasants and townsfolk, were gathered at the verges of the red dirt track, crossing themselves as the black-draped coffin passed by.

A visit from the circus was a huge event in itself for this quiet hill town, but a death at the circus was big news. Children sat on their fathers' shoulders so they could watch the bizarrely attired coffin followers as they walked by. Their mothers, draped in navy blue or black floral cottons, and with their heads covered in lace mantillas pinned on with tortoiseshell combs, cooled themselves with large feather fans. The menfolk of Teguise were dressed in their best black suits, smelling of naphthalene, which protected their clothes from moths.

The local men wore black sombreros to show their respect, even though they had not known the lion-tamer. It was enough that he had died at his chosen work, here in their town. Never would it be said that the hill town of Teguise could not show respect for the dead. There would be tortillas to eat later, and thick brown wine to drink.

The iron gates of the little graveyard clanged shut and the procession made its lugubrious way back to the *terreno*. The villagers dispersed through the barren countryside, the volcanic black ash and molten rock looming like a moonscape around them. They went back to their goat herds or returned to their neat rows of potatoes and their fig trees whose bare branches looked like the arms of ghosts in the black landscape.

The evening performance was due to start in an hour or so but, instead of resting, the whole circus family opened several casks of local wine and drank to the memory of the lion-tamer.

'He was a good man, a lovely man,' said the transvestite wardrobe mistress, crying into her voluminous skirts.

'He owed *muchas pesetas*, though,' a *chamaco* said quietly.

'Yes, he did. To me,' said the ringmaster, smiling with no humour and staring pointedly at the lion-tamer's daughter. 'He owes me for the lion that took his life and two of the others.'

'I will pay you in full, do not fear,' came the clear bell-like voice of Floradora.

'I do not fear,' he said. 'I know you will pay, my dear.'

'I will take my father's place. You will bill me as Floradora, the lion-tamer's daughter. But I will not use Kwasi again.'

'You will do exactly as I tell you.' With a flourish, the ringmaster drew back his long cloak and pulled an envelope from a deep pocket. He handed Floradora the letter and she stood silently and read her father's words.

'I, Horatio de Valencia, being of sound mind, do promise to give my daughter Floradora to Lorenzo the ringmaster, to use as he wishes, if I die before I have paid him the sum of three hundred thousand pesetas.'

Folded inside was a receipt for fifty thousand pesetas signed by the ringmaster.

Floradora stared disbelievingly at the purple ink. 'I do not believe it. He would not have done this to me,' she cried.

'He most certainly did,' said the ringmaster, twirling his waxed moustache.

The circus folk stood around, shuffling their feet uncomfortably. They all had experience of Lorenzo's cruelty and greed. His sensual needs and sadistic leanings were gossiped about and his evil doings were woven into their stories as they sat around their campfires or huddled in their beds. They had known of Horatio's obsessive gambling, and that he had borrowed heavily from all of them, especially the ringmaster. They even knew of the notorious promissory note.

The snake charmer, Salome, smiled lasciviously and placed her long, gold-painted fingernails on Floradora's cheek. 'Come, my dear, let me take you to your caravan. You look exhausted,' she said softly.

The shocked girl was led away by the slender snake charmer, whose breasts were hardly camouflaged by the black chiffon she wore. Her long legs, strong thighs and round buttocks were draped in the semi-transparent silk, held tight round her narrow waist by a silver snake-shaped belt, which ate its own tail. Her long, dark hair was piled high on her head leaving a tail which fell to her waist. Her dark eyes, painted black on the eyelids, glistened with scarcely hidden desire. She led the acquiescent girl away through the silent crowd, and placed an arm around her shoulder.

Isambard scowled but had to go to his duties, as had the other members of the troupe. The evening performance would not wait. There were animals to feed and clean, trapeze wires and ropes to check, costumes to mend, clowns' custard pies to mix, sawdust to spread, and make-up to apply; all before the crowds gathered at the *taquilla* – the ticket office – for the evening performance. The whole island knew about the lion-tamer's untimely death, and many more people were expected to attend that evening, some of them hoping for yet more drama or the sight of spilt blood.

In her caravan, Floradora was being comforted in her grief in the arms of the snake charmer. Salome was older than most of the dancing girls – the *bastoneras* – who were mostly in their teens but she was a sensual creature, strong-muscled and curvaceous. Her sultry, heavy eyelids, fringed with thick black lashes, drooped over green eyes. Her scarlet-painted lips curved in an exaggerated bow. Her breasts were proud, full, jutting from her narrow trunk. Usually she had at least one large snake wrapped around her like a living stole. This week, her image appeared on the posters that proclaimed that Circo Lorenzo had come to the island. Usually the star turn – the trapeze artistes – was the act depicted on the luridly coloured handbills but, occasionally, the artist would paint portraits of the clowns or even the elephants and lions.

Salome pressed the distraught girl to her, holding her close, stroking her hair and hushing her tears. She leant closer and kissed the wet cheeks. At this telling moment Anastasia entered the caravan.

'She is very tired, poor little thing,' Salome said to Anastasia. 'You must look after her well.'

The round-faced, homely Russian girl nodded and bit her lip. Salome said goodnight to them both, and left the caravan and went to her own, where Lorenzo awaited her.

'Well?' he said.

'I could not do anything this time,' said Salome, bowing her head.

'Blast your eyes!' Lorenzo cracked his whip and Salome fell to the floor, sobbing, knowing what punishment was to come.

Chapter Two
Ringmaster

*L*orenzo wore a black rubber mask, which hid his dark bushy eyebrows and the bags under his eyes. He also sported a cloak. Not the usual showman's black silk garment with a silver lining but a full-length, black rubber cloak, which fastened at the neck. Under that he was naked. He had been rubbing himself slowly, languorously, waiting for Salome to finish what he had started. Salome still had the taste of Floradora on her lips when the ringmaster dropped his whip, pulled her from her prone position and passionately kissed her breasts. She succumbed to his caresses, as he tore off her garment and flung it to the floor.

'Now you are aroused, suck me and swallow my come,' he ordered.

'Yes, master,' she said, lowering her head in obedience.

Naked, her full breasts swinging heavily, she slid down his body and took the slender rod into her rouged mouth. He covered her with the cloak and pressed on her head through the rubber. The clammy material, swishing against his writhing buttocks and rubbing against his thighs, chest and shoulders, made him feel safe from the world, in a universe of his own making. As ringmaster, he had power over all his performers, but chose to wield it mostly over the females. They had

9

all fallen prey to his sadistic leanings at one time or another. Even the virgin Floradora's turn would come – whether she complied or not, he thought with satisfaction.

Each of the dancing girls was frightened of him, and for good reason: his whip was not simply part of his big-top persona – it was a necessary part of his private life and his dark needs. Only Salome understood him, he thought, as she sucked. He knew that she too had similar leanings: wanting to hurt, or sometimes to be hurt, and enjoying pain for lust's sake. Lorenzo enjoyed power more than any other thing. It was an aphrodisiac to him. He needed to be totally in control or he could not get an erection. He made sure that he was always the bully, always the one who wielded the whip.

He breathed in the scent of the rubber and relaxed into the rhythm his 'slave', Salome, had set up with her tongue and teeth and the inner surfaces of her soft, caressing mouth. But, before he could come into her throat, she stopped the sucking movement and slowly, carefully, slid away from him.

When Lorenzo roused himself, she was bending over the leather stool, the only other piece of free-standing furniture in the small caravan. Next to the stool, attached to the wall by steel rings, was the snakes' lidded ceramic jar, where the pythons and other serpents slept when they were not in the big top. He heard the gentle hiss of their movements within the giant jar.

Lorenzo, his erection sticking out through the opening of his rubber cloak, took up his whip and set about her raised buttocks. 'Yes, you must be punished for not finishing me off properly,' he spat. 'How dare you disobey me, the Great Lorenzo! You will suffer for this.'

Salome remained quiet, head bowed, while the whip striped her olive skin. He sighed in contentment as she opened her thighs wide at the gentlest touch of the whip. He could see the dark pouch – the red glistening lips stretched open. He flicked the whip expertly, getting it to land exactly where he wanted, and he knew her excitement grew with each stroke. He knew from his own experience that the pain, at first intense, was now mellowing to a humming, warming vibration which, he could see, was making her sex-lips swell and her juices flow. She pressed her belly against the leather stool. She widened her legs and lifted her buttocks high so her brown rose was offered to the whip. He saw the whip mark her flesh all over. He could see her rounded buttocks were on fire. He moved forward and thrust himself into her open flesh, watching the vulva close over his swollen rod and swallow it. He came into her almost immediately, leaving her panting and desperate for release, but he did not give it to her. Instead, he pulled out of her, leaving his emissions dripping down her reddened thighs.

Later, he had a more public act to perform. The Great Lorenzo stood with his silver-lined black cloak thrown over his shoulders. His faced was masked in black; only his red lips and dark, glittering eyes were visible. In each hand he held long-handled knives, their blades shiny and vicious. The drums rolled and the clowns tumbled and somersaulted round the ring. In front of Lorenzo, about three metres away, was a huge circular board, painted like an archery target. Attached by ropes to this corkboard was La Roux, the redheaded *bastonera*, sometimes dancer, and sometimes part of the *equilibrista* – the balancing act. She was practically naked but for leather straps which flattened her breasts and held her to the target. Her thighs and pubis were bound also. Her arms were stretched out on either side and her legs were apart in a V. Her belly was crisscrossed with tight straps which went between and round her long, athletic legs, and pressed into the white flesh. Blue veins pulsed in her narrow wrists. Her pale-blue eyes were glazed, as if she was drunk or drugged. She stared unseeing at the ringmaster. The clowns shouted and tumbled in front of her. One clown, the dwarf, Jellico, splayed himself across

11

La Roux in a laughable effort to protect her from the knives. The ringmaster threw a long, shiny-bladed knife, its handle made of mother-of-pearl. It pierced the trouser leg of the clown, pinning him to the target. He threw another, which attached the clown's voluminous sleeve to the board. The clown pretended fear and cried aloud, water spouting from his kohl-blackened eyes. The audience laughed. The ringmaster swaggered over to the clown, removed the knives, then waved him away, dismissively. Jellico fled, falling over his enormous rubber feet, and the crowd laughed again.

La Roux writhed in a pretended effort to free herself from the bonds that held her. The band played an accelerating, excited phrase of music, the drums rolling faster and faster. The other *bastoneras* appeared, semi-naked in hourglass, boned corsets, which accentuated their curves. The girls began to turn the circular board, which was attached to a wooden easel. The target began to move very slowly as first one knife then another flew threw the air and hit the board either side of La Roux's waist. Then the drumsticks flickered faster, and the target spun more rapidly, and the two girls stood back. The black-gowned, moustachioed ringmaster – knife-thrower extraordinaire – turned his back to the target, removed the voluminous cloak, exposing his slender, lithe body, and threw the knives fast over his shoulder. They landed safely on the board, pinning La Roux's hair to the cork, brushing her thighs, grazing her breasts. The crowd sighed as one. The clowns leapt in the air and threw themselves about, applauding with rubber hands, falling over elongated rubber shoes. The music blared. The *bastoneras* danced forward and flamboyantly untied the bonds that held La Roux to the target.

La Roux posed with her arms above her head and turned slowly so the crowd could see she was unharmed. They could also admire her raised, round breasts, straining from the spangled corset, and her firm, full buttocks displayed in fishnet tights. They roared approval.

Floradora stood in the shadows, her heart beating fast

in her corset-encased body. Even though her father had only just been buried, the show must go on. There was no time or place for sentiment *en circo*. She adjusted her tailcoat and top hat and picked up the whip her father had always used.

The ringmaster blared through his megaphone: 'I present Floradora, the lion-tamer's daughter, and Kwasi and his pride of the most magnificent lions ever seen in the kingdom of Spain. She will thrill you with her mastery over these terrifying beasts; she will excite you with her skill and beauty; she will ensure you go home with wet knickers!' He hissed the last word, and the audience whistled and laughed.

In the front row a moustachioed man in a black sombrero held a wine flask over his wrist and poured a stream of dark-red liquid from his arm's length into his mouth. His wife fluttered her embroidered fan. Elaborate turtleshell combs pinned a black lace mantilla on to her raven hair, which was tied back into a knot at the back of her neck. Peasants crowded forward in the dark to get a glimpse of the lion-tamer's daughter.

The ring was lit with hurricane lamps and flaming torches, highlighting the rickety cage, octagonal in shape, in which paced several lions. Floradora stepped forward into the light and the band started to play loudly. The clapping was subdued. The audience knew it was the girl's first performance since her father's death. The whole island had heard about the interesting event. They did not wish her harm but, at the same time, they had come with the knowledge that she was inexperienced and there would possibly be yet more gore and horror this evening for them to remember. There was a hush as she entered the cage. The lions stood and stared at her. She did not wait for fear to overtake her, but cracked the whip and commanded them to jump on to their stools. She had helped her father with the lions out of the big top, but never in the cage; she had never been part of the lion act until this time. She was an equestrian; she rode bareback, and sometimes almost bare, her black stallion,

Thunderhead, and his mares – Jet, Cornelian, Ruby and Fire in her own act. She was not afraid of the big cats, or she had not been before the mauling.

The big lion, Kwasi, refused to obey her command to sit, and he swished his tail in defiance. What would he do? Would he push her over with his huge paws, claw her face and chest, as he had done with her father? Kwasi was not hungry; rather, he was extremely well-fed. Floradora had seen to that, before the performance. But he wanted to sleep. He was instinctively lazy, had only recently joined the act, and was unsure of what he had to do. He opened his black mouth and yawned. The lionesses were already meekly sitting, watching the whip and the girl who wielded it. She talked softly to them all, then suddenly cracked the whip again and made as if to go towards Kwasi. Surprised, he leapt on to his stool and sat with his tail tucked under him. The applause came for the girl.

She was surer of herself now; she crooned to the cats, and flicked the whip lightly. They rose on to their back legs and pawed the air above them. Kwasi did not; he simply stared at his harem in boredom. She let him be, thankful that he was quiet and sitting still. She kept an eye on the new lion while putting the others through their paces. Floradora was a proud slender shape, with her black tailcoat and white bow tie over the bright-green corset of sateen. Her gleaming fair hair was hidden under the top hat, which she wore to make her appear taller to the lions. Her high-heeled green boots gave her another few centimetres. Despite this, she was barely the size of a fourteen-year-old. But her bearing and stance was mature, proud and beautiful, like a ballet dancer.

Several admirers watched Floradora's maiden performance. The black clown adored her passionately, silently and secretly, and Salome the snake charmer was infatuated with the *guera* and could not wait to get her long-nailed fingers on to that smooth, fair flesh.

Floradora strode around the cage, sending cracks of whiplashes flashing through the air. The band continued to play loudly as she made the lions run in a circle round her. Even Kwasi complied.

The finale was a demonstration of the lions leaping through a blazing ring, which she held high above her. The danger was very real. The lions could easily tear her apart instead of leaping through the fiery circle. Her heart in her mouth, she called each lion in turn to make the leap. There was an expectant hush. One after the other, the lionesses, their stomachs full of specially slaughtered piglets, bounded towards her and leapt through the flames, to climb subdued on to their stools again. Only Kwasi sat roaring and growling on his stool. He pawed the air. He raised his shaggy head and raged. Floradora's arms were getting tired; the fire would burn out in a moment.

'Kwasi, come!' she ordered the beast, looking him in the eye.

To her great relief he jumped off the stool and casually bounded the two steps that separated them. The crowd held its breath and sighed deeply as the lion obeyed, easily flew through the dying flames, and went back to his stool.

The cheers were loud as the lions disappeared into the tunnel and Floradora bowed low. She was sweating profusely, her armpits damp, and her hair stuck to her head. But she had done it. She was a lion-tamer. Her father would have been proud of his only daughter. She cried silently as she walked from the big top, accepting the applause yet sad in her heart. She was still only seventeen, alone in the world, and thanks to the foolishness of her beloved father she apparently belonged to Lorenzo. Her soul railed against the idea of being the property of anyone, let alone the evil authority figure that Lorenzo had always been. She had heard the whispers of the other girls in the circus who had all had intimate experience of his decadence. The smoothly handsome older man frightened her.

Yet, there was something else; there was also an attraction. She had seen him look at her and devour her with his dark eyes. She felt naked when he turned his hard gaze on her body. Her breasts tingled and her blood overheated as she saw his breeches swell with his erection. She was repelled, yet excited.

So, as she left the spotlight and ran to change into her equestrian costume, she was horrified to find herself remembering her father and thinking of Lorenzo at the same time.

She changed out of her top hat and tails and discarded the green sateen corset. Her outfit for bareback riding was far more exotic and daring. Black high boots reached her thighs and dug into her fair flesh. The soles were thin and were more like stockings moulded to her feet. She drew on a black leather strappy garment that showed off her slender frame and small breasts. It was like a corset but it covered only her hips to beneath her breasts. Her private parts and her breasts were covered only by a thin gauze, which shimmered silver and did not hide the beauty beneath but, rather, accentuated it. It was as if she was naked yet strapped tightly around the waist by a wide leather belt.

She ran to the tent and said a quick hello to Olympia at the *taquilla*, the ticket office.

'You look stunning, darling,' said the wardrobe mistress, who doubled as the ticket seller. 'Stunning! Don't let Lorenzo see you, he'll want to pounce on you and eat you.' She laughed wickedly.

Floradora's horses were ready, waiting for their appearance. The clowns held the harnesses. The animals had been brushed and their manes and bodies shone with health. Tonight their headdresses were plumes of black in honour of Horatio. The clowns wore sad painted faces tonight, also in Horatio's memory.

Isambard gave his big hand to Floradora's leather-clad foot and lifted her gently on to her black stallion, Thunderhead. The horse whinnied a welcome to his mistress and she patted his long, proud head and stroked his nose. Her little bottom settled on his broad back for a moment and she felt the heat of him between her legs.

16

As the band began the opening bars of her entrance, she leapt on to her feet.

She led the mares through their paces, riding the stallion before them. They pranced prettily, reared on to their back legs, and danced to the music. The mares finished their turn and obediently went off through the exit, where they were met by the clowns and *chamacos*. Now Floradora and her stallion worked together. The girl and animal were totally in tune with each other; the horse read her thigh movements and those of her feet and knees. She performed a handstand on the horse's back as he cantered around the ring. She juggled while she stood backward on the stallion's back. She climbed under his belly and up the other side.

She was aware that the ringmaster stood close by, near enough to smell the horses and her hot body. She was aware of his closed, humourless, lascivious smile. She did the splits upside down on the horse's back, the dark patch between her legs hardly hidden by the silvery gauze. Lorenzo pressed his leather-gloved hands to his crotch.

Isambard, too, watched her performance, as always. Floradora felt his comforting presence.

Salome was in the wings, watching in the dark. Her crimson costume was practically nonexistent. Her nipples showed over the top of her tightly laced corset and her lower half was bare except for fishnet tights. The bulge of her labia was pouting through the fine mesh. The circus garments were designed to be highly erotic for the wearer as well as the audience. They accentuated the sex, the full bosom, and the proud buttocks. Salome's nipples were rouged and she licked a finger and touched each red peak to make them stand upright. Then she felt between her legs and rubbed the nub of her sex as she admired the bareback rider. Salome's sexuality was a source of delight and everlasting pleasure to her. She loved her own body, its curves and swellings, its secret places. She also loved Lorenzo, or at least was in awe of him, and enjoyed his punishment of her, such as the whippings he regularly subjected her to. She was his slave when he wanted her to be.

She saw the ringmaster rubbing himself as he watched Floradora flash by. She determined to bring the girl to him, as a present. He would surely love Salome for it; perhaps he would even make love to her for once, instead of simply using her. She longed for his long, thick cock to fill her and stay in her long enough to give her the orgasm she desired. Perhaps, soon, it would happen.

Chapter Three
The Aerialists

*L*orenzo cracked the whip to draw the crowd's attention from the clowns' frivolities. While the clowns had been juggling and throwing custard pies at each other the trapeze and high wire had been checked and the two stars *del circo* – the gypsy Rosalita and her younger brother, Rosario – climbed hand over hand up the rope ladder. The drums rolled and Lorenzo called through the megaphone:

'*Mas famoso . . . increible triple salto mortal . . .* incredible triple somersault!'

This was the act the crowd had been waiting for: a breathtaking high-wire and trapeze performance. The circus had drawn crowds from all over Mexico to see the brother and sister act. Now, with the tour of Spain and the islands off the northwest coast of Africa, Lorenzo was sure the siblings would bring fame to his little circus. He was ambitious; he wanted to enlarge the repertoire of the circus and wanted more animals and yet more daring acts.

The dark-skinned gypsy girl looked naked. She had been sewn into a tight-fitting stocking net one-piece. Gold spangles accentuated her small, pointed breasts and her sex triangle. Her thick, curly dark hair was dragged back into a ponytail high on her head. Her slender body glittered on the swinging trapeze. All eyes were raised, all necks strained to lift heads back.

Rosario was a masculine echo of his sister. He too had thick curly hair, only slightly shorter than Rosalita's. His dark, rugged features were a stronger version of her proud, gypsy features. He too was neatly built, nicely muscled with small, taut buttocks. He too wore a garment that barely disguised his genitals. Indeed, his spangled pouch was minuscule, and only a strap divided his buttocks. His bulge was closely wrapped in pink-brown stocking net, its jutting authority clearly defined.

The crowd whispered in their anticipation and waited for the excitement to begin. The trapezes swung and passed each other. Rosalita was swinging from her brother's hands. The two artistes danced together in midair. Their bodies clung and writhed and moved together in an aerial ballet.

Floradora was below in the ring, in the shadows, watching them. A cloak, a *bata*, covered her daring costume, and she stood on her own, staring upward, waiting for the terrifying triple somersault. There was a silence. Even the drums had stopped their heartbeat rhythm. Above the darkened ring, and the upturned pale faces, highlighted by hurricane lamps hung high on the stays of the big top, the trapeze creaked as Rosario swung. There was no other sound. On the top step of the rope ladder the slender figure of Rosalita was poised. She was too high for the crowd to see her face. Only her brother saw her expression – saw the stillness, and the sombre set of her jaw. She quickly covered her hands with chalk and flung herself out on her trapeze. For a moment she disappeared into the dark. Then she reappeared. More lights were aimed at the pair, the arc following the movement of the swing. Rosalita's athletic body, sheathed in nothing but spangled stocking net, shone and gleamed like an angel above them. She swung, once, then again, higher, then higher, until suddenly she was flying through the air, tumbling and spinning, blurring into a silver gleam, an apparition, a ghost, a firefly, speeding, falling, until she fell into the safe hands of her brother and they were swinging together up into the big top.

The crowd sighed and screamed with delight, clapping and whistling. Floradora applauded as loudly as any of them. Suddenly she was aware of hands under her cloak, round her tiny waist. She gasped and turned to see who her assailant was.

'There, there, my dear, do not fear, it is only me,' said Lorenzo, moving his hands down over her exposed hips to her thighs.

She drew away, or tried to, but his grip became insistent. He held her by the crotch at the front and had his other hand under her bottom between her legs. In spite of her horror at the attack, Floradora was excited by his experienced touch. His hands caressed her tender flesh.

'Please do not handle me, *Señor*, I beg you,' she whispered, almost afraid to let anyone know what was happening to her.

'Why not, my dear? You know you enjoy it. I can feel your juices run against my palm.'

She gasped as his hands rubbed firmly on her fleshy pouch. In the dark she could almost imagine it was the young and handsome Rosario touching her. But she suddenly became aware of her iniquitous position. She drew away determinedly from his embrace. He let her go.

The trapeze artistes had climbed down the ladder to the sawdust-covered floor of the central arena. They had to pass by where the ringmaster and Floradora stood. As they ran by, in the dark, there was a sudden flash of Rosario's smile as he saw her. His white teeth were like a shining beacon to her in the darkness of her sexual desire. In that moment she fell in love with Rosario. His gypsy spell was cast over her. Her fairness and blonde-ness, her female sensitivity, were aroused by his dark-ness, his gleaming sensuality. Also, the bulge of his

21

genitals was enticing. She had seen the shape of his organ leaning towards her and she yearned for it, to hold it. Her love juices, already flowing because of the unwonted attentions of the ringmaster, now flooded her, and her heart beat fast.

'Well done, Rosario, Rosalita,' said the ringmaster. He grabbed the trapeze artiste by one arm as she ran by and kissed her hard on the mouth. 'You were superb, my dear,' he said.

Rosario stopped in his tracks and came back for his sister, who was limp in the arms of the ringmaster. 'Let her go now,' said the gypsy, his eyes blazing like Kwasi the lion, or so thought Floradora.

'We owe you nothing. Unhand her, you brute,' Rosario continued.

Floradora stood back in the shadows, admiring the gypsy, loving him *and* his beautiful sister, whose fluid body slumped in the arms of Lorenzo.

'Yes, go now, Rosalita.' The ringmaster's voice seemed to have an energising effect on the trapeze artiste. She raised herself from his arms and shook her head as if to shake off sleep.

Rosario took his sister's arm and they ran off together like sparkling fireworks in the gloom, their sequins catching the lantern light.

Floradora, too, took the opportunity to run from the ringmaster's command. It seemed he could get anyone to do anything he wanted – females, anyway.

Later, after she had helped with bedding down the lions and her beloved horses, making sure of their security and that they had clean straw and fresh water, she slowly made her way to the caravan she shared with Anastasia. The dancer was already in the tiny double cot, her small, neat head visible above the harsh blanket.

Floradora removed her costume and hung it up. She cleaned off her make-up, washed herself briefly and brushed her teeth, remembering her father's words to her: 'Always clean yourself before you sleep.' It should have been her mother's advice, but Floradora had never known her mother. She had died giving birth to her only child eighteen years ago. Horatio might have been a gambler and a weak man, but he had loved Floradora with all his heart and had cared for her all her life. He had taught her all she knew about animals: how to feed them, treat their sicknesses and injuries, and how to master them without cruelty. He had taught her to read and write, too, and she was the only circus performer she knew who could do that. She sobbed quietly as she thought of her father and his beloved features: his large mouth, which she had inherited along with his stubbornness; his deep-blue eyes, and his bushy eyebrows, which he had wiggled at her to make her laugh when she was little.

Floradora climbed into the hard bed, which had a mattress of straw, and cuddled up to the warm, naked back of Anastasia. Their bodies were like joining spoons tucked together, the round buttocks of Anastasia pressing into the small concavity of Floradora's belly. The other girl stirred and Floradora hushed her with gentle murmuring and, as her own head touched the hard pillow, she fell immediately asleep.

In the caravan which La Roux and Gina – the other dancer, who was half-Italian, half-Chinese – shared, no one slept yet.

The two girls were servicing Lorenzo. Gina was a contortionist, and not only in the big top. She was twisted now in a position where her elbows were spread on the floor, her hands clasped. Her breasts pressed into the floor, her waist was bent and her lower half was thrust forward over her head. Her knees were bent, her feet either side of her face, and her toes were tucked under her wrists, which left her vulva high and open. She was, of course, naked, so Lorenzo could stick his cock first in her mouth, then in her adjacent vagina.

Meanwhile, La Roux whipped the ringmaster's

exposed buttocks. His rubber cloak was lifted high over his back, and held with straps. The contortionist was like a strange statue, an erotic ivory carving, with her black hair in tight braids close to her small head, and her small breasts flattened. Her red mouth opened in an O, and her vagina flared in a V.

Lorenzo was in a frenzy of lust, his long wand of a cock pushing in and pulling out of her orifices, his hands shifting it from one to the other. He pulled her open, thrusting himself ever deeper. Gina remained unmoved, her eyes glazed like a china doll. La Roux wielded the short whip, which made a sharp crack as it struck the ringmaster's flesh. She was also naked, except for a rubber *bata*, like Lorenzo's cloak, long and flowing, silkily caressing her overheated flesh. Her nipples were taut against the rubber, her thighs heavy with desire.

She watched the sexual congress of the ringmaster and the contortionist and touched herself between the legs, wanting his cock there. She saw the dark rod thrust between the red sex-lips then emerge, glistening, to disappear into the other, open red lips. She thrust the whip handle between Lorenzo's taut buttocks and rubbed it back and forth. She leant on him, rubbing herself over his rubber cloak. Her spasms went unnoticed by the other two.

Gina moaned as the pressure inside her built to a climax. Her small round face reddened, and the irises of her almond eyes dilated. She sucked with both mouths. Lorenzo spurted his white foam into her yielding flesh and fell down, exhausted.

Rosalita and Rosario slept in each other's arms, as they always had. Rosalita was two years older than her nineteen-year-old brother and had looked after him since they had both run away to join the circus in Mexico five years before. Their violent father had never even bothered to look for them, and the circus left their village with them hidden in the clowns' caravan. The gypsy children soon learnt to clown and tumble and do acrobatics. They were naturally agile and very nicely made.

The high wire had enticed them, and they had been taught by the Inimitable Czychosky, who had fallen to his death after an unfortunate lapse of concentration only a few months after they had joined Circo Lorenzo. It was said that he had been in love with Rosalita and had fallen because he had been staring at her instead of concentrating on his trapeze. This was not hard to imagine.

Rosalita was a captivating beauty when she allowed a smile to light her sombre face. She loved only her brother, and lived for him. Rosario was a fickle youth, only now becoming aware of his beauty and the power it gave him. He was in the thrall of his older sister, and always did as she said. She had been his protector and mother substitute since he was three years old. He did not remember his real mother, though Rosalita did.

Their father had killed their mother in a jealous rage. He had ignored his children, mostly, except that he had sent them out to beg from an early age and beat them when they came back empty-handed, which they often did in the poverty-stricken area where they lived. This was why they had run away with the circus, or why Rosalita had run away, and her brother had followed. They had sat with the other young people of the dusty, windswept village in the magic of the big top, the canvas singing around them. They had lost themselves in the music, the excitement, and otherworldliness of the colours and sparkling costumes. They had held their breath as the lions roared and the white horses had galloped around the ring. They had wanted to be a part of all that magic. And now they were star performers, expert in their chosen trade, high-flying trapeze artistes.

Rosalita was secure in the knowledge that they would always be able to earn their own living if they stayed together, worked together, kept the discipline of fitness and exercise, and looked after each other. Rosario was easy: he always did as she told him. He was lazy in his animal strength, happy to be alive and swinging high over the clowns of the world. He wanted nothing more out of life. It was she who insisted on them getting out of bed early each day to practise their act and strengthen their muscles. Rosalita was the driving power behind the siblings' success.

Now, as his sister slept, Rosario remembered the pretty face of Floradora, the lion-tamer's daughter, her admiring glance, adoration for him clearly shining from her blushing face. He saw again Lorenzo's hands on his sister's body, her slumped against him. He understood the desire that Lorenzo felt for his sister. He too knew the power of lust. His young body called out for physical contact with female flesh. He pressed closer to his sister in the dark warmth of the small caravan. His naked thighs wrapped themselves round hers. He felt his cock rise to his stomach. He rubbed gently up against her, careful not to wake her. He thought of her lithe body in the trapeze costume, the nipples taut against the thin sparkly gauze, the bulge of her pubis, the slit defined by the clinging fragile fabric. He rubbed more firmly against her buttocks. She stirred and he turned over, away from her. He held his sturdy erection between his eager fingers, rubbing up and down, stretching the skin over the head and down again.

Rosario would have carried on in their dull, half-starved existence in the small village but for Rosalita. It was she who had found the way into the big top without having to pay the two pesetas it should have cost them. It was Rosalita who had planned the escape from their father. But now, after several years of eating regularly, keeping fit, travelling with the circus, Rosario felt he was a man of the world. He was bigger than Rosalita, sturdily made, with big shoulders and upper arms, made strong by the high-wire act. He and she had a family now – the circus family. He was liked by the clowns, adored by the wardrobe mistress, admired by the *bastoneras*. He was a handsome lad, and full of sexual vigour, as yet

26

unleashed on the world. He saw himself winging through the air; he imagined his sister, naked, her legs wide, and he spurted his juices over his belly and moaned quietly into his straw-filled pillow.

Chapter Four
The Great Lorenzo

The Great Lorenzo twirled his moustache – a habit he had when deep in thought. He legally owned the lion-tamer's daughter, but he had not the stomach to force her to be his. He flattered himself that he did not need to use brute force. He was not a bad-looking man, indeed, his darkly brooding face was considered very handsome by many middle-aged ladies throughout the Americas and beyond. He kept himself trim. As well as his knife-throwing act he was an accomplished mesmeriser. He had started on the boards as a hypnotist and only in recent years had turned his many talents to the circus. During his youth he had successfully mesmerised many middle-aged ladies into giving him their gold and rubies. He had hoarded the fortunes until he came across the travelling circus he had his mind set on. It was in Mexico, in a sleepy town, where spiny cacti flowered with bright-pink edible blooms, and the heat blistered the faces of the wet-whited clowns.

He had bought the whole circus from a drunken Hungarian, who was homesick and maudlin for snow and windswept tundra. The Hungarian was satisfied with the deal and Lorenzo became owner and ringmaster, delighting in the exhibitionism this entailed. Many of his performers were odd misfits, runaways from cruel families or the law. Some had had a violent past. He asked no questions. He wanted quality acts. Who cared if a laughing clown had killed a man in anger? If a *bastonera* had been a prostitute? If the fire eater was a sodomite? Lorenzo lent money to the feckless gamblers in his troupe; and there were many. The *chamacos* spent all their wages on card playing. So he accrued riches and was powerful in his own world. He had plans to expand, maybe to go to Paris and Vienna with his circus, but first he had to find more acts, and spend wisely on new animals and equipment. However, his acquisitive nature was such that he became less and less inclined to spend money, and more and more inclined to hoard it. His ambition was thwarted by his own avarice.

Meanwhile, he enjoyed the sexual sway he held over the females of his circus.

He twirled his moustache, painting the ends with black pomade so they were stiff and curled upward. His red lips parted and his sharp white teeth gleamed in an evil smile as he evolved a plan to win the heart of Floradora.

Floradora knocked on the ringmaster's door. It was just before the evening performance was due to start. The dwarf clown, Jellico, had given her the message that the Great Lorenzo wanted to talk to her immediately. She was dressed in her equestrian costume, her sex parts barely hidden by sequins on the tight-fitting garment. She had thrown her *bata* over the top to hide herself from his gaze.

'Come!' he commanded.

She entered with trepidation. His caravan was larger than any of the other performers' and elaborately decorated with swagged, scarlet velvet curtains and gold-painted walls. He had not changed the Hungarian's baroque surroundings, having no preference of his own. Heavy, ornate mouldings of gilt mirrors gleamed from the walls, and the tasselled, emerald velvet upholstered bed and sofa transformed the caravan into a miniature

Bavarian castle. The bed was a four-poster, with green damask curtains hanging round all four sides. He sat at one end of the sofa, his eyes painted with kohl, his lips naturally red, and his black moustache bristling in anticipation.

'Sit here, Floradora, my dear,' he said, patting the upholstery next to him.

There was nowhere else to sit except the bed, from which she kept her eyes averted. She perched on the edge of the sofa, alarmed at her own anxiety, her heart pumping hard. Her lips moved dryly, in fear.

'Now, my dear, do not look so frightened. I shall not eat you, you know. In fact, I have good news for you. I feel you are not happy with the arrangement your late father made with me concerning your future.'

Floradora raised her frightened eyes to his. The room was lit with candles in brass sconces. The little flames flickered in his staring eyes.

'You are right, sir, I cannot accept that I am your property.' Her lips trembled.

'Of course not, my dear, I see that. Your father was wrong to have given you to me.' He reached forward a narrow, long-fingered hand, which was covered in black hair, and touched her gently on the knee – which invited his caress, exposed as it was at the opening of the black *bata*.

'I release you from the unfortunate bargain.'

'Oh!' Floradora had not expected this sudden change of fortune. She had been expecting him to insist on her carrying out the first of many iniquitous obligations. Who knew what disgusting habits he had? Part of her was relieved, yet another part of her was disappointed that he had not demanded some immediate physical payment. Was she not attractive enough for him?

'I do not want to spoil your innocence and virginity, my dear,' he whispered, and put out his tarantula-like hand to stroke her blonde hair. 'Think of me as a father, Floradora, in place of your own dear papa. I mean you no harm, you know. However, I shall consider the lions

30

my property, Floradora, from now on. You will continue to pay for their food and keep, but they are all mine to dispose of as and when I wish.'

His caress fell to her soft cheek and the peachlike bloom of her skin. She was flustered and flattered and cross all at the same time. She crossed her spangled legs and thrust out her little breasts, wishing she had not worn the camouflaging *bata*. He leant into her and kissed her forehead, gently, like a fond parent.

She closed her eyes, expecting a more telling embrace, but suddenly she was left sitting on the sofa, alone. He stood, tall above her, and clapped his hands. She came to herself, shocked at her naughty thoughts, and rose also.

'I must finish my dress and make-up,' she blurted, and hurried out of the ornately painted door.

The Great Lorenzo smiled to himself and rubbed his hands together. He followed Floradora out of the caravan into the bustle of the circus ground. There were crowds of Canarians gathered at the ticket office. Children ran about in the dark, their excited faces glowing in the moonlight. Fires blazed, and almonds burned. Sombreros and mantillas flashed in the night, castanets crackled. A high-pitched male voice keened a sad, deeply passionate flamenco. A smell of tortillas and popcorn cooking could not mask the overpowering stench of lion.

Lorenzo swept past the peasants in their rags, the grandees in their sombre black merino wool, the ladies in their black silks and lace.

In the big top the sawdust settled, the lights were lit, the rickety lion cage assembled, the trapeze wire tightened.

The parade began. First the clowns – Isambard, the black clown, painted in wet white, his handsome features disguised behind the large, white, sad mouth, the pointed stars of his eyes. He wore a harlequin costume, striped and diamond, in red and yellow. His strong calves swelled under the short breeches. The ballooning

31

sleeves accentuated his massive shoulders. His eyes, reddened by smoke and kohl, were like those of a caged animal. He laughed and tumbled mirthlessly. The other clowns leapt and flew and threw coloured flags and balloons at the audience, whose pale faces were laughing and excited.

Alphonso, the sword eater, was tattooed all over, or so it looked, his mosaic skin exposed to the wondering masses. Purple dragons and sea serpents, sea-green mermaids and black eagles, swam and flew over his muscles and veins. A sea battle raged on his broad back, galleons ablaze, dying in a turbulent ocean. Even his face was etched with strange foreign words. He ate fire as he walked, casually dipping the flaming stick into his open throat and swallowing the blue-green yellow flame. The dwarf clown, Jellico, lit Alphonso's flame each time it was consumed, jumping up to reach the torch.

Gina, the contortionist, leapt by on her hands, her legs hanging over her head, her bottom painted with a grinning face. She writhed and twisted, turning herself inside out, it seemed, knotting her hands and feet and thighs. Suddenly she jumped into a tiny box and twisted herself into a space only big enough for a baby. The clowns closed the lid and carried her off.

Hannibal and his elephants came next – a matriarch and her baby, gently swaying, looking from side to side, their solemn heads decorated in feathered plumes. The mother trumpeted loud and her little one followed suit, and the children ooh-ed and aah-ed.

Salome, with a necklace of striped snakes, led the dancing girls and *bastoneras* into the ring, each one dressed provocatively, their bosoms and buttocks practically exposed, their nipples taut under spangled net. The males in the audience hissed between their teeth at the sight of so much young flesh. Their wives sighed and shifted their well-fed bulks beneath dark silks and satins. Children picked at *palomitas*, 'little doves', paper twists of fresh popcorn, and licked their sticky fingers.

Next came the horses, plumed in white feathers.

Floradora rode Thunderhead, the black stallion, his long mane gleaming in the coloured lights. She stood on his back in her long, soft leather boots, her reedlike body sheathed in gold. Her golden hair was held high on the back of her proud little head, and it bobbed, as did Thunderhead's tail as he cantered round the ring followed by his beautiful white wives.

The high-wire artistes, shrunk to less than heroic size in the sawdust ring, strode by, arms held high, holding hands. Rosario was dressed in a thong of tigerskin, which flapped over his bulging prick, and his sister wore a minuscule tigerskin shift, which covered one breast. She wore a flesh-coloured body stocking, but her other breast was clearly visible, the dark peak of her nipple poking through the fine gauze. The siblings looked so slight and fragile on the ground; not like the gods they became when they flew.

The ringmaster cracked his long, black whip, the parade withdrew into the dark recesses of the tent, and the show began.

The natives of Teguise were filled with the magic of the circus. Their humdrum lives were transformed by the unusual excitement. The children planned to run away and become high-wire artistes or ride horses bareback.

The men, their gold teeth glinting, sucked their wooden toothpicks and thought of squeezing the narrow waists of the *bastoneras*. They imagined the contortionist's legs round their necks. Their wives fell in love with the tattooed man who swallowed swords and ate fire, or the loinclothed trapeze artiste, whose flashing smile was like sunlight on their boring domestic lives. They imagined themselves in the arms of the dashing ringmaster, whose black-rimmed eyes and gleaming teeth seemed almost to mesmerise them. They watched the turn of his fluid hips as he wielded the whip; saw his bulging crotch under the long red-lined cloak. They yearned for the dark caress of his spider-like hands.

No one fell in love with the clowns.

* * *

After the performance the *chamacos* cleared up the drop-
pings from the lion cage, the elephant shit from the
sawdust, and the horse dung. They swept between the
seats of the audience, finding the occasional peseta
dropped in the dark. The clowns and other performers
all had their tasks to complete before they were allowed
to collapse where they could. Only the main performers
had caravans, or shared a caravan. The others slept in
boxes, or the stable truck, on straw, or in the big top,
when it was standing. When they were on the move, *en
gera*, on tour, they roughed it, snatching sleep where
they could.

The wardrobe mistress had closed her ticket office and
hung the costumes on hangers in the aisles of spangled
garments of her caravan. She slept there, in a feathered
corner, surrounded by sweat-stained satins and bruised
velvets. Her life was costumed. She chose each night to
be a different woman. Tonight she was Delilah, dressed
in a silk toga, her nipples painted red, and her balls and
cock tied between her legs. She went to the caravan of
the tattooed man and knocked gently on his door.

'*Quien es*?' he hoarsely whispered, his throat blistered
and burned.

'It is Delilah, your wife,' said the transvestite,
winningly.

'Enter, my dove,' said the sword swallower.

Olympia climbed the steps into the tiny caravan, full
now the two of them sat on the bed. She pouted her
painted lips at the tattooed man and he planted a tender
kiss thereon. She sighed contentedly as the man's G-
string came off and the large penis swayed towards her.

'Oh, keep your pet snake under control, dear, look at
it!'

'Yes, my *palomita*, it wants you to kiss it,' the man said
huskily.

Olympia bent her bewigged head to the swaying
snake, for that is how it was tattooed, with a zigzag of
purple and green around its formidable girth. Its head
moved in a serpent-like manner and she willingly

34

steered it to her red lips, where she sucked and licked.
The fire eater lay back in a voluptuous enjoyment while
he was eaten. He tenderly caressed the large-limbed
wardrobe mistress, slipping his big hands under her silk
skirt and feeling between her thighs. He rubbed the
camouflaged bulge, pretending it was a pouting vulva.
He grabbed the hidden cock, unwrapped it from its
bonds, and rubbed it between his patterned fingers. The
two lovers writhed together in blissful joy, each in his
own heaven.

After she had made all her animals comfortable for the
night Floradora had gone quietly to the caravan she
shared with Anastasia. She was dog-tired and had
wanted only to sleep. After washing herself at the little
basin in the corner, flushing the soapy water between
her breasts and thighs and under her arms, she cleaned
her teeth. As always, she remembered her father's words
about cleanliness.

The night was chill and she slipped a white cotton
nightgown over her head. Its crisp cleanliness rasped her
breasts. She thought of her poor father and began to cry
quietly to herself. She wished Anastasia were there to
comfort her.

There was a knock at the door and the snake charmer
entered.

'Oh, Salome, I am so unhappy,' Floradora whispered
and drew close to the older woman. In her sorrow,
Floradora clasped her arms around the warm, womanly
hips and leant towards the snake charmer. Salome,
moving her hands to stroke the girl's breasts, kissed her
on the lips as if it were the most natural thing in the
world. In her distress and need for comfort the lion-
tamer's daughter allowed herself to be thus used, letting
the snake charmer wrap her in her arms as if she was a
snake curling round her. Salome's sly fingers dipped
under the young girl's white shift.

'Look at your white skin!' She clasped the fair-skinned

thigh in her red-nailed fingers and pinched the white flesh firmly, seeing it flood with colour. She smiled.

'Be gentle with me, Salome,' said Floradora, feeling desire pumping inside her, filling her virginal mind with strange longings.

'Don't worry, my *chiquita*, I will be gentle with you . . . this time.' Salome pushed the girl back on to the cushion-bedecked bed and lifted her skirt to her thighs. Floradora lay still, acquiescent, breathing quietly, her arms above her head, her eyes chastely closed. Salome shoved the cotton nightgown above Floradora's waist and straddled her. She leant over her, kissing her mouth, pushing her insistent tongue inside the soft lips.

Floradora felt as if her legs would melt. Her thighs parted under the pressure of Salome's legs. She was suddenly wet, and felt long fingers firmly touch her soft sex-lips. The strokes were firm, sensuous, and rhythmic. Her whole body felt softened, turned to fire, melting, liquid. Salome's firm breasts were pressed hard on her own small buds. She felt the large nipples digging into her like buttons. Her mouth was full of the other's tongue. It invaded her. She could not resist the snake charmer's love-making. Her desire sparked and flamed and Salome's fluttering fingers pressed into her body and gave her release. She sighed and sobbed and pressed the snake charmer close.

'There, now you will sleep, my little one. Rest, rest easy.' Salome drew reluctantly away from the young beauty – the *guera* – the fair-skinned girl – and covered her with a blanket. She smiled a secret smile to herself, unlocked the caravan door and went out into the crisp, already dark evening. Stars shone like beacons in the cold black sky. She drew her *bata* round her and hurried to her own caravan, which she shared with six snakes, her husbands, as she called them.

The next night, when Floradora went to her caravan to sleep, a dark-haired figure was in the cot. But, when Floradora had finished washing, put on her night shift and climbed into the cot, she was surprised by the identity of her bedfellow.

'Yes, you little goose, it's me,' said the naked snake charmer.

'Where is Anastasia?'

'She is with the ringmaster,' the snake charmer whispered into her ear, kissing it and caressing her on the breasts.

Floradora felt her nipples harden.

'Why are you wearing so much?' said Salome, laughing quietly.

'I was cold,' Floradora answered demurely.

'Take it off, darling.'

'No, I would rather not,' said the virginal equestrienne. She was not being overly prim; she simply enjoyed the feeling of the snake charmer's hands caressing her through the rasping cotton.

Salome pressed a hand between Floradora's legs and cupped her pubis. 'There, is that good?'

'Mm, comforting.'

'Comforting? I do not wish to comfort you; I wish to excite you.' And, so saying, she rubbed hard and pressed a finger into Floradora's cleft.

The lion-tamer's daughter caught her breath. Her sex juices began to flow and she felt her thighs soften and open. Salome's hands lifted the long skirt of the nightgown and caressed her belly. Floradora felt the hot breath of the snake charmer on her mouth and then the pressure of her lips force her own open. They kissed and Floradora's senses reeled. Salome writhed on top of the younger girl, and Floradora realised the snake charmer still wore her wide leather belt. It clasped her round her narrow waist, pulling it in tightly. It flared her hips and made the soft flesh above and below even more silklike. Salome placed Floradora's hands on her breasts.

'There, feel my *chichis*, aren't they soft?'

'Oh, yes, beautiful and so full and round,' said the admiring girl.

Salome sat astride the other's hips, her bare sex –

shaved, as all the female performers' were – touching the other's belly. She leant back, away from Floradora, but her belly and sex were pushed towards her. Floradora relinquished her hold of the jutting breasts, with their extraordinary swelling areolae and brown nipples, and stroked the offered sex. Salome's sex parts swelled and pouted, her labia full and plump. Floradora gazed at the ripe fruit and stroked it wonderingly. The lips parted and she saw the wetness within; the darker flesh, red-brown and glistening. Her fingers inevitably moved to that moisture, to dip into the pool of honey.

Salome moaned as the girl's fingers slipped inside her and discovered the contours of her inner flesh. She leant back on her hands, her breasts pointing to the ceiling, her belly thrust towards the girl. Floradora complied, agreeably surprised that she could cause the older woman so much pleasure. She dipped and stroked, learning her body's responses. She listened to Salome's moans and whimpers, and pushed several fingers inside the dark cave. With her other hand she stroked the pouting belly and pudenda, and raised her own belly towards the other. Salome remembered herself and began to caress the girl again, dipping a hand beneath her bottom to stroke the tender flesh between arse and sex. Floradora could not move her closed legs, trapped as they were by Salome's thighs. She ached to have fingers inside her. Salome's red-nailed fingers caressed firmly and slipped into the wetness of the closed slit. They stroked each other tenderly, then faster in a passion which flared and grew tumultuous.

Outside the wind moaned loudly and the fig trees sang.

Salome and Floradora at last lay quiet in each other's arms.

Chapter Five
Antonio Valera de Teguise

*T*he next day was a rest day, and there were no performances. Instead the performers washed their hair, took a bath, laundered their costumes, or walked to Teguise market and spent their earnings on women, cards, tortillas, wine, and fripperies – gaudy ribbons, baubles, Moroccan leather slippers, Arabic coffee.

Floradora took her horses out for a gallop. She rode the black stallion and led the mares behind her until she was out of sight of the town. The landscape enthralled her; it looked like a picture from a childhood bible. The green-sloped hills, terraced and planted with olives and vines, had on their summits tall slender palms, like date palms in Palestine. The land opened out into black-earthed prairie, and she allowed the mares their freedom. She sat astride the stallion, cantering him, breathing in the cool, fresh air of the high land, gazing at the far horizon, the volcanoes, the cobalt sky. This was a beautiful, mysterious island, unlike any place she had been. There were little enclosed fields with walls made of black volcanic lava rock, each rock piled on the one below, balancing precariously in the strong wind. In the fields were rows of low green shoots, onions and *papas*, the Canary potato, covered in the black volcanic ash, which kept the precious moisture in. Spiky aloes and agaves flourished. Some fig trees were in leaf; some were bare, white skeletons. Prickly pears grew in large, succulent clumps. They were grown as food for the cochineal beetle which, when crushed, was used to make a red dye.

The horses were sure-footed Arabs and they whinnied as their hooves felt the bare earth and rock, the rough mossy herbage beneath them. Their white manes arced in the wind, their black nostrils flared, and they threw their hind legs up and danced for the joy of freedom.

Floradora felt, for the first time since her father had died, a sense of life, a reason to live. She was, after all, a healthy young woman, pretty enough, and full of vigour. Her life was just beginning. And, now the threat of Lorenzo's lustful power was lifted, she had no reason to fear anyone. She was surprisingly grateful to the ringmaster for having let her off so easily. She willingly gave up all claim to the lions. It was a small price to pay for her honour, she thought. All the same, it niggled at her, the idea that he had not wanted her. Why didn't he desire her? She thrust out her small breasts and held her blonde head high, her back straight in the saddle. Her hair flew in the wind; the stallion galloped with his mares each side of him.

She had been out for an hour or so when she came across a settlement, a farm of sorts, she supposed. The low stone buildings looked like part of the rocky landscape. The black ashy earth spread around the perimeters. Giant cactus plants decorated the front entrance, where two enormous aloes stood sentinel at the metal-studded door.

She needed water. She dismounted and knocked at the door. An old man appeared and beckoned her into the entrance hall.

'*Agua, por favor, señor. Quiero agua.*'

'*Si, si, si, uno momento.*' He disappeared into the gloom and she peered after him. Her eyes had difficulty focusing after the bright sunlight. There were brasses and copper pans hanging on the walls. All manner of silver plates and china sat on wood shelves. She was in a kitchen. A smell of herbs and aromatic meat wafted around her head.

'*Señorita*, I am at your service.' She heard the soft melodious voice before she saw the man. She turned from the large dresser, which was filled with hand-painted china, and looked up into deep-brown eyes, shaded with smoky lashes. He was a tall man, about six feet three, and powerfully built. He smiled and she noted his even white teeth and his sad mouth. His nose was straight, long and aristocratic. He wore riding breeches of brown suede and a full-sleeved white cotton shirt, open at the neck to show a strong column of tanned flesh.

'*Buenos dias, señor.*' She smiled up at the good-looking man. 'I beg your pardon, I only wish for fresh water, for my horses and myself.'

'Your horses? May I see them?' Without waiting for a reply he strode to the door and went out. Floradora followed in his wake, feeling like a small pilot fish following a shark. His hips and buttocks were firm and strong; his long legs like trees. She felt a *frisson* of excitement.

'They are magnificent beasts, you have,' he admired. 'But you must excuse me, I have not introduced myself. I am Antonio Valera de Teguise.' He bowed low and she noted his thick, brown curling hair. He was about thirty years old, she guessed.

'And I am Floradora de Valencia.' She smiled and bowed her head.

'Ah, the circus! You are from the circus!' He clapped his hands and two servants appeared. 'Lead the horses to the water trough,' he ordered.

The men obediently led the stallion away and the mares dutifully followed.

'And now, permit me to offer you the hospitality of *mi casa*. Would you like wine?'

'Could I please have water first, then perhaps a glass of wine?' she asked.

Floradora sat in the heavily carved chair that he beckoned her to. They were in a large, dark-panelled room with oil paintings on the walls. Through the open shutters of the wide glass doors she could see the shady courtyard outside. She stood and walked over to the doorway.

'Would you like to go outside?' he said.

'Yes, please, it looks so cool and beautiful.' Floradora was uneasy indoors, being used to the life of the circus, the constant travel, living in a humble caravan.

The courtyard was full of potted palms and fig trees, giant ferns and orange trees. A trickle of water drizzled from a small fountain into a pond full of golden carp.

'It's beautiful!' she approved, and sat in a large wicker chair at a metal circular table.

'Thank you,' he demurred. 'Was it your father that was killed the other day?'

'Yes.'

'I heard about it. A terrible thing. I am sorry.'

'Thank you,' said Floradora, bowing her head to hide the sudden tears.

'How long is the circus going to be with us?'

'Who knows? It is not something the ringmaster feels he has to tell us.' She smiled. 'No doubt when audiences dwindle we will move on to Spain.'

A manservant, dressed in a long white apron over dark breeches, carried a tray with a jug of water and a jug of dark red wine and four glasses.

'Are you a good horsewoman?' Antonio Valera de Teguise's eyes twinkled and he smiled.

'I hope so, *señor*. Have you not been to see the circus?'

'Not yet, but now I have met Floradora de Valencia, I know I could not miss it.'

'Well, I shall expect to see you in the front row, sometime soon,' she said, cheekily.

This was the first time in her short life that she had been exposed to society, and been alone with a man. In the circus, where the circus family looked after one another, it was like a closed world, a village community.

Meeting normal people from the outside world was difficult, if not impossible. She had only met clowns and trapeze artistes, elephant trainers and strong men, *bastoneras* and *chamacos*. Her experience had been limited by her birth.

Floradora finished her glass of water and began sipping the glass of wine.

'To your very good health, *señorita*.' Antonio Valera de Teguise lifted his glass to his smiling lips and drank.

He helped her up on to Thunderhead, noting the slender shapeliness of her legs in the tight riding breeches. Her heart beat fast and her head felt light. She threw her head back in a familiar gesture, pushing her heavy hair over her shoulders.

'Thank you for your hospitality, *señor*.' She nudged Thunderhead with her knees and moved off at a trot, the white mares keeping pace beside her.'

The man stood for a long time and watched the vision disappear over the horizon.

'Well, well, well,' said the old woman, who had been hiding in the gloom of the hacienda, 'and what have you found there?'

Floradora positively flew back across the volcanic landscape to the *terrano* outside Teguise, where the circus folk were enjoying their rest evening. Fires blazed and rabbit stews were sending out aromatic smells. Men sat in circles laughing and drinking. Women washed clothes and hung them to dry on washing lines outside the caravans. The cool night was falling fast, and the evening star twinkled above the hills. Floradora hurriedly rubbed down her horses with the help of Isambard, who had been patiently waiting for her return.

'Your lions are fed and watered, Floradora,' he admonished, quietly.

'Oh, Isambard, am I that late? I am sorry. Thank you for doing that.' She threw him a morsel of a smile, which he caught and treasured in his poor clown's heart.

43

Later, in the limited privacy of her caravan, she described the man to Anastasia.

'He is so handsome, Anastasia, you would not believe a man could be so attractive. His teeth are gleaming and his nose is so straight and fine, and his legs so long. He is a real gentleman.'

'Is he married?' asked the girl.

'Goodness, I shouldn't think so, I saw no sign of a woman,' she said, thoughtfully.

'Will he come to the circus, do you think?' asked Anastasia.

'I hope so, I do hope so.' Floradora cuddled up to the dancer in the hard little bed and thought of the tall dark stranger. Her life was suddenly full of interesting developments. She thought of Lorenzo and his sensual lips, his hand on her sex. She thought of Salome and the secret things they did together. She thought of the trapeze artistes – their beauty and charm – and she wanted Rosario to touch her the way Salome had, and wanted his hand on her pubic mound, pressing into her cleft.

There was a knock at the caravan door, a gentle tapping. Floradora rose, put on her nightgown and tiptoed to the door, being careful not to disturb her sleeping companion.

'Salome!' Floradora was gratified that the older woman had come looking for her. Perhaps she wanted to make love to her? Her heart fluttered.

'Follow me, darling child,' said the snake charmer. Her voluptuous body was wrapped in a black rubber cloak, like the *bata* she usually covered her circus costume with, but this rustled and fell in deep dark folds around her curvaceous figure. Floradora followed unquestioningly. Salome almost ran between the dark shadows of the caravans. Here embers still burned, a yellow dog barked, a guitar twanged soulfully. Behind closed curtains shadows danced, amorous shapes clung and writhed.

'Where are we going?' Floradora asked as she ran to keep up, but she knew where she was being led.

The ringmaster opened the door of his caravan – his Bavarian castle, his baroque harem. Salome stood back and pushed the girl forward, following her up the steps.

The Great Lorenzo stood silhouetted against the hissing naphtha lights, his cloak wrapped close about him. He opened it and Floradora was shocked at the sight of his large erection raising its massive head.

'Come in, dear child,' he said, enveloping himself once more in the rubber cloak.

Perhaps she had imagined it? She sank into the plush armchair, almost pushed there by Salome.

'I hope I did not disturb your beauty sleep, Floradora,' said the ringmaster. 'I need you, you see. You are a charming girl, is she not, Salome?' He drew the snake charmer closer to him and opened her cloak. He casually caressed her naked breasts and flicked the nipples to erection. Floradora gazed at the ringmaster. His eyes, outlined in kohl, seemed to draw her gaze. She felt hot and dizzy. It was the naphtha, she thought. He held her gaze as he stroked the brown bullets of flesh. Salome sank to her knees and opened his cloak. Floradora could see nothing except the two black-cloaked figures, clasping and moaning like giant bats engaged in some animal ritual. In spite of herself she rose and drew closer to the lustful pair. Lorenzo's stiff rod was held in Salome's red mouth. It disappeared into her throat and withdrew, like one of her beautiful snakes. She knelt, her bare knees on the Brussels carpet, her dark ringlets fallen over her sensual face.

The Great Lorenzo moved away from her and clapped his hands. Salome rose and turned towards Floradora and, wordlessly, she undressed the girl, removing her white, virginal nightgown.

'Now, the rubber cloak,' commanded Lorenzo.

Salome undid the clasp that held her cloak around her shoulders and placed it round the fair-skinned shoulders of Floradora. The lion-tamer's daughter shivered as the

45

silky stuff caressed her back and buttocks, her arms and belly.

'There, that's better,' said Lorenzo.

Floradora felt she was in a dream, that this was not really happening to her. But it was; she knew it was.

'No, what? Why are you doing this?' she complained.

'Ah, reluctance, disobedience! Right, Salome, fetch the cane.'

The naked, voluptuous woman, her full breasts swinging on her narrow frame, her fleshy buttocks trembling, turned away from them both to find the short, whippy cane he had asked for. Floradora's lips trembled in anticipation and her sex grew moist. The caravan was full of animal scents. Floradora could smell the lust of the ringmaster, the snake charmer's musk, and her own sweat. She felt faint, yet oddly excited and wanted to continue this bizarre introduction to the ringmaster's fetishistic desires.

She knelt on the sofa as Salome showed her, her bottom up high, her head held low. The cloak still covered her, and she already breathed deeply of its warm, darkly erotic fragrance. It clung to her buttocks, defining her bottom cleft. She felt hands lifting up the cloak and restraining it with straps round her waist. Her bottom was exposed to the ringmaster. She felt wet. She writhed on her elbows.

'Keep still. How dare you show such lasciviousness!' Salome, give me the cane and handle me.' Lorenzo's prick grew at the pretty sight of young buttocks writhing welcomingly.

Floradora dare not look behind her as the blows fell on her bare flesh. But she could imagine what took place as the ringmaster beat her with the schoolmaster's weapon. Salome was massaging his fleshy weapon, she felt sure.

She was surprised at how the hurt disappeared after the first few blows. Her flesh was not sore, just burning, and her thighs felt soft as silk. She accepted the 'punishment' as if she had deserved it, and understood the pleasure that the caress of rubber could bring. The ringmaster – or was it Salome? – slipped a hand between Floradora's legs and stroked the swollen fleshy purse. Floradora closed her eyes and pressed back on to the kind hand that brought her pleasure. She moved slowly back and forth on the fingers that caressed her. They withdrew and the blows were renewed. The constant repetition of blows and caresses confused her flesh and her brain. She enjoyed the sensations equally. The whippy cane smacked her genitals and made the flesh sing. Her climax came suddenly as he touched her, the thwack of the cane still ringing in her ears. She moaned aloud. She felt his cock press against her buttocks and then the spurt of his juices over her.

Chapter Six
Floradora's Birthday Celebrations

The next day, Floradora could not stop thinking about her introduction to the bizarre, erotic entertainment she had taken part in. For, she admitted to herself as she cleaned out her horses with Isambard's help, it had been entertaining, and enjoyable. Her blood moved faster in her veins, her cheeks were flushed pink, and her lips were softened, fuller.

Isambard noticed the change in the girl. He said nothing that was not necessary. He loved her dumbly, wanting no reward. But instinct made him ask her if the ringmaster had been bothering her.

'No, of course not, Isambard, don't be silly. I really am capable of looking after myself, you know.' The blushing girl could not look him in the eye as she spoke, and Isambard was hurt that she barked at him. She forked more hay on to the bedding and strode out of the stable. The mare, Ruby, nickered softly and the clown stroked her nose.

Rosario was waiting outside the stable, hoping to see Floradora. His sister was busy trying on a new costume, and he had left her in the wardrobe mistress's care and made his way to where the horses were kept.

'Floradora, come with me, I have a surprise for you,' said the young man, and she blushed pinker than ever.

'Rosario! For me? A surprise?'

'Yes.' He grabbed her hand and ran with her to the edge of the circus compound, past strings of washing and cauldrons of stew, curs snapping at their heels as they ran. He led her through a gateway and sat down with her by a low stone wall. White daisies with yellow hearts and yellow daisies with white hearts fluttered like little flags in the wind.

He leant over her, held her close and kissed her lips. She was so surprised that she allowed the caress, her whole being melting in desire with his proximity. She smelt his youth and freshness and she wanted him.

'Is this my surprise?' She smiled between kisses.

'Yes, and there is more if you want,' he whispered.

He took her hand and pressed it on his crotch. She felt the hardness under his breeches, and left her hand there a second before drawing away.

'Rosario. What are you saying?'

'I love you, Floradora, I want you.'

This was the very first declaration of love she had ever had in her eighteen years. Her first love. 'Oh, Rosario, I love you too,' she declared naively, meaning every word.

He kissed her more passionately, rubbing himself against her, pulling her close to him. The lust transferred itself to the girl and she felt the need to be joined with him, and wanted to be part of his body. They writhed together, still clothed, on the bed of wild flowers; the mustard-coloured pollen powdered their limbs, dyed their clothes, and spattered their hair.

'Oh, Rosario!' She opened her thighs and he touched her. She smelt hay and horses.

The two young lovers were trying to remove each other's clothes. He had her shirt buttons undone and his hands felt the first clasp of her nubile breasts. He almost came there and then. He groaned.

'Oh, Floradora, if you love me, please hold my cock,'

he implored, and undid his flies, whereupon his heavy prick slid out, rudely pink, and swayed towards her.

'Oh! It is beautiful!' She took it delicately into her small, capable hands. She was surprised at its sturdy girth, its superior length to Lorenzo's prick. Her willing hands stroked the rearing beast. The youth was too far gone in his passion to remove Floradora's riding breeches. He still held her breasts, rubbing them furiously. Her hands held tight the beast with one eye and she watched curiously as it swelled even thicker, hardened, and a white foam spurted high on to her chest, covering her little peaks with snow.

'Oh! Rosario, did I do it right?' she asked, for the youth was flat out, exhausted, and at the moment of truth a look of agony had twisted his charming face.

'Oh, what? Er, yes, it was exactly right, Floradora. But I must go now. Rosalita will be wondering where I am.' He struggled to his feet, tucked his shrivelling cock back into his breeches and, without a backward glance, hurried off.

'Well, if that's love, you can keep it!' said the affronted Floradora, her maidenly innocence still intact but her pride pricked and deflated like a balloon left in an aisle of the big top after the children had gone home.

When she got back to her caravan there was a small posy of yellow and white daisies waiting for her. She smiled forgivingly, thinking that Rosario must have left them for her. But, when Anastasia saw her later, the dancer put her right.

'Isambard brought the flowers for you, Floradora, isn't he sweet?' the dancer said.

'Isambard?' Floradora blushed in annoyance. Had the clown been watching them in the meadow? What had he seen?

Anastasia was a simple girl, a Russian gypsy, whose parents had worked in circuses all their lives and brought her up to do the same. She had no particular talents, but could put her lithe, dancer's body to many uses. She took part in the *equilibrista*, the balancing act, and could juggle and tumble as well as the clowns. She was engaged to one of the *chamacos*, a swarthy, handsome Hungarian, with a square jaw and brown curly hair. He was one of half a dozen young men who followed the circus, erected the big top and took it down again, and helped with all the practical work around the place. But that did not stop her having fun with any other man who took her fancy. She, along with all the females of the circus, regularly took part in Lorenzo's real-life fantasies. It was a pattern that had been established right from the beginning. When her parents died, Lorenzo had taken her on and fed her and clothed her. In return, he expected her total obedience. If any of the girls misbehaved or made mistakes in the ring, they paid for it later, in the Great Lorenzo's caravan.

Her fiancé, Yulias, was a bear of a man, big-boned and broad-shouldered. He was a meek soul; his strong visage belied his gentle nature. He owed money to the ringmaster, as most of the casual labourers did, so he too had to toe the line and take part in the various displays of lewdness that Lorenzo insisted on.

That night, Lorenzo and Salome were occupied in a little voyeurism. Yulias and his fiancée were making love vigorously, the dancer on top, her little breasts bouncing up and down. Lorenzo flicked a riding cane at the bare buttocks of the chained and naked Salome. He wore riding breeches and his rubber cloak, but his flies were open and his cock stood upright, a dark pink stalk with a purple bulging head. The ringmaster watched the tableau in front of him: the sweating, writhing lovers, and the bound, enslaved Salome. His erection withered and he looked at it in displeasure. These days it took increasingly bizarre situations to make his excitement last. It was probably his age, he thought. He stopped flicking the riding crop at the ripe, reddened buttocks, and clapped his hands.

At once the other participants stopped what they were doing and looked questioningly at the ringmaster.

'Go away, the two of you, you bore me, get out.' He casually hit the dancer and her consort with the crop's leather loop. 'Find Floradora and send her here, immediately.'

Floradora had been in a state of mild sexual excitement ever since her arousal in the meadow. She was aware of unfinished business. Her new-found love with the pretty youth was a disappointment to her. Why, he had not even kissed her afterwards! He was nothing but a brute. Salome had told her that all men only wanted one thing, and would do anything to get it. Perhaps she was right.

When the nocturnal knock came at her door, Floradora was ready. She had lain awake waiting for the summons, and she was prepared for it. Before she had gone to bed she had washed carefully, shaved off all her pubic hair, smoothed herself all over with aromatic oil – bought for her by Anastasia in Teguise market – and washed her hair. She was dressed in her most becoming gown. It had a long, white lace skirt hanging from a tight-waisted corset which laced at the front. Her little bosom was pressed upward to peep over the top, her tiny waist was constricted further by the corset, and her legs, hips and buttocks glimmered pale through the transparent lace. She wore no knickers.

Olympia had made Floradora this garment today. She had found the lace in the market. The corset had been a separate item until the wardrobe mistress had seen its possibilities. She had given the girl the dress as a gift for her birthday. The occasion had been missed in the shadow of her father's funeral.

Now, Floradora answered the gentle knock at the door. 'It's your turn, Floradora,' said Anastasia, dragging her fiancé behind her by the hand. At least they could make love in the comfort of her bed, its rough blankets warmed by the lion-tamer's daughter.

Floradora wrapped her *bata* around her shoulders and held it tightly to her chest. She ran barefoot through the dark, being careful to avoid guy ropes and wires. Foul-smelling rubbish burned on a smouldering bonfire. She heard the wind screaming through the volcanic valleys and pulled her cloak closer. A dog howled and inevitably started off all the dogs for many miles around. The far-flung farm and vineyard curs spoke to each other across the miles and keened their love, losses and desires in the wind-filled night. A bat flicked by Floradora's head and she felt its leathery wings lift her hair.

As she reached the ringmaster's caravan, she saw Salome coming through the night towards her. Behind her, two dark shadows, slight, slender.

Floradora went in through the low door first and turned to see Salome smiling at her. Behind her, wrapped in their *batas*, were the aerialists – Rosario and his sister, Rosalita.

'What is this?' asked Rosario. His sister stared solemnly at the ringmaster.

'An exclusive little celebration for my star performers,' said Lorenzo. He was dressed in leather breeches with high, black boots and a white linen shirt, loose at the neck. On his dark hairy chest shone a large medallion of gold hanging from a gold chain. He poured Spanish brandy into small, green-glass tumblers on a silver tray. The trapeze artistes looked surprised.

'A party?' said Rosario. He looked pleased. He had been too restless to sleep after his naughty earlier rendezvous with Floradora. His sister had been cross with him when he had returned, powdered with pollen, his dark hair stained yellow. She had noticed the dark stain on his crotch, too, and wondered who he had been with. She was jealous of any and all females who took an interest in her brother. He had always attracted feminine attention. Men, too, loved him from afar. His looks were darkly handsome; his brown eyes smouldered, or so he hoped, narrowing his eyes.

'She is not a star!' Rosalita stared haughtily at Floradora as she spat the words.

'Oh, I think she is,' said Lorenzo. 'Anyway, it is Floradora's birthday and she should celebrate it.'

'How did you know that?' asked the surprised Floradora.

'Isambard told me.'

'Isambard?' She remembered the bunch of wild daisies, and Rosario's kisses.

'Drink up, all of you, there is plenty more,' said the ringmaster, twisting his moustache.

Salome was attired in more than she had been wearing earlier, but her costume was designed to show off her round, pointed breasts and her narrow waist. Her hips flared beneath the wide, shiny black belt, which held the short-skirted rubber dress round her waist. The silky material had been treated with some sort of oil to make it shine. Her breasts pushed against the stuff, her nipples little peaks straining the rubber. Her arms and shoulders were bare under the halter-necked dress. She took Floradora's cloak from her shoulders and displayed the girl to the ringmaster. She twirled her round, making chirruping noises of admiration for the girl's dress.

The trapeze artistes removed their cloaks, exposing the costumes from the last act they had performed. Rosalita wore a scarlet body stocking spangled with orange sequins. Her small, round breasts gleamed in the candlelight. Her brother wore only a G-string of red with orange sequins, outlining his sturdy cock and the firmly pouched balls. His hairless chest showed clearly defined pectoral muscles rippling in the flickering light. His belly was flat as an ironing board. All the gathered guests stared longingly at the youth. His face was more beautiful than his sister's, which was marred by her fierce expression, the low, gypsy brows gathered in a perpetual frown. Rosario always had a smile for everyone.

'To Floradora on her eighteenth birthday!' said Lorenzo, raising his glass.

'Floradora!' They drank and drank again, as Lorenzo filled the tumblers with the blood-red brandy. He dangled his medallion as he drank, swinging the chain so it glinted in the candlelight.

Floradora felt sleepy and deliciously light-headed. Rosario swayed close to her.

'Kiss the girl on her birthday,' commanded the ringmaster.

Rosario pushed his face into Floradora's and breathed brandy fumes into her mouth. His lips felt soft and pliant. She returned the kiss. Lorenzo and Salome clapped their hands and laughed. Then, Salome bent over the girl and kissed her hard on the mouth, leaving traces of red lip colour.

Floradora was hot. She sat on the green sofa, her transparent lace skirt raised to her thighs. Lorenzo pressed her side and licked her cheek before kissing her on the mouth, snaking his tongue behind her teeth, curling it round her tongue. She felt faint and hot.

Rosalita was nearly asleep, her eyes half-closed, the smoky lashes casting a purple shadow on her downy cheek. But she moved her head slowly from side to side, hypnotised by the gold medallion which swung in front of her.

'Kiss your sister. She will miss the party if she slumbers,' hissed the ringmaster at the youth.

Rosario did as he was bid, his cock bulging inside the flimsy covering, stretching the elastic waistband. His sister groaned as he kissed her and she returned the caress, slowly, with sensuality, lifting her arms round him and stroking his naked back. Salome watched with narrow eyes, smiling her slow smile. The ringmaster stopped swinging the gold medallion. It had done its work.

Floradora sat on the couch, her legs splayed, between Salome and Lorenzo. Her lacy skirt was up round her waist now. Salome and Lorenzo dipped their fingers in her honey and licked them and leant over her to caress her. She was in a stupor of arousal, her eyes dark, her lips swollen. Her sex was exposed to the gathering, but Rosario did not see it yet, as he was too busy caressing his lovely sister. Salome knelt on the floor in front of the ringmaster and the snake charmer took out Lorenzo's flaccid cock from the fly of his leather breeches. She drew her lips to the pink stem and kissed it, then held it in one hand while her tongue crept up Floradora's legs. The lion-tamer's daughter arched her back and pushed out her pubis towards the coming caress. Salome's long red tongue lapped at the font of pleasure and Floradora moaned and writhed.

Lorenzo stroked his cock and pushed Salome away. He stood, still regarding the entwined siblings, who were now on the floor, kissing each other passionately, their legs wrapped round each other.

Rosario's G-string had come undone and sat ridiculously on one hip. He thrust himself up against the flimsy fabric, which covered his sister's crotch. Rosalita covered her brother in passionate kisses.

Lorenzo stroked himself, and casually reached for a small, black-plaited whip which hung on the wall. He lifted Salome's black rubber skirt up over her wide hips to reveal her dark-skinned round buttocks, the cleft wide as she crouched to suck and explore Floradora's virginal purse.

Floradora opened her eyes to see Lorenzo bring the whip down on Salome's generous buttocks. The snake charmer did not flinch. The next stroke was aimed at the slender bare buttocks of Rosario. He yelped like a puppy and looked around to see what was happening. Floradora saw him take in the erotic scene of Salome kissing her between her thighs. She also saw that the ringmaster was rampant now, his slender cock firmly held in one hand.

'You young hound, unhand your sister. I'll horsewhip you for that.' And Lorenzo set about the boy again. His sister and Salome, who had risen from her delightful pastime to restrain the youth, held Rosario. He was upturned neatly over a leather stool and immediately the whip fell on his backside. Floradora was deeply aroused by the developing orgiastic scene. The ringmaster now had Rosalita holding his cock and Salome stroking his balls. He whipped the youth, and the youth did not flinch. Floradora knew that Rosario's cock was nicely rubbing the leather stool every time the whip fell. Her eyes were on his delectable flesh; she could see his balls as his bottom lifted and fell with each stroke of the whip. She could hear kisses, lapping tongues, smacking of lips; she could smell sex, sweat, brandy, and musk. Floradora saw Rosalita now enjoying the caresses of Salome, who reached behind the rampant ringmaster and stroked her between the buttocks. There was a hole in Rosalita's costume where Rosario had tunnelled and Salome pressed her fingers inside to reach the wetness of the swollen sex. Lorenzo stroked himself and forced the female trapeze artiste to hold him more firmly; to rub harder and faster. She complied, her own climax close as Salome stroked and dipped her fingers into her.

Floradora, meanwhile, was alone on the sofa, watching the erotic display. Her eyes were drawn to the trembling limbs, the reddened buttocks of the boy, his balls squashed under him. She could see his enjoyment was great, his penis rubbing on the leather upholstery. He groaned, oblivious to the others. Lorenzo wielded the little whip, flicking the striped bottom that was raised to him. Floradora saw his penis swell under the tender ministrations of the prim Rosalita and the sly hands of Salome. Floradora rose from her lonely sofa and positioned herself in front of the ringmaster, so he had to notice her. She lifted her lace skirt and bent over, raising her bare bottom to him. He took up the invitation and whipped her white skin. Then he dropped the whip and leant forward, releasing the hands of Salome and Rosalita from his genitals.

He grabbed the round buttocks of the virgin, Floradora, and the taut small bum of Rosario, and pressed himself between the cleft of each in turn, his penis appearing and disappearing into the thrusting *derrières* to the delight and enjoyment of both prone young people. Rosalita fell into the round arms of Salome and they soon writhed together on the sofa. Rosalita's red costume was torn to shreds by the enthusiastic snake charmer.

Her little breasts bulged from the ragged stretchy stockinet. Her buttocks stuck out from two large holes. Her sex was totally exposed, the lips swollen and red. Spangles from her costume were stuck around Salome's mouth and in her hair. She voraciously tongued the trapeze artiste's sex parts and cupped her little breasts. Rosalita cried out in her little death. Salome withdrew her caress and went to finish her work. She took up the crop and laid into the slender buttocks of her master, the Great Lorenzo, who was still thrusting and dipping his cock where he could between the raised buttocks.

'Oh, Lorenzo, what a naughty boy you are,' she whispered, so only he could hear. She rubbed him between the legs and slapped his balls with her hands, then continued the whipping.

He moaned loudly and spent his seed he knew not where, only that it was in young, soft, eager flesh, reddened by his whip. Floradora sighed and smiled.

Chapter Seven
The Horse Breeder

A ntonio Valera de Teguise sat in the very front row in the big top. His mother, Señora Octavia Valera de Teguise, sat next to him, resplendent in black silk with a black lace mantilla decorating her tightly knotted black hair. She cooled herself with a black feather fan and watched her son carefully. She had not seen him so animated in a long time. He had been a worry to her for several years, ever since his fiancée had died in a riding accident. He had given up horse breeding, and had sold all his brood mares, keeping only the one stallion, Bandito, that he had ridden since he was a child, and a couple of geldings who pulled the carriage. He hardly ever rode out these days, keeping himself busy in the vineyard and with the production of the wine. His heart had been broken when his beautiful sweetheart had died. That was five years ago and his father had died three years after that, leaving Octavia bereft once more. Mother and son lived together in the large, old farmhouse, surrounded by relics of their family history. They had cut themselves off from humanity, only hearing of what happened on the island from the farm hands.

When Antonio had suggested they visit the little ramshackle circus that was at Teguise, his mother's first instinct was to say no. Then she remembered his face as he had watched the circus girl ride away. Yes, she did resemble his lost love, in a way – the lithe, small, childish figure, the blondeness. But his fiancée, Señorita Carlotta de Cadiz, had been a well-born lady with riches of her own and a castle on the mainland. His future had crumbled in a heap of ash, like the volcanic ash which covered half the island, and he was burnt out, grieving still for his lost love.

So, his mother had agreed to accompany her son to the event. It would be the first time she had travelled further than the chicken run at the end of the paddock since her husband had died.

And so they sat, mother and son, and the townsfolk saluted them when they saw them there; the son so austere in his black suit, the proud *señora* in her widow's weeds. *'Buenas tardes, señora, señor,'* came the greetings from the farmers and the tradesmen. *'Como esta usted?'* and the answer – *'Muy bien, y usted?'*

And Antonio felt lighthearted and gay, as if a page had turned in his sad life to show a picture full of hope and sunshine.

The parade began. There was always a grand parade before the show, in which the entire circus took part. They paraded the streets of Teguise and then, followed by ragamuffin children, the trail of elephants, horses, clowns and dancers, jugglers and tumblers, made their way through the scrubby lichen and low thorny shrubs to the big top, which blossomed white in a black field. The crowds still queued at the *taquilla,* where Olympia, dressed tonight in emerald satin and red feathers, her skirts full and pleated, her wig red and curly, sat in splendour and sold tickets to the populace.

Antonio sat forward in his seat as he saw the girl ride by on the splendid black stallion. Her face was pale in the glow of the naphtha lights and her slender body looked as if it would snap with one squeeze of her waist. He had no eyes for the snake charmer who paraded with her boa constrictors wrapped round her body like feather boas. Salome was dressed in a black rubber tight-fitting all-in-one garment which showed every voluptuous curve of her generous body. The audience clapped in pleasure. The *bastoneras* were attired in little more than short red tutus with flimsy bodices, their yellow stockings held up with gold ribbons. The girls were all erotically clothed in garments that would have been banned from the streets of Teguise, where girls were kept hidden from the male gaze, behind shutters in dark rooms, and never allowed out without a chaperone. Most of the men in the audience had come purely to feast their eyes on female flesh.

After the grand parade, the audience thrilled to the sight of the elephants, the mother and her young one, who bowed and stood on two legs and balanced on stools and blew water over the clowns and generally amused everyone.

The ringmaster did his terrifying knife-throwing act, with La Roux wearing next to nothing, tied to the revolving target. Every time the wheel revolved and she was upside down, her short skirt fell up over her breasts and her pink, transparent knickers were revealed, her legs apart. The knives landed between her thighs, between her arms and body, either side of her golden-crowned head. It was obvious that her red hair was natural as only she, of all the girls in the circus, was unshaven.

Antonio watched avidly for the moment when the horses entered the ring. He did not have to wait long. After the clowning and the fire-eating act, the black horse entered the empty sawdust ring, seemingly alone. He circled the ring several times before Floradora drew herself up from underneath his body, climbed up, and stood on his back. She was dressed in black leather, a very short, fringed cowgirl jacket and thigh-high chaps over a black leather G-string. Black leather gauntlets completed the image. Her hair was tugged back in a long ponytail. Her circus make-up was more subtle than that worn by most of the girls. She wore scarlet lip colour and black eye make-up which highlighted her blondeness. She rode backwards, on Thunderhead's back, underneath him, on his side; she rode on her head, her legs in a split.

Antonio was bewitched. His eyes never left the girl. His mother watched him and fanned herself. As Floradora brought in the mares and put them through their paces she noticed Antonio sitting in the front row. She threw a kiss and a smile in his direction and he caught it and held it in his frosty heart, where it burned and melted the stony organ.

Her performance was stunning that evening. She and her horses could do no wrong. Thunderhead obeyed her every thigh movement, and the delicate touch of her hands or her leather-bound feet. The mares were glossy, white as first snowfall in the high Pyrenees. Her lovely young face shone with enjoyment as she leapt and did daring acrobatics on her horses. The crowd loved her.

When Floradora returned, half an hour later, for her lion act, she looked for him, but he was not there. She was disappointed that he had not stayed to watch her brave mastery of the fierce beasts that had killed her father. She got through the act, aware of the gap in the row where he had sat with the fiercely beautiful old woman next to him.

Isambard was there to help with her lions, as always, and he put the cloak round her shoulders as she left the cage.

'Did you like the daisies?' he asked her, looking into her eyes.

'Daisies?' She blushed. 'Oh, yes, thank you, Isambard. It was kind of you.' Her feelings of *joi de vivre*, and her new-found sexuality, were so strong in her, and in such need of expression, that she kissed the clown on his wet-whited cheek, leaving a scarlet stain which burned into his ebony skin. She ran off into the night to dream of Antonio Valera de Teguise.

Chapter Eight
Isambard

*T*he snake charmer was practising a new act. It was
morning and she had the big top to herself apart
from a few of the circus hands who were doing running
repairs to tears in the fabric of the big tent. The snakes
were in two large stone jars which had to be carried in
by two of the *chamacos*. Salome wore one of her performance costumes: a black strappy arrangement which con-
sisted of a studded leather brassière which buckled at
the front and a wide strap which encircled her hips and
went between her legs. Her arms were covered by long
black leather gloves and she wore a studded leather
collar round her neck.

Salome removed the lid of one jar and dipped a hand
into the dark. She drew out a small black and yellow
snake; its cold eye regarded her. After she had performed
the morning ritual of milking the poison from its fangs
she wrapped it round one arm. She drew out another,
similar, serpent and wrapped it round her waist, where
it hung, its darting tongue on one thigh. A third snake, a
python, she threw round her neck, and a fourth she
placed round a leg, where it slithered slowly upward.
She began to gently writhe and dance, and the snakes
seemed to dance with her. They twisted and curled

outward, then swept their long bodies in towards her, caressing her with their cold skin.

She quietly hummed an Arabic melody and did a sort of belly dance, kneeling and thrusting her belly forwards. The snakes were like dance partners holding her and taking her weight as she leant far back, her head nearly touching the sawdust, her knees wide apart. The humming stopped and she rose to her feet. The snakes slithered downward, all ending in a writhing heap at her bare feet, before they zigzagged their way to their jar, climbed its orange exterior and disappeared inside. Then Salome went to the other jar, removed the heavy lid, and whistled into the interior. She stood back as the boas slid out, looked around them with alien eyes, and headed straight for her. She had a flute which she played solemnly while the snakes curled up over her muscled calves, up her legs, round her hips, round her waist, her breasts, completely covering her. They were heavy and she had to move her feet to take the strain. The two snakes met round her throat and hissed at each other. She stopped the music and pursed her lips first at one then the other, receiving their cold kisses. Then she opened her mouth and let one snake head enter. Its dark scaly head was enveloped by her red lips. She sucked the snake and let it go, and then welcomed the other into her mouth. Her body was practically hidden by snakes. They slid down again and she watched as they went back to their jar.

'Good!' She clapped, and two circus hands came and took the jars away.

Isambard was attending to the horses, combing their long tails and manes and singing softly to them. He helped each day with Floradora's animals. It was his favourite task. He was a private man, in spite of his calling as clown. His massive frame hid a sad, poor heart, which fluttered feebly at times. He had had a hard childhood with beatings and starvation and no parents to care for him – only a slave owner who had been

64

terribly cruel. Isambard, at sixteen, prematurely grown and strong for his age, had killed him. He had run away and had fallen into the life of the circus, literally, when he jumped from a hayrick, where he had been sleeping for days, on to a circus train which was taking the troupe of animals and performers from Alabama to Mexico. He had been adopted by the clowns and taught his trade, and he was grateful to his circus family for his salvation, as he saw it. He had travelled across the Americas with the same people, learning as he went the various skills of tumbling and balancing. He had been with the circus in the days before Lorenzo had bought it. They had been happier days, more innocent, though the performers often had no pay and slept where they could in the big top, or, when they were travelling, in trucks or in piles of corn. With Lorenzo came more prosperity and, for a while, the circus was thriving. But soon the gambling, which Lorenzo encouraged but did not take part in, was an all-consuming passion for many of the circus hands, including Isambard. Most of them owed Lorenzo money. One or two of them had died because they could not pay. The ringmaster's knife-throwing act was an indication of his skill with the dagger and stiletto.

Isambard had had various love affairs in his years with the circus. There had been a Russian *bastonera*, a fair-skinned blonde with large breasts and big hips. She had arrived one day on foot, having run away from a brutal husband, and persuaded Lorenzo to hire her. Isambard fell in love with her at first sight. He had been a young man then – only twenty – and she was at least twenty-five. She had taught him so much. As he brushed the horses' tails he thought of Raisa's long blonde hair. She used to tie it round his cock, pull it tight, and suck his cock until he came into her mouth. She had left with a roughneck Greek *chamaco* who had hair all over his back and arse. God, she had such appalling taste! Isambard finished with the horses and left the stable. He wondered where Floradora was.

* * *

65

The lion-tamer's daughter sat in the wardrobe caravan surrounded by lace and leather. She wore only a chamois leather G-string and her little breasts jiggled as she talked excitedly to Olympia.

'You must have noticed him, Olympia. He was so distinguished-looking and handsome. And his mother – such a lady. They have a wonderful *finca* in beautiful countryside, and he was so polite and gentlemanly.'

'Mm, well, you sound smitten, *chicita*.' The wardrobe mistress tut-tutted as she sorted through the rows of exotic garments that were her territory. Olympia wore a short black wig today, cut to her chin, and she looked very chic. Her pleated skirt was neat and her white cotton blouse was draped over her false bosom and had a bow tied at the neck.

'I don't suppose I will ever see him again,' the girl sighed, slipping on the chamois slip that Olympia offered her.

'Oh yes, I like that. You look just like a squaw. Do you want a black pigtail wig and feathers, dearie?'

'No wig, just the feathers, please,' said Floradora, admiring herself in the mirror. The short, fringed garment, honey-coloured like her hair, was stretched tight over her breasts and hips and showed off her nubile curves.

Olympia found a bunch of feathers from a drawer full of accessories and quickly sewed them on to a red headband. 'There!' She slipped the headband on to Floradora's forehead and stood back to admire her work. 'Yes, perfect!'

'And what about your other *amoroso*?'

'Who do you mean?' said Floradora, smiling.

'*El gitano*, the gypsy, Rosario. He is very handsome, isn't he?' The transvestite smirked and put her head on one side.

'Oh, Rosario, he is just a boy,' said Floradora disdainfully. 'I am more interested in men.' She flung her cloak round her shoulders and made her exit, leaving a bemused Olympia, who was more of an age to appreciate boys than mature men.

'Well, throw his remains this way when you have finished with him,' Olympia called after her.

Floradora looked in vain for Antonio Valera at the afternoon performance and the evening performance. She was very disappointed. Her pride was hurt. She had assumed that her youth and beauty would be irresistible to him. She was proud that her lion act had developed into her own rather than an echo of her father's. She was less afraid of Kwasi now; he seemed to have settled down.

After that night's performance she bathed, cleaned her teeth, dressed in her white lace birthday dress, and waited for the expected summons. At a quarter to midnight the knock came on the door. She left Anastasia asleep in their shared bed and crept out into the dark. She was surprised to find Alphonso, the tattooed sword eater, waiting to accompany her to the ringmaster's caravan. She drew her *bata* close round her and had to run to keep up with him. He held the door of Lorenzo's caravan open for the girl. Her cloak brushed his chest as she went past him.

'Come in, *chica*, come in and join the fun.' Lorenzo was naked except for his rubber cloak and an array of leather straps holding his buttocks apart and dividing his breasts. He was standing, his back to the door, obscuring the view of Salome, who was tied to the four-poster bed, spread-eagled and naked. Alphonso came into the caravan behind Floradora, and stood, arms folded over his massive chest. His loincloth of tigerskin showed his tattooed buttocks and solid thighs. Floradora had never been so close to the man before. He seemed a giant to her. His sweat was strong but fresh, and not unpleasant. She felt his hands on her shoulders as he removed her cloak. She stood with her long white dress and her flowing blonde hair like an angel in the devil's bedchamber.

67

The smell of sex was overwhelming. She breathed it in deeply. Lorenzo flicked his whip at Salome's buttocks and thighs and stood to one side so Floradora could see the erotic scene. His balls and cock were hidden behind a black leather pouch held on by leather straps. There was no perceptible bulge, she noticed. Her eyes were drawn to the striped flesh of Salome. She looked beautiful in her bondage, her arms and legs stretched wide, her curvaceous bottom and narrow waist looking so desirable. Floradora licked her dry lips.

'Alphonso, look to it, do your duty, man,' ordered the ringmaster, and the tattooed man pushed past Floradora and eased himself on to the helpless snake charmer. She grunted and pressed her bottom upward to help his progress into her. He removed his loincloth with one movement and shoved into her. Floradora saw the red rod of his flesh push into the open pouch. The sight moved her and she found herself breathing fast. Lorenzo wrapped his arms round Floradora and drew her to him. He kissed her lips and she closed her eyes. He lifted her long lace skirt and she felt the cold rubber of his cloak pressed into her slit and rubbed up and down. Suddenly, he twisted her arm behind her and shoved her towards the leather stool, which he made her kneel over, her bottom high, and her head away from him. He pushed the skirt up over her shoulders and she felt totally naked. He stroked her back and the dark cleft between her moons, and she shuddered with pleasure.

'Look at them!' he ordered Floradora, and she looked up at the thrusting figure of the massive Alphonso, galleons rising and falling on the giant waves of his back. Mermaids swam furiously over his muscled arms and eagles flapped their giant wings on his pectoral muscles. Under him Salome drowned. She writhed against her leather bonds, her whole body wracked as if with electric shocks, each time Alphonso plunged into her. Their cries and moans excited Floradora, as did the scent of their hot bodies, and their sex juices.

Lorenzo said, 'Do you enjoy the performance of lasciviousness, my dear?'

'Yes,' whispered Floradora.

'Well, that is very naughty of you, very wicked, and you will be punished. I told you to think of me as your father, Floradora. As your father I will spank you, to teach you not to be lascivious.' So saying, he spanked her with his leather-gloved hand and the sharp pain made her cry out in surprise. He held her hip with one hand while he spanked with the other. The slaps came fast and furious and she began to sob, but suddenly she felt warmth and wetness flow into her genitals. Her sex-lips swelled and she lifted her buttocks to meet the caress of his hand. He shifted so he could rub himself against her flesh while he spanked her, lifting his cock from its leather pouch.

She was aware of softness, of firm flesh pushing at her, and the sharp sting of his hand on her tingling flesh. She wanted the gaping purse of her pussy pounded by his hand, hammered by his cock. One leather glove covered her mouth and the other pressed between her legs. She cried out and the sound of her climax was muffled in the gauntlet. She was barely aware of his throbbing penis pressed between her buttocks, but she felt the wet stream of his eruptions run down her thighs.

On the four-poster bed, Alphonso was untying Salome and, after she had rubbed life back into her wrists, she kissed the giant on the mouth and slapped him on the buttocks.

When Floradora went back to her caravan, Salome went with her, holding her arm tight. They giggled like schoolgirls in the dark and breathed out white breath into the cold night air.

'Did you enjoy that, Floradora?'

'Yes, I did,' she said quietly, 'and did you?'

'Oh, yes, I enjoy a good seeing to now and then, especially by Alphonso, though you know he not only loves women, don't you?'

'What do you mean?' said the girl.

'He does it with men, too, usually. Only when Lorenzo tells him will he fuck women.'

'Oh, I see,' said Floradora, though she did not.

'I want to cuddle you. Throw out Anastasia!' said Salome, kissing the girl's ear as they drew close to her caravan.

'I can't do that,' said Floradora.

'Very well then, good night, little goose,' she said, and kissed her on the lips.

Floradora melted under the older woman's caress, and said, 'Let me come back with you.'

'All right, if you like,' she said, making Floradora feel that it had been her idea, not Salome's.

They turned away from Floradora and Anastasia's caravan and stumbled through the dark to Salome's home on wheels. Inside, there was a faint smell of raw meat. Salome threw the dead mice into the snake jars and washed her hands.

'Come to me, my little darling,' she crooned to Floradora, as if she were one of her snakes. She almost sang her caresses into the girl's ears as she lifted her skirt up to her waist and drew her head down to kiss Floradora's jutting hip bone. Floradora held the dark head to her belly and stroked her hair. She loved the way Salome took her time licking and kissing her belly, stroking the silky skin, pressing and touching her bottom, her inner thighs. She moaned imploringly as Salome's long tongue slithered down the naked slit to her labia. She opened her thighs imperceptibly. Salome pushed the girl back on to the edge of the narrow bed and knelt between her legs.

She wet her fingers and pressed them under Floradora's body, in the gap between anus and vagina – that tender flesh which is so sensitive. She moved them back and forth, stroking first her anus then her pussy, slipping a finger in, dipping it in the young-girl honey. She lifted a wet finger to Floradora's mouth for her to taste herself. Floradora was in a haze of desire. Her legs were open wide; she wanted something inside her, filling her empty purse. The snake charmer saw the girl shiver with cold, and rose, urging her into the bed to keep warm. Floradora did as she was bid, still wearing her white lace dress.

When Salome drew back the blankets to get in with Floradora, the girl saw she was holding something. Salome blew out the candle and snuggled down next to Floradora. She put the thing she was holding up against the girl's belly and pressed it between her legs. It felt like a snake, a thick silky snake, its skin smooth and firm, a solid rod of cool leather. Salome drew it back and forth across Floradora's genitals and the girl gasped at the exceedingly pleasant sensations she experienced. Salome withdrew a hand from the bed to lift a phial of scented oil from the shelf. She tipped the oil on to the girl's belly and massaged it into her pubic mound and between her legs. Then the rod slid into her, slowly, slyly, a slithering of leather. Floradora could not believe the wonderful feeling the rod imparted. Her whole body felt full, whole, made complete by the insertion of the snakelike object. She felt her internal muscles gather round it, press it from all sides.

Suddenly there was an intense, sharp sensation. Salome hushed her with a soothing, gentle kiss.

'Do not worry, Floradora, darling, that is just your maidenhead. It must be broken, so that you can take the penis into your depths.'

Floradora relaxed, trusting the experienced woman's firm touch. The dildo hit the top of her channel, pummelling her, making her gasp with excitement. She felt as if she would wet herself if she just let go, relaxed into the sensations, and did not hold anything back. She suddenly went with the feeling, and it was as if she had launched herself from a rooftop and wings had spread and she was flying. It was the most wonderful feeling she had ever had.

Chapter Nine
Sibling Affection

*T*he trapeze artistes had finished their act and descended the rope to the sawdust ring. They were doing the triple somersault every night now, and were quite confident that they could do it without a safety net. When the show was over Rosalita went alone to see the ringmaster to suggest the new innovation. The caravan was full of his foul-smelling cigarillo smoke. She coughed and flapped her hands.

'You think you can do the *triple salto mortal* without a net?' He was incredulous.

'Yes, but we want more money, for the danger,' she said.

'Well, I could give you a little more, I suppose,' he said as he twirled his whiskers, thinking of the poster declaration of the daring and dangerous act.

'No, if we do it, it will draw many more people. We want double our usual wage,' she said, determinedly.

'Double! Are you mad?'

'Double, or we leave and take our act elsewhere,' said the gypsy girl.

'Elsewhere? Where, elsewhere?' he sneered.

'That is not your business,' she said haughtily.

'Let me think about it,' he said, angry to be talked to in this way.

'Tomorrow. We want a decision tomorrow.' Rosalita turned her straight little back on the ringmaster and left his caravan.

Rosalita had not told her brother that she would threaten to leave Lorenzo's circus if he did not pay them double. She had in fact heard of a bigger travelling circus that was at the moment in Cadiz, on the Spanish mainland. It would not be difficult for them to get to Arrecife and from there take a ship to Cadiz. She had it all worked out. She was more ambitious than her young brother, and had more on her mind than where the next kiss would come from. Rosalita had her brother's well-being at heart, but she did not want him to follow his heart's desire and chase after the lion-tamer's daughter. She had seen him watching the blonde's bouncing breasts; seen his eyes gleam and his tongue slide over his lips as he watched her ride Thunderhead.

She got back to the caravan she shared with her brother and went in. He was lying on the bed, naked, his belly pressed to the rough blanket, his triangular back gleaming in the candlelight.

'I am sore tonight,' he said, after greeting her. 'I ache in every limb and muscle.'

'Let me massage you with oil,' said the kindly Rosalita.

'Mm, please, Rosalita, that would be wonderful.'

She discarded her cloak and removed her trapeze costume. She washed hurriedly and put on a bright Japanese silk kimono over her nakedness. She looked in a drawer for the oils they used on their hard-worked muscles. The essential oils were scented like the wild flowers they came from, and the small room was filled with the perfume of violets, dog rose, and thyme.

Rosario stretched himself on the bed, his arms beside him, his legs a little apart. He closed his eyes as his sister's hands began to work their magic on his muscles. She knelt astride him and, pouring the oil on to her hands first, pressed firmly in rhythmic strokes along either side of his spine. She worked at his shoulders and neck until he moaned in appreciation. She moved her

73

hands down towards his hips and buttocks. He had the most delightful bottom, she thought, slapping it playfully. It bounced, the flesh so young and firm.

'Ouch!' he said, and she giggled.

She continued the massage, her strong hands finding his aches and pains and rubbing away the tight knots that developed from their strenuous activities. His thighs were pummelled and stroked, and he opened them instinctively at her touch. She pressed sly fingers to his inner thighs and imperceptibly, tenderly, touched his squashed balls, which were brown, hairless, and in the trap of his upper legs.

She felt him flinch slightly at her initial caress. He stretched out his arms and opened his legs a little more. Her fingers, silky with the oil, stroked his scrotum, and slipped down the crack in his buttocks, opening him. Her lips caressed his backside; her tongue licked between his cheeks. Her fingers did not stop the gentle caress, the insidious assault. She knew that he was used to her caresses, and welcomed them. He would know nothing about his own sexual nature if it had not been for her tuition. She had learnt what pleased him. Now, she was determined to show him how to please her.

She had, up until now, steered clear of complete sexual connection with him, knowing it to be wrong, forbidden, but their recent activities under the wicked influence of the ringmaster had left her sexually unsatisfied, and she needed release from her own tensions. Perhaps she could keep him from the arms of the lion-tamer's daughter if she let him make love to her. Taboos fell away from her mind as she felt the stirring of his cock under her hand. He was a very charming and beautiful boy. She could just play with him a little. He turned over slowly and she shifted a little, her kimono opening to his gaze. Her small, firm breasts bobbed out and her belly pouted at him. Her legs were open. Her shaved pubic area was smooth and the slit, which went from her Mount of Venus to her vagina, was dark and inviting. He touched her. She shivered. He stroked her slit and belly. His cock,

74

caught under her bottom, was stiff. She felt it rise against her flesh. She pretended to carry on with the massage, rubbing more oil into her little hands and rubbing his chest and belly. She loved his flat stomach. It was hairless and the colour of dark honey. Her hands made poetry on his flesh. He sighed and shifted so his cock leapt up between them. It looked like it came from her loins, and she moved slowly up and down, watching the growing, thickening rod of dark flesh sticking up from between her legs. She pressed herself on to him, on to the base of his root, rubbing him. The cock rubbed her clitoris in a most delightful way. She could not stop the rhythmic swaying, the caressing of his cock with her cunt. She held the cock between her fingers, squeezing firmly. He moved up and down also.

He pressed his fingers on top of hers, aiding her caress. She led him to touch her labia, stroke the swollen flesh, and slip into her with his oily fingers. She closed her eyes and did not know if it was his fingers or his cock that drew the passion from her loins. Was he inside her, or simply pressing on the outside of her sex parts? She thrust against his touch, desperate for the final climax. She writhed on his hands and cock and pressed his balls with her plump little buttocks. Her moans and breaths came faster and she relaxed into her release, shouting out. He yelled at last as his sperm spewed over her belly and thighs and she fell on to him, exhausted and happy.

'You were very good, Rosario. You will be a great lover one day, little brother.' She smiled her thanks and approval, her usually hard mouth soft and full.

They were not the only performers enjoying after-show relaxation. La Roux was strapped to the target in the big top. Lorenzo, instead of the knives, had his cock drawn out of its sheath, and aimed at the girl's breasts. She was upside down and spread out, naked. Her face was red. He stood close to her, his cock pressed between her round breasts, his hands holding them close to it. Then he pressed his erection between her red lips.

'Suck me,' he ordered. The staring eyes of the redhead showed no emotion. She sucked. His rubber cloak was wrapped around him and he moved the circular target slightly so as to place her mouth in the best position for his cock. He moaned and leant into her. Her hands and thighs and ankles were tied and her waist was held tight to the target by means of leather straps. He pulled out of her mouth, spun the target, and pushed his cock between her sex lips, which were surmounted by a little bush of natural red hair. His dark cock plunged beneath the ginger nest and into her pink purse. He tied a piece of rubber ribbon around her eyes and ears.

Her sensations were concentrated in her flesh. She could not hear his cries or see his evil eyes. She enjoyed only the pressure of his flesh on hers. Her body became all sex. He suddenly withdrew and she felt the spurt of his sperm over her breasts. She trembled with unsatisfied desire. A few minutes later she was untied by one of the *chamacos*, the dwarf.

'Ah, he is so cruel to you, my beauty. Won't you let me caress you? I am more virile than the ringmaster is – see!' And the dwarf showed her his enormous erection. La Roux smiled demurely and let him caress her quickly.

'Go, get on with you, you rascal. I need to sleep.' She did not want to hurt the dwarf's feelings and she knew he was a randy opportunist, taking advantage of a situation for his own purposes. She admired his erection, but did not like his foul breath and unwashed sweat. She wrapped herself in her red *bata* and walked out of the sawdust ring.

Floradora dreamed of a man in black. She was tied up and being whipped by him. She was naked and her sex parts were hugely swollen, like a baboon's bottom. The man's enormous cock, which was purple and brown and red, was pummelling her. It glowed like a torch and grew to fit her huge sex parts. She woke in a sweat and found her inner thighs wet with her juices. Anastasia was next to her, and she woke as Floradora cried out.

'What is it, darling?' Did you have a nightmare?'

'Sort of, I suppose it was, except that it has left me with a longing to love,' said Floradora.

'Well, I am here, darling, cuddle up to me,' said the dancing girl, sleepily.

'Will you hold me?' said Floradora.

'Of course,' said Anastasia, and held out her arms to the hot body of the lion-keeper's daughter.

Floradora thought how different the dancer felt to Salome. Her body was softer, plumper, and lazier. Her plump fingers were slow and soft. She stroked gently and languidly. Floradora was so aroused by her dream that she opened to her touch immediately and the girl's fingers slipped right into her juicy pouch. Floradora needed more inside her. She cried in frustration.

'What is it, darling?' said Anastasia.

'Have you anything bigger to go in me?' she begged.

'Wait,' said Anastasia, and the girl slipped out of bed and felt around in the dark.

'Here, will this do?' she giggled, and pressed a banana against Floradora's slit

'Yes, push it in me,' she begged.

Anastasia was excited too now and led Floradora's fingers to her open legs. Floradora readily complied with her desires and the two friends were entwined and writhing under the rough blanket.

Anastasia drew the long curved fruit in and out of Floradora's pussy. Soon Floradora cried out and clung to the girl.

'My turn for the fruit,' said Anastasia, and gave the sticky banana to Floradora to manipulate. The dancing girl eagerly took the yellow fruit into her sheath and clung to it with her internal muscles before releasing it. Floradora was immediately aroused again as she watched Anastasia's athletic thighs clutch the fruit. She put one end into herself and the other into Anastasia and they rocked together on it, pressing each other voluptuously. The pale dawn light bled through the small window with its ragged curtain held up by a ribbon on a hook. The two friends fell asleep at last, holding each other tight, the ripe banana squashed and limp between them.

Chapter Ten
An Invitation

*A*t the *finca* Señora Octavia Valera de Teguise fed her scrawny chickens copious sprays of grain. They ran to her, frantically pecking at the corn. The brightly coloured fancy cockerel and his brood of feathery-footed hens were a small consolation in her widowhood. She had enjoyed a life of luxury, with fine wines, exotic food, and plenty of amusing company when her husband had lived. Now, alone in the farmhouse, apart from her bereaved son and a servant or two, she had few pleasures. She had not wanted to leave the circus when they did, before the end of the show, but her son had been so agitated by the girl's equestrian performance that he had insisted they go.

'Why leave?' she had asked him, as they mounted the horse-drawn carriage with its canvas hood.

'I have seen enough,' he said, mysteriously, and she knew better than to press him.

She thought of his moods now, as she fed the cheerful, uncomplicated birds. She understood his misery and grief about his fiancée's awful accident and death. He had felt that it had been his fault. It was a new horse she had been riding that fateful day. A horse that he had broken and trained. But the horse had been scared by a lizard or something at the edge of the track and had reared, throwing her into the deep crevice of the fiercely sharp and ragged volcanic rock. She had been cut to pieces and died horribly of poisoned blood a week after the accident. Antonio had not been with his fiancée when it happened and they had found her, badly cut, unconscious, after the horse had returned to the *finca* alone. The land was treacherous in that vicinity, wild and rocky, with deep volcanic caverns and fissures. Nothing grew except the beautiful scrubby lichens of yellow and gold, grey and white, like alien flowers on a moonscape. He had worn black ever since, and had sold most of his wonderful horses.

His mother had her own grieving still to do, as she had loved her wild husband more than life, but she carried on living for the sake of her unhappy son. She sighed and clucked her tongue at the chickens, smiling at their strutting prettiness. She gathered the brown eggs from the straw of their bedding and took them back to the kitchen in her apron.

'Mother, I am going into Teguise, can I get you anything?'

'Really, are you, Antonio?'

'Yes, Mother, alone, on my horse.' He smiled at her uncertainly.

'That's good, my son, go. No, no, thank you, I need nothing.' She smiled reassuringly at him. To ride his horse to Teguise! It was a breakthrough. 'I am going to make a tortilla,' she said. 'Don't you want some first?'

'No, Mother, I will have something there. It is market day.'

'Oh yes, of course it is. I never know what day it is, these days, they are all the same to me.' She patted him on the arm and he kissed her cheek and left.

Antonio Valera saddled his stallion and mounted. The horse nickered, pleased to be ridden after such a long time, and excited and frisky.

'Come on, boy, we are going to see a very beautiful

young woman,' he said to his horse, pulling his ear caressingly. And they rode off into the cool bright day.

The clouds skittered across the bright blue sky and eagles soared. The dirt track under the horse's hooves was dry from weeks of no rain. They kept to the main track and, after a hard canter and a steady trot, soon came in sight of the white town with its red roofs. Circo Lorenzo had been there for two weeks and small tents had been erected here and there. Fires burned, cooking pots were kept hot on charcoal, and washing lines had been attached to adjacent caravans, joining them together in a display of flaglike brilliant clothes in gold and emerald, silver and scarlet, like a gypsy encampment. Dogs ran free and barked at the caged lions. Hannibal, their trainer, was washing down the elephants. He wielded a long-handled stiff broom and scrubbed their backs with warm water. The matriarch trumpeted happily.

Antonio dismounted and led his horse through the noisy, malodorous scene, marvelling at the clowns practising their tumbling. He stopped and asked one of them, a handsome black man, where he could find Floradora, the lion-tamer's daughter.

'Over there.' Isambard pointed to a blue-painted caravan in the middle of the encampment. He gazed suspiciously after the man with the fine horse. He had seen him before, in the audience, in the front row, with a fine old lady. He had seen him leave suddenly, after Floradora's equestrian performance a few days before. Yes, he had noticed the man's hot eyes on his Floradora. He gave his excuses to the other clowns and followed the gentleman to Floradora's caravan.

Antonio knocked at the door and there was no answer. Anastasia suddenly appeared, looking flustered and hot, tugging her *bata* over her shoulders yet showing that she was naked underneath.

'What do you want?' she said, staring rudely at the good-looking stranger.

'I am looking for Floradora, the lion-tamer's daughter,'

he said, quietly, looking away from her naked breasts which fell out of her cloak.

'Oh, you have just missed her. She has gone to the market today.'

'*Muches Gracias, señorita*.' He bowed and clicked his high-heeled riding boots.

Anastasia raised her eyebrows in amazement at the stranger's proud demeanour and his gentlemanly manners. She knew he must be the *señor* that Floradora had enthused about. However, she knew that Floradora had gone with Rosario to the market that day, unbeknown to Rosalita, who would have been furious. Anastasia gazed lustfully after the gentleman before returning to her lover.

Rosalita was busy cleaning the caravan, which was a task she could only tackle on the day of so-called rest. She was glad to be rid of Rosario, who, she thought, had gone to Teguise with some *chamaco* friends. She did not want him under her feet.

The wide clean streets of Teguise rang with the tinkers' cries: 'Leather belts and bags, the best leather in the world,' sang the Moroccan traders. Drums and hats, ribbons and harnesses, cooking pots and utensils changed hands. The air was suffused with the scent of freshly dug potatoes, almonds just gathered, saffron and aromatic spices, herbs such as thyme and sage, and the perspiration of Spanish gypsies from Andalucia wearing red and purple garments like bold banners. Turbans and veils, lace mantillas and sombreros sat on proud heads. The populace bustled and shoved, and begged and persuaded in honeyed tones and raucous cries. Everyone loved the market. Antique guitars were twanged by happy boys, and mothers bought castanets and ribbons of silk in bright yellow, red, green and purple for their little girls. Frilly dresses spotted in red and yellow, blue and pink, hung from rails, their cut indicating the fluid shape of flamenco dancers.

Floradora hung on the strong arm of Rosario, who

looked splendid in yellow chamois breeches and a black shirt, his throat brown and hairless at the open neck.

When he had asked her to go to the market with him she had said no at first, then, with his cajoling whispers and promise of a silk ribbon, she had capitulated to his youthful charm. They sat in the shade of an old olive tree and drank a glass of the local sweet brown wine. Shrimps were served with the drink, and a plate of *papas* – the salted tiny potato of the island. Floradora wore her white dress, her birthday frock, with a petticoat of cotton underneath so it was modest and becoming. Her blonde hair was covered in a straw hat, very ladylike, and she took it off to tie the promised blue ribbon round its brim. She looked up just as she finished tying it and saw, across the crowded little square, Antonio Valera de Teguise talking to a stooped old man. He was dressed in black, his sombrero like an umbrella shading his face from the sun. He looked kind and his sad smile was directed only at the old man. He suddenly looked up as if feeling her gaze on him and their eyes met. To Antonio and Floradora the crowded square was empty except for the two of them. He excused himself and headed towards the two young circus performers.

Rosario had drunk several glasses of the powerful wine and he was flushed and perspiring. He had brought Floradora here on a whim. Asked her in a sudden surge of youthful confidence. He had flashed his white teeth at her, smiled and twirled a little pirouette at her. He showed off his muscular arms in his rolled-up sleeves, lifted her in his arms and literally carried her through the crowds at one point to impress her with his strength. She was amused and flattered at the handsome gypsy's attention and forgave him his recent awkward attempts at love-making in the daisy field.

She found herself at a café table in Teguise with the handsomest youth in the circus, and approaching her was the most interesting and desirable man she had ever met.

'*Señorita, señor.*' The man stood, his sombrero in one hand, and bowed to Floradora.

'Oh,' she said, 'Señor Valera. This is my friend, the aerialist, the famous Rosario.'

Rosario did not stand, as he should have to a gentleman, but leant back so that his bentwood chair was on two legs. He looked hard at the man. He lifted his glass of wine and said, 'Salut!'

'Your health, *señor.*' Antonio kept his head bent and then looked into Floradora's eyes with a lingering, smouldering gaze. 'I have come to ask you to my *casa* for dinner tomorrow, *señorita*. Will you come?'

'We work tomorrow, *señor,* and then we are moving on to Arrecife for a week, before heading for mainland Spain,' she replied.

'You are leaving Teguise so soon?' He looked shocked.

'Yes!' She laughed. 'We have been here for ages and have run out of audiences.'

'Then come tonight,' he said, ignoring the obviously put-out Rosario, who was fuming at the audacity of the well-dressed stranger.

'Tonight?' She laughed again.

'My mother will be there to chaperone you, *señorita.*'

'But . . .'

'I will fetch you in my carriage at six o'clock. Please.'

'Very well!' She smiled flirtatiously at him but he did not smile.

'Six, at the circus ground,' he reiterated.

'Yes,' she said, frightened at her decision.

Antonio bowed, clicked his heels, and turned away. He was soon lost in the crowds.

'Well, what about that!' said the trapeze artiste. 'Who is he, anyway?'

He is Señor Antonio Valera de Teguise; that is all I know about him,' she answered, shrugging her shoulders.

'He is a bit old for you, isn't he?' The boy bristled, jealous of the man's sophistication and Floradora's obvious interest in him.

'Oh, I don't know. He is younger than Lorenzo. I expect he is about thirty-two or three.'

'Old enough to be your father,' said the youth, and spat on the cobbles.

'Oh, Rosario, don't be silly. What harm can it do to have dinner with a gentleman? Anyway, I will do it. Come on, let's get back, I have to find something else to wear.'

'Don't you love me, Floradora?' said the unhappy youth.

'I don't know, Rosario, if I love you like that. I think I love you like a brother.'

'Huh! If you only knew,' he said as he followed her through the crowds.

Floradora opened the door of the wardrobe caravan. Olympia sat on the floor, surrounded by yards of cotton net and bright satins, with a pair of scissors and needle and thread in her large, capable hands.

'Hello, little chicken,' said Olympia, smiling at the sight of the flushed Floradora.

'Oh, Olympia, you must help me!' exclaimed the girl.

'What's up?'

'I need a stunning dress for tonight, something special.'

'And what is wrong with the white lace?'

'He saw me in it today. I can't possibly wear it tonight.'

'Who is this honoured lover, dearie?'

'Oh, he is not a lover, Olympia, he is a gentleman who has asked me to dinner. The gentleman I told you about.'

'Goodness me, that gentleman, is it? Well, what can we find?' said the wardrobe mistress, throwing bales of cloth into the air and watching as the misty nets floated down in clouds around them.

They held cloth up to Floradora's chin and draped it around her waist – grey satin, blue cotton, yellow leather. In the end they decided on navy-blue velvet embroidered with tiny white flowers. Floradora watched as Olympia speedily cut and sewed the lengths together.

She told the girl to search for a suitable petticoat to go underneath the full-length skirt and Floradora chose from a rail of frilly garments a scarlet froufrou of layered net. The wardrobe mistress sent her to her caravan to bathe and said the costume would be ready in an hour.

Floradora kissed the transvestite and ran back to her caravan. She needed to organise a bath. Isambard was hanging around looking worried.

'There you are, little dove,' he said. 'There has been a stranger here looking for you.'

'A handsome stranger?' She laughed at him and gave the astonished man a kiss.

'Well, a local gentleman, I would guess, very rich-looking, on a spotted horse.'

'Yes, I know, Isambard. Will you fill the bathtub with hot water for me?' She ran inside, not even waiting for his reply. She could depend on Isambard to do whatever she wanted.

The black clown, divested of his clown costume and looking very much like one of the *chamacos* – strong, big-boned, and tough – sighed and did as she bid. He carried large enamel jugs of hot water from the cauldron to the bathtub, which was in a separate tent close by. After fifty trips with the ewer he had filled the tub sufficiently for his Floradora to have a deep soak, and he banged on her door. She swept past him in her *bata* with a large towel and a bag of soap, waved him a brief salute, and went to the bath tent. There, she scrubbed her feet, her knees, her elbows, her fingernails; she smoothed her skin all over with a large loofah and a pumice stone. She washed her hair and piled it high under a small turban of a towel, wrapped herself in the large towel and left the tent, a whirlwind of steam following her. There was a queue of dancers waiting outside to use her hot water.

'Lend us your soap, Floradora,' begged Gina, and La Roux said, 'Yes, and me, please,' and the lion-tamer's daughter threw her soap bag to the line of girls.

When she entered her caravan, there on the bed was the navy-blue two-piece costume. The skirt was wide, flared from a tight, broad waistband and long enough to reach her ankles. The little jacket was cut to fit her like a glove, and flared from the waist to just below her hips. The embroidery was of small white flowers and the pattern was sprinkled over the garments like stars in the velvet night.

'Oh, it's lovely,' said Floradora to herself. She plunged into the skirt, tying it at the waist. She pulled on the scarlet net petticoat to make it stand out. The little jacket fitted her perfectly and was cut low at the bust to show the rise of her breasts. She twirled in the narrow aisle between the bed and the mirror, admiring herself. She brushed out her hair and put a red comb in it, high on her temple, holding the wet blonde mass back from her face. She examined her pale face in the mirror. Should she use lip colour? No, she bit her lips to make them red. There, that was good enough. Shoes! Olympia, bless her heart, had thought of shoes and there under the bed were a pair of red leather boots with little heels. She slipped them on. Should she wear stockings? Yes. She found her black stockings she had worn to her father's funeral and was suddenly sad. She removed her boots, put on the stockings, and held them up with elastic bands above the knees. Now the boots again. She raised her skirt with both hands, exposing the flame-red petticoat and black stockings with the delicate, soft-leather red boots which went up to her calves. Oh yes, she was perfect! Or so the black clown thought as he peered through her open curtain.

She was ready for whatever the evening would bring.

Chapter Eleven
True Love

*A*ntonio had had to canter practically all the way back home, tell his mother he had invited the girl, listen to her complaints and exclamations: 'What shall we eat? We can't eat fowl, they need hanging for a day or two, and what about my hair and my dress? Why have you invited her? Are you insane?' and so on until she calmed down and had come to terms with the sudden dinner party. Then he had to groom his tired horse, water and feed it, get the carriage ready, harness the two carriage horses and wash and dress himself.

At six o'clock precisely Antonio knocked on the door of Floradora's caravan.

She did not want him to see the squalor of her living conditions and so she opened the door to him and stepped out into the evening.

He could not believe it was the same girl. She looked stunningly beautiful and very ladylike in the dark, velvet fitted jacket and full long skirt. She lifted her hem and he saw the brilliant red petticoat and her red boots. His eyes were drawn to her bosom, gleaming pearl-like above the *décolleté* neckline. He took her hand, bowed, and handed her down the three steps as if she were a grand lady. She smiled cheekily at him and said, 'Do you like my dress? I had it made this afternoon.'

'I think you would be beautiful even in a sack,' he said, huskily.

'You are too kind,' she said.

'Before we go to my *finca*, may I see your horses, if it is not too much trouble, *señorita*?'

'My horses? Of course, if you wish. Follow me.' And Floradora picked up her skirts, making her petticoat swish deliciously against her stockinged legs, and led him through the circus encampment to the stables.

'They are all very good animals,' he said, running his eyes over each of the mares before admiring the stallion, Thunderhead.

'Yes, my father had a good eye for a fine horse. He would have been a breeder, if he hadn't got into circus life.'

'I was once a horse breeder,' said Antonio, somewhat sadly.

'You are no longer?'

'No, no longer. Come, *señorita*, let me take you home to meet my mother.'

Floradora was suddenly nervous of this adventure she had entered into. His mother! She would not know how to behave. She remembered the fierce, proud woman who had sat next to Antonio in the big top. She was bound to make a fool of herself with the *señora*.

She allowed him to help her up into the carriage, though she could easily have climbed up on her own. She enjoyed the strong arms lifting her, the big hands circling her waist. The hood was down, as the evening was mild and windless. The evening star glowed in the west in a sky the same colour as her costume. Gradually other twinkling stars appeared and Antonio looked at her and thought she was like a small scrap of sky that had fallen into his carriage. The horses trotted through the darkening valleys. Glow worms flickered like tiny candles. Fig-tree ghosts loomed up at them from the fields either side of the track.

Floradora was so excited she kept quiet in case she said something stupid. He had become silent too. They travelled on in a companionable silence and she was aware of his strong, big shape next to her on the padded wooden seat. He crooned and clicked his tongue at the horses and urged them on through the gathering dusk. It suddenly occurred to Floradora that she would have to return to the circus later that night. The drive back in complete darkness would be hazardous for the horses. However, she kept quiet, not wanting to disturb or spoil the atmosphere of peace and calm that had come over her. Not since before her father had died had she felt so safe and unafraid.

The dark square shape of the *finca* buildings was lit at two windows. Antonio stopped at the big, studded door and got down to take her arm as she stepped out of the carriage. A manservant appeared out of the dark and took the horses and carriage away and Antonio opened the door for her. She walked in, her skirt sweeping the stone-flag floor. The lobby led into the kitchen and there they found the cook – a robust dark-skinned woman smiling and stirring a large pot.

Was this his mother? she wondered, not recognising the woman.

'This is my mother's best friend, our cook, Carmen Maria,' he said to Floradora.

They went through a long passageway and into a large room she had not seen before. There was a large stone fireplace and in it a wood fire was blazing. Moroccan rugs in reds and yellows covered the tiled floor. The room felt warm and welcoming in spite of dark, large pieces of heavy furniture, which cluttered the space.

The *señora* sat in a large high-backed rattan chair, close to the fire, her hands busy with a tapestry. She was dressed in black silk and her hair was pinned low on her neck, in a tight bun, with a turtleshell comb holding it. She looked up as Antonio entered, and smiled.

'Do not get up, Mother, we are here at last. This is

Floradora de Valencia. Floradora, this is my mother, Señora Valera de Teguise.'

Floradora gave a light curtsy to the old woman who was regarding her curiously.

'Give me your hand, girl,' commanded the matriarch, and Floradora held out her hand.

'Yes, good, strong hands, practical hands.' She patted Floradora's rather rough-skinned hand and smiled at her. The smile transformed her severe face and the girl could see that she had been a very beautiful woman. 'I saw you the other night; you are a fine horsewoman,' said Antonio's mother, and went back to her sewing.

'Mother, will you have a drink? *Señorita?*' Antonio went to the cut-glass decanter and poured them all a draught of *fino*.

The glasses were like melting ice: smooth, thick shapes which held the heavy golden liquid. He held his glass up to the oil lamp and it shone red-gold like Floradora's lions' eyes.

Floradora took in her rich surroundings with sparkling eyes. She threw back the *fino* quickly and her cheeks were flushed.

'Sit by me, child, and tell me about yourself,' said the *señora*, patting the low footstool.

Floradora did as she was bid, feeling an immediate affinity with the old woman and wanting her approbation and approval.

'What do you want to know, *señora*?'

'Well, how long have you been with the circus?'

'Circo Lorenzo? For all of my life. Eighteen years.'

'Are you Mexican?' the older woman asked, raising her eyebrows.

'No, *señora*, my father is – was – from Argentina and my mother was from Brazil. I was born *en gira*, on tour in the Americas. I am Argentinian, I suppose.'

'Hence the horsemanship.' The *señora* nodded to her son, who had sat in another chair, away from the fire, quietly watching the two women.

'Oh, we always had horses. I could ride when I was

two. I had my own horse then.' Floradora laughed at the memory. 'He was called Button, like my father called me – Little Button. I rode him in the ring.'

'And what happened to your mother?'

At that moment the cook appeared in the doorway and announced that dinner was ready. The three arose and the *señora* led the way through to the dining room, which was lit with candles. Books and pictures filled the walls and a log fire blazed.

'There, child, sit between us, there is no formality here at Finca de Valera.'

The meal was good and hearty: a rabbit stew with fresh vegetables from the garden and dark, heavy bread. Floradora tucked in as if she had not eaten for days.

'Tell me about your mother,' urged the *señora*.

'She was very beautiful, or so I was told. I have a photograph of her. She died when I was born.'

Señora Valera de Teguise had never had a daughter. Her childbearing days had finished with Antonio, for health reasons. She had had two stillborn babies, both boys, before she gave birth to Antonio and she had been ill for months after he came into the world. She patted Floradora's hand.

'What a shame, child, that you never had a mother!'

'Oh, my father was everything to me. I did not know what I was missing, I suppose. My childhood was very happy, *señora*, do not worry for me.' But suddenly the tears came, for her lost father, her smiling, cheerful father, who *had* been everything to her.

'Oh, you poor child, now I have upset you. Antonio, fetch a large handkerchief from my room, quick, my son.'

Antonio rose and hurried off to do as his mother asked. He felt a stab in his heart as he saw the tears fall, and for once the feeling of sorrow was not for him, but for another – for the lion-tamer's daughter. He gave her the large white handkerchief and she blew her nose loudly and wiped the streaks of tears from her face. He poured her more wine and she drank it, hiccuping a little in the aftermath of emotion.

They ate *flan*, crème caramel, the *señora*'s speciality, and withdrew to the sitting room for a glass of brandy.

Floradora felt warm all over, but she could not remove her fitted jacket as she wore nothing under it. Her neck and bosom were pink and she used a white-feathered fan to cool herself.

'Tell me about your horses, *señor*,' she said.

'My horses? I got rid of them. There was an accident, a fatal accident, concerning the woman who was to have been my wife, and I could not bear to see the horses after that.'

'She fell while riding one of your horses?'

'Yes, she fell.'

'I see. But how can you bear not to have your horses? I would give up anything rather than my horses,' she said.

'I still have my own horse, which I need to get me here and there, and the two carriage horses.'

'I saw your horse. It is a Lippizaner, isn't it?'

'Yes, that is what I bred, Lippizaners.'

'They make wonderful circus horses, you know,' Floradora enthused. 'My father told me he had seen the best in Lippiza, near Trieste. He loved them. But, once we started buying Arabs, we continued with them. They are sturdy and have level action and canter, just right for the liberty and ballerina acts. They can jump without breaking tempo and have broad backs.' The girl came to life when she talked of her horses; her features were animated and she smiled happily.

Antonio leant forward in his chair and the two began to talk, unhampered by shyness. Antonio's mother looked on, approvingly, and smiled.

'I must go home,' said the girl at last, her eyes shining and her glossy hair gleaming in the firelight.

'I will take you,' said Antonio, and he got up.

'No, she cannot leave. How will you drive in the dark? And listen, the wind has risen. Why don't you stay the night, my dear, and Antonio will return you early in the morning?' The matriarch was determined.

'Well, I suppose Isambard will look after my animals,' Floradora said. 'But I have nothing with me.'

'I will take care of that,' said the *señora* and, rising, she went upstairs to find a nightgown and towel. 'Antonio, you will give her your bed, the sheets were changed this morning, and you can sleep on the day bed.'

'Oh, I couldn't put you out,' said Floradora.

'Nonsense, I often sleep there,' he said.

Floradora tucked the cool, white cotton sheets around her. She felt very strange in a real bed, with a sprung mattress and a feather pillow. It was wonderful, and Antonio's room was so big and had shelves filled with books. There was a chest of drawers and on it several silver-framed photographs of a very pretty young woman – his dead fiancée, she supposed. Floradora had a carafe of water next to her bed and she lay listening to the howling wind blowing in through the open window.

Would he come to her in the night? Did he think her beautiful? He had made no move, no effort to seduce her. Did he think her too young, too simple? She was a mere circus girl, how could she hope to win his heart? She fell asleep, her heart fluttering in happiness, but aware that she would soon have to say goodbye to the handsome horseman.

He lay on the narrow, hard day bed, tossing and turning, thinking of Floradora. He had only just met her, but he wanted her. He needed her strong little arms round him, her tinkling laughter in his ears. He thought of the swell of her breasts, like twin moons rising from the midnight-blue velvet. His cock rose and he stroked it. He wondered if she was a virgin. What about the callow youth he had seen her with at Teguise? Had she slept with him? He grew cold at the thought. He must have her. His cock ached and he slowly massaged it to release the tensions that would keep sleep away. He realised that he loved this circus performer. She had ignited the flame of enthusiasm for life in him – a feeling of positivity and optimism that he had not enjoyed since before his fiancée had died.

As he rubbed his large organ he thought of Floradora in his bed – that slight form in the huge bed – and he desperately wanted her, but he would never abuse her trust and his mother's hospitality. She would remain unviolated while she was a guest in his house. He stroked his plump balls and thought of Floradora's red boots and the rustling petticoat. He imagined putting his hands up inside her skirt, raising it over her thighs, and seeing the pink mound that had been visible in her equestrian costume. That was why he had had to leave the circus performance. His erection had hurt so much at the sight of her round buttocks in the tight costume, the spangled pubis, the rise of her pudenda, the defined split of the peach.

He reached for a silk kerchief and wrapped it round his cock. It became her silky sheath, clasping him tight. He thought of his hands under her skirt, feeling between her slender thighs, and white spume spurted into the silk.

Chapter Twelve
A Proposal of Marriage

Came the dawn, and Floradora awoke to the sound of the *señora*'s cockerel crowing and a feeling of exhilaration. Never had the pink sun shone so cheerfully. Never had the morning mists drifted so prettily and woven such thoughts in her mind. She had never had a real window to look out of before. The vista was of pink mountains and mauve skies. Turquoise shrubs and pink-gold waves of rocks shimmered in first light.

Her heart felt as light as a skylark. She stepped down from the large white bed and went to the window, put her head out, and breathed in the cool, herb-perfumed air.

The manservant knocked at her door and told her there was a bath waiting for her if she wanted it. She did. She luxuriated in the deep hot water. Her second bath in two days! She examined her perfect toes and her slender legs, admired herself in the full-length mirror, which she had to wipe with the towel to remove the condensation.

Breakfast was dark bread and tortilla and strong Arabic coffee, served in tiny cups with a glass of water. Antonio was there, but his mother was still in bed.

'She is tired after last night's excitement. She wishes you well and says goodbye,' said Antonio.

'Oh, I see,' said Floradora, disappointed that the old woman was not there to say goodbye in person. At the same time, she was pleased to have Antonio to herself.

They ate in silence, he looking at her and about to speak but unable to, and she doing the same. They smiled, recognising each other's nervousness.

'I must go,' she said, reluctantly.

'Yes, of course.' He stood and went before her to the door, where the carriage was waiting.

'I am so sorry not to have said goodbye and thank you to your mother,' she said.

'Do not worry about it,' he said, handing her up into the carriage.

The journey back to the circus was quicker than the outward journey had been. They saw foxes and hawks hunting, rabbits and hares fleeing. The mists rolled through the mountain valleys and lifted, giving to a clear blue sky. The Lippizaners trotted, their spotted coats gleaming with perspiration; they snorted and snickered.

Antonio was aware of the lion-tamer's daughter next to him, her hip pressing on his, the scent of her clean skin in his nostrils. He took a hand from the reins and pressed it on hers. She shivered in the warmth of the morning. He took her hand in his and held it tight.

They reached a pass in the mountain where the light was pale and peach-coloured on the volcanic rocks. They waited while a goatherd passed over the track with his hundred goats, their bells clanging and tinkling, their long, thick tails dragging behind them, and their teats heavy with milk. He waved to Antonio and they exchanged greetings.

'Do you know everyone on the island?' she asked Antonio.

'No, only in our part,' he said.

'May I drive for a while?' she suddenly asked.

'Of course, if you wish,' he said.

He watched her every hand movement, her animated

expression as she drove the horses to Teguise. He smiled and said nothing. She was an excellent equestrian.

'This is such a beautiful island. You are very lucky to live here,' she said.

'Yes, I know I am. Could you ... could you think of living here?'

'Me? I have to go where the circus goes.'

'Of course,' he said, sinking in his seat. 'Floradora, would you stop a moment, please?' he asked.

She halted the horses and turned to look at Antonio. He took her in his arms and kissed her – a long, passionate kiss that had her gasping for breath.

'Floradora, I love you. I want you to be my wife.'

'But ... your wife? Me?' She could not believe what he was saying.

'You could bring all your horses. We could breed Arabs and Lippizaners. What do you think?' He was holding her close, and all she could think of was his lips on hers, the passion he had awoken in her.

'Oh, Antonio, to be your wife and live in a house with a bath? Yes! Yes! Yes!'

They held each other tight, laughing into each other's face, then kissing again.

'But, the circus?'

'Can you bear to leave it?'

'Yes, of course. But I must explain to Lorenzo, and say my goodbyes to my friends.'

'Yes, I understand. But I want you to come to me as soon as you can.' He wrapped his strong arms round her, squeezing the breath out of her.

She laughed, in a haze of disbelief and joy. 'Come on, let's tell the ringmaster straight away,' she said.

'Let me take the reins and you can hold *me*,' he said.

They changed places and she clung to him as he trotted the pretty horses along the dirt track.

'Shall I come with you to tell the ringmaster?' Antonio asked her.

'No, thank you, I can tell him myself,' she replied.

When they reached the circus, Isambard was cleaning

out the lions' cage. He said nothing but looked angrily at the horse breeder.

'Isambard, thank you,' said Floradora.

'I will come and collect you later today,' said Antonio, then kissed her and rode away.

'What did he mean?' said Isambard, closing the cage door behind him.

'I am leaving the circus, Isambard. I am going to be married.' She hugged the clown and kissed his cheek.

'To him?'

'Yes, to a gentleman. Would you believe it?' She was not at all put out at Isambard's obvious disbelief. 'And we will breed horses.'

'So, you will take the horses?'

'Of course, Isambard. Where is Lorenzo? I must go and tell him I won't be travelling to Arrecife with the circus.'

'He is organising the dismantling of the big top,' he said.

Floradora did not bother to change out of her smart clothes, but hurried through the dusty *terreno*. The enormous tent was collapsed on the ground and the *chamacos* were folding it neatly and coiling the guy ropes. The ringmaster was wearing a black suit and his wide-brimmed black sombrero.

'Señor Lorenzo, may I talk with you in private, please?' she asked.

'Not now, my dear, I am very busy, as you see.'

'But, *señor*, it is very important.' She felt like a naughty girl about to admit to some childish crime. Suddenly she was nervous of his reaction.

'Very well, tell me,' he barked.

'I am leaving the circus to be married. I want to go today.'

'Impossible. The posters say you are appearing in Arrecife tomorrow night, and you will be there.' He turned away from her.

'Oh, but I have made arrangements to go today.'

99

'You forget your debt to me, my dear,' he snarled at her.

'I have no debt. You said it was null and void.'

'I have changed my mind.'

'But you cannot do this. I will not stay.' She turned, sobbing, and ran back towards her caravan.

Lorenzo stared after her, anger in his eyes, and called to one of the *chamacos*.

Floradora wished she had asked Antonio to stay and talk to Lorenzo with her. But she was determined not to be cowed by him. She would be with Antonio.

Anastasia was at the caravan and she knew something was wrong when she saw Floradora's determined, tear-stained face.

'What is wrong, Floradora? Didn't your gentleman treat you right?'

'Oh, Anastasia,' Floradora flung herself into her friend's arms. 'He loves me and we are going to be married, but Lorenzo will not free me of my father's debt to him. He says I must go to Arrecife with the circus.'

'Married? Oh Floradora! What will you do?'

'I will leave today. I will not go to Arrecife.'

'But, can't you leave after Arrecife? We must have a goodbye party for you. You can't just leave.'

'No.' She was frightened. 'I think Lorenzo will not let me go.'

'What rubbish, darling, of course he will. He is not a monster.'

'Oh, Anastasia, I love Antonio so much.'

'Did he make love to you?'

'No, he did not – not really. He only kissed me. But he loves me, Anastasia, he loves me.'

'Come to Arrecife with us, Floradora, and we will all say goodbye to you properly there. Rosario and Rosalita are going to do the triple somersault without a net for the first time. You cannot miss that.'

'No, I cannot explain, but I think that Lorenzo will not

give me up. I do not trust him. I am going to get my horses ready.' She had changed her clothes as she was talking and now she wore her oldest breeches and shirt and riding boots. As she stepped out of her door she saw two tough, suspicious-looking *chamacos* waiting for her.

Two hours later, the circus was ready to move on. The caravans, pulled by horses over the rough terrain, stretched in a long trail. The elephants walked, the young one holding its mother's tail. The lion cage was covered at the front so the horses would not see the beasts. Floradora's horses were ridden or led by Isambard and another *chamaco*.

Isambard was concerned at Floradora's sudden illness. Salome had told Isambard that Floradora had become sick and she was looking after her. She said she thought that she had eaten something that did not agree with her.

Isambard was sullen with misery at the idea that his beloved girl would be leaving the circus. He trotted along on Thunderhead, his head full of Floradora, his heart aching.

Chapter Thirteen

Lorenzo the Mesmeriser

*F*loradora had been set upon by the *chamacos*, who had held knives to her throat. Then she was hidden under a *bata* and bundled off to Salome's caravan, where the snake charmer had received her, tied her to the bed and waited for her master, the ringmaster, to come to her as he had told her he would.

Floradora writhed in frustration under her bonds. Salome tried to soothe the girl. 'Don't be silly, little one, you will be set free soon, but you must wait for Lorenzo. He is our master, you know, and we must do as he says.'

'He is not my master. He is not! You fool, Salome, how can you love such a man?'

Salome smiled and stroked the helpless girl's breasts. Floradora's shirt had been torn in her fight with her captors, and her naked breasts were caught under the ropes that held her, and were red from her struggle against the bonds.

'Drink this, Floradora, it will calm you,' Salome said, putting the cup to her mouth.

Floradora drank the milky liquid, so thirsty was she, but after swallowing a little of the strange beverage she spat the rest out, suspicious of the contents. Was Salome trying to drug her?

However, she had swallowed enough of the sedative

to quieten her and, eventually, Floradora stopped struggling and slept.

The caravans moved slowly through the valley towards Arrecife. Lorenzo, after checking that everyone was there in the procession, went to Salome's caravan. He climbed on to the step and opened the door. He saw Salome sitting by the narrow bed, her hand delicately tracing Floradora's hips and waist. 'I am here,' he said. 'Let her be.'

Salome reluctantly rose and let him sit in her place.

Lorenzo slapped Floradora's face twice, sharply.

She opened her heavy-lidded eyes and stared unseeing at him.

'Good. You will stay with the circus and play at Arrecife, will you not, Floradora?' He swung the metal pendant that hung on a string round his neck. It flickered in front of her, swinging rhythmically, shining.

'You will do what I want you to do, Floradora, until I release you. You are my slave now, as Salome is, and Anastasia, and Gina, and Rosalita and La Roux. You will enjoy being my slave, believe me, my dear. It will be a delightful experience for you, and your new sisters will help you settle to your bondage, won't you, Salome?' His words were soft, caressing, dangerously quiet.

Salome nodded her head and smiled.

'Come, sit next to me, Salome, and help me make her comfortable.'

Floradora had closed her eyes again and seemed to be asleep. Salome slid into position on the edge of the bed and helped untie the girl's bonds.

'Look at the marks on her little breasts,' she whispered.

'Mm, delightful, charming. Kiss her, Salome.'

Salome leant over and caressed the bruised bosom with her lips. She held the breasts gently and kissed them both. Then her caresses became more passionate and she tugged at the girl's breeches and pulled them down to her ankles, not bothering to pull off her boots. She stroked the flat belly and slid her fingers down between the tightly closed legs. Floradora's pink pubic mound rose like a perfect hillock and split like a peach. The snake charmer licked the girl's stomach and thighs and insinuated her tongue into the dark channel.

Lorenzo had undone his breeches and had his half-erect tool in his hands. Salome removed her own clothes and bent over the sleeping girl, exposing her voluptuous buttocks to the ringmaster. He pressed his penis between her white globes and clasped her round the hips. Salome was concentrating on making love to Floradora, who was flowing into consciousness, aware of a licking and sucking at her private parts. She slipped back into a dream where Antonio made passionate love to her in a big white bed.

The ringmaster urged Salome to push her buttocks higher, and he slapped them with one hand, marking the firm full globes with red slashes. She yelped as he hit her, but pressed into his hand. His cock grew at her cries, and the marks darkened. He watched the semiconscious girl, whose blouse was torn and whose breasts glistened with perspiration and the red marks of her recent bondage, and whose breeches were caught around her ankles, breathe heavily and open her eyes. She stared in sleepy understanding at what was happening to her.

Floradora's sex-lips were parted by a clever tongue, which slipped inside her and twisted and churned. The lion-tamer's daughter breathed faster and raised her thighs, trying to open them to the sly caress. Her nipples were hard as buttons and she tried to caress them. But her hands did not do what she wanted them to do. They fell at her sides. She let the spasms flow through her body, bucking as the orgasm struck. Her mouth was dry and hot, her face and chest flushed, her neck exposed to the pair of seducers. Lorenzo seemed excited by the girl's throes and noisy release. He pushed hard between the full buttocks pressed up to him. Salome sobbed and Lorenzo cried out as his sperm rushed out of him and splashed over Salome's buttocks and down her thighs.

* * *

104

When Floradora came round properly, two hours later, she had been washed and covered with a clean blanket by Salome.

'Where are my clothes?' she said, calmly. She did remember, vaguely, what had happened, but she thought it might have been a dream.

'Oh, you are awake, darling,' said Salome, who was feeding day-old chicks to her snakes.

'Are we there yet?' said Floradora. She seemed to have forgotten her promise to marry Antonio; she remembered only that there had been a beautiful interlude and she remembered the bath and the large white bed and a kiss. Her body was still languorous from Salome's lovemaking. She wanted more of the snake charmer's caresses. Her skin still sung and tingled with the memory of the gentle, subtle tongue and the passionate mouth. She gazed lovingly at Salome, and smiled at her.

'Oh, darling, yes, we are nearly there, and you will appear in the big top later. Lorenzo is very pleased with you.' She patted the girl's cheeks, and gave her clean clothes to put on. Anastasia had brought them over earlier, giggling with Salome when the snake charmer told her what had happened.

Floradora dressed slowly, wondering briefly how she had got the vivid marks on her breasts.

'I will go back to my own caravan now, Salome, I feel better now,' she said.

'Yes, darling, of course, but come back later, won't you?'

Floradora kissed the snake charmer on the lips, quite unembarrassed. Salome returned the embrace with enthusiasm, smiling and holding her tight.

'Until later, dearest,' she said.

The caravan had stopped for a rest to feed the animals. Isambard was glad to see Floradora. She had been sick for a day and a half, he had been told, during the long journey to the harbour town of Arrecife. He had attended to the horses and the lions, uncomplaining. She greeted him with affection and set about helping to feed the horses.

'I'm sorry I haven't been much help on the journey, Isambard,' she said, 'but I am fine now.'

'Good, I am happy for you,' he said. He waited for her to mention the gentleman of Teguise, but she did not. It was as if he had been wiped from her memory. Perhaps she had only joked about leaving the circus, he thought. His misery dropped slowly from him as he realised she would stay.

'Rosario and Rosalita have been asking for you,' he said.

'Oh, yes, they are going to perform without a net, did you know?' she said, excitedly.

'Yes, I did know,' the strong man said. Without his clown's wet-white make-up he was a very handsome brown-skinned muscular man. His arms gleamed with sweat, and his soft lips pouted in concentration as he swung hay from a fork into the stable truck. Floradora lifted a hand and touched his arm lightly. He froze, and she stroked the muscular upper arm. He stood still, a statue, as she stroked his arm and felt its roundness and hardness. She drew even closer to him and stretched up to his face and kissed his lips.

'What are you doing?' he said, aroused by her caresses.

'Kissing a lovely man,' she said.

He moaned and drew her into his huge arms where she shrank, a tiny slender shape hidden in the cage of his dark limbs.

He tenderly kissed her face and neck and pulled her into the darkness of the stable. The horses were outside, feeding and stretching their legs, tethered to the truck. The clean straw rustled as Isambard and Floradora fell into the golden mass. Her pale limbs flashed and clung to his huge body. Her fingers tugged at his buttons and pulled at his trousers. When he was naked she pressed his pectorals and pinched his rubbery buttocks. His penis was hidden against her belly. She pushed away from him and looked at it. It leapt up towards her. His searching tongue invaded her mouth.

He lifted her on top of him, sliding her up and down his body – the little breasts squashed against him, the flat belly, the rounded thighs. He held her by the buttocks, slid fingers down her cleft and under her body between her legs. He put each breast into his mouth and sucked hard on the nipples, stretching them. He sucked his fingers before flicking them on her shaved pubis and sliding them into her. He felt her thrust herself on to him, as if desperate for the voluptuous caresses. His lips found hers. He moved her around so her belly was on his face, and her face was close to his thighs. He urged her to suck him. He licked her naked sex-lips gently at first. She held his cock between her hands and slid it over her lips. Then the huge purple head filled her mouth. She licked it and flicked her tongue around it and sucked.

He groaned in disbelief. Was this really happening? He could not believe it. His beloved Floradora, making love to him!

She caressed his buttocks and held the root of his big cock, behind his balls and in front. Her body wrapped round his, lying on him, and her breasts rubbed his balls. He licked her thighs and slid his tongue between her sex-lips, sucking and tasting her fresh virginal juices.

'Are you a virgin?' he suddenly asked her.

'A virgin? I suppose I am, but I don't want to be, Isambard, I want you inside me.'

He breathed heavily, excited beyond belief at her words. He turned her back so their faces were close together, and whispered, 'I love you, Floradora.'

'Oh!' Floradora screamed, suddenly trying to get away from his embrace.

'Love me?' She sounded strange and Isambard pulled away from her to look at her face. Tears were streaming down her cheeks and her eyes were wild and unseeing. She began to laugh, hysterically. 'Love me?'

He kissed her stricken face gently, and found that his erection had shrunk. She was beside herself with a sort of grief, he could see. Perhaps her fever had done something to her brain? He stroked her face and shushed her, holding her gently and comforting her. She probably still grieved for her father, he thought. The illness had weakened her reason. She sobbed into his shoulder and he gently held her. Eventually, she stopped crying. They became aware of the straw around them, the horses stamping and snorting outside. Reluctantly he let her up, and she brushed herself down and dressed. He did the same and, embarrassed, went outside and looked around to make sure no one had seen them. She did not seem to care or notice him, but placed blankets on the horses' backs and saddled up one of the mares to ride. She ignored the black clown, as if their love-making had not occurred. His balls ached with the unfinished act, and he sadly walked away to attend to the lions.

Chapter Fourteen

The Triple Somersault Without a Safety Net

*T*he big top had been set up with the help of all the young men and boys in the area, who had turned up to see the circus arrive in town. They did as they were told and pulled on ropes and tugged at canvas, unfolding it and arranging it neatly on the cleared ground. Yellow curs barked and snapped at strange ankles. Donkeys brayed. Goats bleated. Children ran in and out of the caravans, trying to see circus animals. Small boys hid under the cage truck and looked up at the yellow lions through the cage floorboards. A large lion pissed on the straw and one boy yelled and scrambled out of the way of the strong-smelling urine. But he wasn't fast enough. His tattered shirt was ruined, and his mother would beat him. His unsympathetic friends screamed with laughter. Isambard appeared and chased them away.

The ticket office had a queue waiting already, although there was an hour and a half before the first performance. The wardrobe mistress, dressed to the nines in feathers and furs, in high heels and a tight skirt, smiled lasciviously at the young men who pressed together and pushed and shoved and laughed.

'Give us a kiss, darling,' she said to one low-browed and dark-complexioned brute.

He blew a kiss at the outrageous transvestite, and Olympia leant over the desk and took his chin in her hand. 'Come and see me after the show at my caravan – the blue one close to the entrance,' she whispered to him.

'I might do that,' the rude youth replied, smiling.

The *chamacos* were making last-minute adjustments to the ropes and wires of the trapeze. This night, for the first time, they did not have to put the safety net up. The space seemed empty without it; the high wire was exposed and naked. It looked a long way up.

The trapeze artistes stood underneath, gazing up. 'You are sure you want to do this?' said Rosario.

'Of course, we will be paid twice as much, my little brother.' She smiled at him, confident in her youthful power.

'Yes, the money will be good,' he said. He had in his hand a handbill proclaiming the circus and its performers. The artist had drawn the trapeze artistes swinging high above the upturned faces of the crowd, their mouths all open in astonishment. The trapeze artistes looked like gods, flying through the sky, muscular and beautiful. Rosario was pleased with the picture of himself. He looked very handsome in it. He knew there would be many people admiring him, wanting him. He felt secure in the knowledge that he was a beautiful young man and he knew his art. He glanced at his sister. She looked slightly strained, her thin lips closed tight.

'Come back to the caravan, Rosalita, and rest until the circus starts. Everything is all right here.' He took her hand and led her away. 'I know how to make you relax,' he said, quietly.

At their caravan, he undid her *bata* and removed it from her shoulders.

'Put on your new costume,' he said. 'I will help you with it.'

She unfolded the brief two-piece costume, which

110

would leave her belly button bare. This would be the first time she had worn this daring costume in public and it looked very fetching on her, he thought, proudly.

She slipped off her old clothes and placed the bra top over her breasts. Her brother did up the fasteners behind. She stepped into the flimsy panties that were spangled with silver and red, but not before he had admired her bare sex. The female performers all shaved between their legs and under their arms. She was smooth all over, and he sucked in his breath as he saw the split of her peach. His erection pushed against his tight trousers and he shifted his legs.

'Do I look pretty?' she asked, coquettishly.

'Very,' he said, taking her into his arms and kissing her lips.

She pressed against his rough, woollen trousers. She pressed a hand on his curved prick through the cloth. He pushed against her. She opened his flies and the cock sprung out and upward. He looked down at his straining prick, brown and thick. She stroked it, holding it firmly in one hand. He groaned and kissed her again. She rubbed her belly against him, and he felt the soft hardness of his fleshy rod on her silky knickers. Her belly button held the tip of his cock for a moment. He slid up and down, bending his knees and pulling himself up and down her belly. She pressed on his head, and he went on his knees and nuzzled between her legs. He pulled the crotch of her panties to one side and licked the sex-lips with his long pink tongue. He held his cock in both hands and rubbed at it furiously. She writhed on his mouth, gyrating her hips as his lips and tongue slithered over her mound.

Later, refreshed, they emerged from their caravan pink-faced and ready to perform on the trapeze. They hid their spangled costumes under the ubiquitous *batas,* and slipped through the crowds who still queued, the children with *palomitas*, paper twists of popcorn, in their little fists.

111

People pointed at them and a young woman thrust a handbill at them and asked them to autograph it. The siblings smiled and waved to their audience as they ran into the big top. The clowns were tumbling and the band played loudly and discordantly, and the crowd applauded loudly. The inhabitants of the port had come out in their hundreds to see the semi-naked artistes and to get a thrill from the excitement of possible disaster. Soon, Lorenzo chased the clowns out of the ring and announced Floradora and her lions.

The rickety cage rocked as the lionesses leant against the bars, scratching their fleas. Floradora, looking stunningly pretty in her white full-sleeved open-necked shirt, black suede breeches and high boots, cracked her whip at the lions and put them through their paces without mishap. She bowed and saluted to the appreciative crowd before Isambard plucked her from the cage. On came the clowns again – Ilia, Pedro and Jellico – leaping and tumbling, throwing buckets of water at each other and pulling down their trousers to expose green balloon buttocks and orange balloon balls to the laughing crowd. Lorenzo whipped them off and shouted through his megaphone:

'And now the *mas famoso . . . increible triple salto mortal* – the famous triple somersault, which will be performed for the very first time without a safety net. I present Rosalita and Rosario, the *magnifico Mexicanos*!'

The crowd's murmur was loud, the tension increasing as Rosario and Rosalita climbed the rope ladder up to the trapeze. Rosalita's daring near-nakedness was fascinating to the stolid Lanzarotians who were always modestly attired. The matrons hid behind their fans and fluttered them excitedly. The men flashed gold teeth and drank brown wine from bladders of skin, which were decorated with tassels.

The high-wire artistes reached the top of the ladder and Rosario undid his trapeze and swung out on it into the darkness. His sister sat on her trapeze and swung out too, passing her brother above the middle of the ring. Their legs swung and pulled at the air, and they arced higher and higher. The crowd fell silent. Only the creak of the trapeze broke the quiet. Rosalita swung herself back on to her little platform and rubbed chalk on to her hands while her brother swung in a lonely arc. At last, Rosalita reached for her trapeze and launched herself into the void. The crowd gazed at the blade of her slender body, her naked belly, her spangled panties flashing in the spotlight. They watched her swing, again and again, higher and higher, until suddenly she flew, spinning and tumbling into a white blur of light, like a lightning flash. Then her hands came to rest in her brother's safe grip and they swung together, a perfect pair, up into the roof of the big top.

The crowd exploded in applause.

The trapeze artistes slithered down the ropes to the sawdust floor and bowed, holding each other's hands and throwing kisses to the tumultuous crowd.

Lorenzo patted Rosalita on the bottom as the siblings ran past him. She smiled, triumphantly.

The circus ground rang with the sound of flamenco music, dogs barking, fires crackling, and arguing, shouting performers. It was midnight and the show had finished, but life continued, food cooked on charcoal fires, wine was enjoyed, and the circus folk could relax after a show well-performed. The trapeze act had been a great success and Lorenzo knew his audiences would grow when word got around.

They gave their own performances to each other. The contortionist ran around like a crab, upside down, her head between her legs, belly up, pubis pressing through the thin stuff of her tight costume. Isambard stared at Floradora through the gloom, watching her every move. She had put her horses and lions to bed, and was enjoying watching Rosario dance flamenco with his sister. She clapped her hands to the fast music, feeling the lust of the dance, their bodies close to each other,

113

their dark eyes glazed. She lusted after both of them, wanting to be within the charmed circle of their love.

Salome stood close to the girl and held her round the waist, rubbing her belly with one hand. Floradora took the bottle that Lorenzo offered her and drank deep. Wine ran down inside her white blouse, trickled down between her breasts. She wiped her mouth with one hand.

La Roux and two *chamacos* writhed together in the dark shadows of a caravan. The wardrobe mistress and her *amoroso*, the local lad whom she had propositioned earlier, were entwined in an intimate embrace in full view of everyone. The boy was drunk and the lascivious Olympia dragged him off to her quarters. Her wig was awry, and she stumbled in her high heels as she climbed the steps, pulling him with her.

The boy found himself on his stomach, his trousers down by his ankles. Olympia fondled his balls and cock from behind and the boy groaned in appreciation. He roused himself and turned to face the seductive wardrobe mistress. Her lipstick was smeared over her large-featured face, but her smile was friendly and welcoming, and her large hands were sensuously knowing. Olympia held the boy's swollen cock and stroked it lovingly. The boy reached out to pull up the long skirt and slipped his hands under it. He felt the unexpected erection and balls, hanging free under the silk skirt. He gasped in shock. The wardrobe mistress held his hand on her very masculine cock and encouraged him to rub it. After a moment or two the boy relaxed and began to enjoy the novelty of the situation. He had his hand up a woman's skirt and was masturbating a large erection. The transvestite murmured love words into his ear and caressed him firmly. She turned her back to the boy and lifted her skirt. The boy found his cock was pressing into the buttock cleft of a large man.

'The grease is there, in that tub. Use it,' whispered Olympia.

He did as he was bid, taking a handful of the gooey stuff and wiping it over her bottom and the brown rose of her anus. He pressed into the widening hole with his fingers, spreading the buttocks. His prick was huge now and needed to be held by something soft and tight.

'Fuck me, go on, do it!' said Olympia, writhing her large hips at the randy youth.

Oh, heavens, why not, he thought, drunkenly. He felt the slippery silk of the dress against his balls as he slipped into the puckered hole. The immediate feeling of warmth and delight that filled him made him cry out. Olympia groaned and shoved against him. The wardrobe mistress reached behind her and found his hand. She pulled it to enclose her cock. So, as she was milked, the youth was also satisfied.

'Come back tomorrow if you want, and bring your friends,' said Olympia, pulling her skirts down and adjusting her crooked wig. She kissed the exhausted boy on the cheeks and helped him do up his trousers. Then she shoved him gently out of the door and went out into the night herself to see what other naughtiness she could indulge in.

The ringmaster had planned his own private party with Floradora and Salome.

Salome half-carried the lion-tamer's daughter to Lorenzo's caravan and pushed her up the steps into the candlelit, rich interior. Floradora undid her blouse and took it off, standing with bare breasts in her tight breeches and high boots. She felt hot and feverish but very aroused. Lorenzo entered the caravan as Floradora knelt to lick the sex of the snake charmer, who stood before her, naked from the waist down apart from a leather strap which circled her body and divided her buttocks and sex-lips.

Salome still wore a strappy leather bra which exposed her large dark nipples. Floradora did not notice the ringmaster's entry. Her little breasts hung down before her and her bottom strained at the suede of her breeches.

Lorenzo sucked in his breath and touched the lion-tamer's daughter's bottom. She did not flinch as the whip came down on her buttocks. He did it again. She carried on sucking at Salome's swollen sex-lips, which were divided by the strap. She rubbed her fingers over the strap, pushing it into the snake charmer's sex.

Salome held the girl's head close to her crotch. Lorenzo took out a knife and cut Floradora's trousers from her body. He tore at the suede, pulling it away from her white bottom, like peeling a fleshy peach. He set about the white flesh with the whip again and she wanted more, pushing her buttocks up towards the caress of the leather. Floradora kissed Salome and pushed her fingers inside the leather strap, into her fleshy pouch. Salome sighed and panted and came again and again on the girl's mouth and fingers. Floradora was aware of the lasciviousness of her companions but became as lustful as they were.

Lorenzo wrapped his prick in the thin end of the leather whip and pulled it tight. He ordered Salome to hold the whip. She pulled away from the continuing caresses and did as he asked, standing behind him and holding the erection firm in the grip of the leather. He pushed the lion-tamer's daughter on to her knees, grabbed her hair and made her take his cock head into her mouth. Salome drew the leather whip tighter round the base of his thick rod and Floradora sucked the top of his throbbing cock. She had her eyes chastely closed, but her nipples were hard and her sex tingled. Her torn suede breeches were tight around her crotch, where a fragment of material remained pressing into her sex. She touched herself, feeling the wetness, the full lips swollen and engorged. She pushed fingers into the secret place and her muscles tugged at the slender digits. She pretended she clutched Isambard's cock, and came, shocked at herself.

As Floradora sucked harder, he came. She swallowed the spurting foam, let go of the shrinking cock, and began to laugh. Lorenzo flew into a fury at the girl's derisive laughter. He dragged her up by her hair and told her to get out. She grabbed her *bata* and fled, without a backward glance.

Chapter Fifteen
Señora Valera to the Rescue

*A*ntonio had ridden into the town of Teguise after he left Floradora. He was elated. He wanted to arrange the wedding ceremony for as soon as possible so he headed for the church of San Miguel in the town square. He did not know or guess that he was being followed. The *chamacos* who were in the pay of Lorenzo did what they had to do. They waited until he had left the horses and carriage in the cobbled street and gone down a narrow alley to the church's side door. They hurried after him, tackled him to the ground, and drew knives on him. He shouted instinctively before he was knocked senseless and tied up. The *chamacos* bundled him into the side door of the church and left him hidden behind a pew.

No one was in the church at that hour, usually, except the priest, who had been encouraged to take another glass of wine with his very good friend, the owner of the wine store. The priest left the shop at last, not too steady on his pins, and staggered to the church, where he found the most comfortable seat and fell asleep.

His snores were still echoing through the high-ceilinged church when Antonio regained consciousness several hours later. It was dark and Antonio knew he should have been at the circus to pick up Floradora. He tried to call but found he was gagged. His hands were tied behind his back and his legs were tied together so he could not shift on to his knees or stand. He lay under a dark blanket, coughing and spluttering under his gag. He did not know where he was, but he could smell beeswax and guessed he was in the church. He struggled in vain against his bonds.

His mother had risen late that morning, knowing that her son had wanted to be alone with the girl. She bathed and dressed unhurriedly, then went to his room and picked up the silver frame with the photograph of his dead fiancée. She had been a beautiful young woman and would have made a good wife to her son, she was sure. She sighed. Marriage had been a great joy in her own life – the love of a good man, his protection, the safe feeling she had had when she was with him, the romance that had been in his soul. She sighed and put the photograph back where she had found it and wandered back into her own bedroom. Her late husband's clothes still hung in the wardrobe, his scent still in the folds. She touched his serge suit gently, as if it were his flesh.

She spent the day alone, assuming that Antonio would spend the day in Teguise after he had delivered the girl back to the circus. When Antonio had not returned at dusk she began to worry. What about the horses? He should know better than to keep them out all day. They would need their feed by now. Where was he? It became dark and still he did not return. She called her manservant and made him saddle her horse.

'But, *señora*, you cannot travel in this dark,' he begged her.

'Something has happened to him,' she said. She walked her horse slowly into the dark night and he watched as she disappeared into the bleak volcanic countryside.

Señora Valera had been a good horsewoman always, like her husband and son. She had not ridden far on her own since the death of her husband, but something drove her now. She knew something had happened to Antonio and could not bear to stay there in the stone *finca* and wait for his broken body to be brought to her. She hurried the horse on, taking care to remain on the track, which gleamed in the moonlit night. At least the moon was up, she thought.

An hour later, she arrived in the town, her horse clip-clopping through the empty streets. She looked for the horses and carriage and eventually found them, standing, shifting from one leg to another, snorting with tiredness. She jumped down from the saddle and went to them. They raised their heads and whinnied at her, thrusting their ears forward. She talked softly, stroked their noses and tied her own horse to the railing. She went down the alley to the church door. Why had he come here? Was her son praying? She opened the heavy studded door and it creaked loudly as she swung it back. She saw him immediately, nearly fell over him. He was unconscious again. The blow to his head had been overly vicious. The snoring priest woke suddenly as she shook him and battered him about his cheeks.

'Help me, you old fool!' she hissed.

'My goodness me, what has happened to Antonio?' said the befuddled priest.

'How do I know, you idiot! Untie him, will you? Get water to bathe his poor head.'

Antonio's mother took control of the situation and soon he was in a warm room with blankets over him in a house next to the church. The doctor had been called and the priest sent home. Antonio's head ached badly. He could not move it without pain. She bathed the wound and covered it with lint. The householders knew of the family and were amazed that such a perfidy could have occurred in their quiet town.

She arranged for someone to take in the horses for the night, and feed, water and groom them. Then she slept, next to her son's bed, on a chair. She would not hear of the householders giving up their bed to her. She was a strong woman who had given up comforts many times in her life. There had been the dreadful volcanic eruptions in the south, the poor villagers fleeing the fire and molten rock. The great clouds of choking dust had hung over the island for months, years. This was nothing. But she worried about her son. He could not tell what had happened to him. He had not seen his attackers; their faces had been hidden under black masks. He only knew they wore blue overalls. He fell into a troubled slumber again, and she slept also.

He dreamed of Floradora, tied and beaten black and blue, and he tried to raise himself to go to her, but he could not. His legs were heavy. He could not move. He cried out in his sleep and his mother went to him. She hushed his moans, wiped his sweating brow, and gave him a sip of cold water. He slipped into sleep again. Then, at dawn, he woke refreshed and remembered where he had seen blue overalls. The *chamacos* all wore them at the circus. He could not know that Floradora had been abducted, did not guess that it was possible, but he knew he had been attacked for some reason. His money had not been taken.

Over a fierce Arabic coffee he told his mother of his proposal of marriage to the lion-tamer's daughter. He told her of his fears for her safety. Why had the circus hands attacked him? It must be for some reason connected with Floradora, he argued.

She could see he was determined to follow Floradora but she was relieved that he was recovering from his injury, and was not seriously hurt.

He urged his mother to go home in the carriage and he decided to take her horse. Luckily, his mother had always ridden astride, not side-saddle. He saddled up the Lippizaner, adjusted the saddle and girth and set off, waving to his mother as she drove the carriage in the opposite direction, to their home.

He cantered out of the town and into the red-earthed countryside, breathing in the early-morning scents of herbs and flowers. The mists withdrew from the valleys. He was confused about what day it was. Was it the night before that he had been hit on the head? Would the circus have arrived in Arrecife yet? Had Floradora waited in vain for him to fetch her, and would she have thought he had changed his mind about marrying her? His mind was full of unanswerable questions. He kicked his mother's courageous little mare on and she cantered through the rough terrain, stepping over sharp rocks as if she was a sturdy Welsh mountain pony. His head hurt again and he cursed his attackers. Why had they done it? He suddenly felt frightened for Floradora. Perhaps she was in danger. He hurried the mare even faster and she grunted and sweated under the warm sun. He let her walk awhile and they stopped at a farm and he asked for water for her. The farmer's wife was in black widow's weeds, like his mother, and he thought how so many of the women suffered bereavement on this island of hot summers and dry winters. They carried on without their menfolk, doing the same hard, back-breaking work their husbands had done, until they could do it no longer.

He came in sight of the sea at last, and the white town with its harbour and old stone bridge. He could see from the high ground where the circus tent had been set up, on the outskirts of town. Please, God, let Floradora be safe, he silently prayed.

The circus posters were all over town – some showed the aerialists flying through the air, some showed the equestrian riding bareback, and some showed the snake charmer, nearly naked, her magnificent body wrapped in serpents. Antonio passed one or two of these garish posters on his way through the daisy-scattered lanes. The sun was hot and he stopped to let the horse drink at a water trough. He had set off with no real plan of action. He simply knew he must find Floradora and make her his wife. Now he was nearly at the *terreno*, he began to have doubts about his impulsive behaviour.

Perhaps he should have brought help with him. If she had come to harm, what would he do? Should he tell his fears to the local police before he went to the circus ground?

His fears were well-founded, for Lorenzo had *chamacos* waiting for him in case he dared to follow Floradora. The rough characters that had attacked Antonio in Teguise were at the crossroads. He saw them too late, turned his horse and galloped off, but they were after him on their sturdy ponies. They were from the Americas and they were used to lassoing cattle and horses. He felt the rope tighten round his chest, holding his arms down at his sides, and he fell heavily on the stony path. His mother's brave little mare fell also.

In Arrecife, at the circus, life went on for Floradora. She did not forget that she had known Antonio, but she was confused. Had he said he loved her? Had she dreamt the kiss he had given her? It seemed a long time ago, though it was only a day or two. She did what she had to do, fed the horses and lions, practised her acts with them, laughed with the *bastoneras*, smiled at Salome, but she occasionally had a glimpse of something else in the corners of her mind – something that might have been.

Safe in the knowledge that the horse breeder was tied up and guarded well, Lorenzo continued educating the lion-tamer's daughter. He reinforced his power over her. She was quiescent, and welcomed the sexual attentions she had now from Lorenzo, Salome and, as and when Lorenzo wished, from other members of the circus.

She learnt that if she made fun of Lorenzo he punished her. If she objected to his treatment of her, he punished her further. But the punishment was always of an erotic nature, and her arousal was more intense each time.

On the third night in Arrecife, she discovered the erotic power of rubber. Lorenzo called her to his caravan where the aerialists were already naked and engaged in mutual masturbation, to Floradora's delight. They were lapping at each other like randy dogs, and Rosalita's sex was flared and her sex-lips full and swollen. Her brother had eyes only for his sister. He stroked her little breasts and belly and grasped her muscular buttocks, ramming her pelvis into his face. His magnificent erection was kept hard by his sister's expert manipulations, but he was not allowed to come.

Lorenzo took Floradora into his arms and lifted her white transparent dress to her waist. He held her buttocks to his groin and made her watch the trapeze artistes perform. He wore, as usual, the rubber cloak, voluminous in its drapes and folds. He wrapped it round her, so she could smell the rubber and feel its softness touch her intimate parts. She moved against him, enjoying the feel of his hardness on her bottom.

La Roux entered with Alphonso, the tattooed sword swallower and fire eater. La Roux was dressed in a short rubber dress that stopped at her thighs, so that her red-haired pubis was just visible. Her breasts were pressed hard against the rubber but her nipples and areolae were exposed through holes specially cut in the material. Olympia had made these naughty clothes for the ringmaster. She designed new ones all the time and he readily gave her money to buy the best-quality latex which came by ship from the Americas.

Alphonso had leather straps round his waist and chest and wore a small apron-like loincloth of leather, which drew attention to his magnificent thighs and buttocks and the hefty bulge of his privates.

Floradora watched through narrowed eyes, her thighs melting under the tender ministrations of the ringmaster, who had his whip-end between her legs. She saw the tattooed man flex his muscles and make the inked galleons toss and roll on giant waves. She saw La Roux stand on her hands while he nuzzled and licked her pink purse. She smelt the warm rubber grow more aromatic with her own love juices, and thought how lovely it would be to wear a short rubber dress like La Roux's; how flattering it would be on her slight, ballet-dancer's figure.

The leather whip handle rubbed her voluptuously, and Lorenzo's cloak enfolded her in its scented magic. She automatically reached behind her to hold his erection but found his cock had not risen.

'Leave it,' he said. 'Bend over that stool.'

She did as he said, lifting her skirt up high so her bottom was exposed. She felt the leather upholstery caress her open flesh. She lifted her buttocks high to meet the welcome thwack of Lorenzo's rubber-gloved hand, and she sighed as it went between her legs to press the soft purse. She strove to see the aerialists still pleasuring each other, and the massive hulk of Alphonso eclipsing the white-skinned little *bastonera*. La Roux's red hair shook like a horse's mane as the tattooed man rode her. At the moment of his climax, Floradora was certain a flame had come from his open mouth.

The circus had been in Arrecife for six days and tonight was the last night they would perform here. The next day they would dismantle the big top and set sail for mainland Spain.

Lorenzo had made sure that Antonio was tied securely and kept in a stone shed on the outskirts of the encampment, guarded by a *chamaco* ruffian. The prisoner was given bread and water once each day, and beaten if he made any effort to move. He was tied and gagged and blindfolded, except when he was fed. Lorenzo had killed men when he had had to in the past – and would not hesitate to do so again – but his plan was to keep the Lanzarotian gentleman away from Floradora and, to this end, he would hold him captive until after they had set sail for Spain, when the ruffian had orders to set him free or do what he wanted with him. Lorenzo did not care.

Antonio was now definitely fearful for the safety of Floradora. He felt so stupidly helpless. When his guard untied the gag so he could eat and drink, he tried to talk to him, but the man spat in his face and showed his blade. Antonio was alone, in a strange town, where no one knew him, or cared that he was in danger. He thought of the beautiful equestrian, her shining face, her golden hair, and the bulge of her pubis. These thoughts of her kept him sane during the dark hours alone in the hot filthy shed, but also drove him mad with desire and frustration.

Meanwhile, back at the *finca*, his mother, Octavia Valera de Teguise, was more than worried at his continued absence. He had been gone four days.

'Paco,' she said to her manservant, 'I want you to take me to Teguise. Will you do it?'

'Of course, *señora*, if you wish, but it will be a hard journey for you. Let me take my son and we will look for Señor Antonio.'

His strong son, a young man of twenty, was fortuitously visiting from the mainland. He was only too pleased to join in the adventure. He had strength and muscles enough to make up for the failing powers of his ageing father.

'No, Paco, I cannot stay here while I think my son is in danger. I am coming, too,' said Señora Octavia.

An hour later, armed with provisions for the journey and what weapons the *finca* had to offer, the three of them set off. The carriage was drawn by the two geldings and was driven by Paco, and his son, Jaime, rode Antonio's own horse.

Chapter Sixteen
The Circus Moves On

*A*ll was bustle and furious activity at the *terreno* as the *chamacos* and all the circus performers helped to dismantle the big top and pack it away, with all the paraphernalia that went with it: the guys, wooden pegs, wires, ladders, trapezes, seating, lights, the lion cage, costumes and boxes of make-up, the bags of sawdust, food for the animals, pots and pans, instruments and whips, and the clowns' apparatus. It took several hours for the team to pack it all away neatly, ready for the voyage. The circus had been set up close to the port, so there was not far to go to embark. The caravans, pulled by sturdy little ponies, were on the way.

Lorenzo, in his travelling suit of black serge, a bowler hat on his head, a silver-topped cane in one hand, walked round the perimeter of what had been their home for a week, to check that nothing had been forgotten. Especially, he was making sure that Floradora's would-be lover was still a prisoner. He saw the stone shed, its ramshackle exterior reinforced with a makeshift door. Sure enough, the ruffian was on guard. Or rather, he slept in the shade under a fig tree. The Lippizaner was tethered close by, disconsolately cropping the dry, yellow grass. Lorenzo started when he saw the animal. He had better take it with him, he thought. It would make a good circus horse. But then he thought better of it, for Floradora would surely recognise it and her memory would return. The hypnosis was only good while he reinforced it regularly, and anything from before he had hypnotised her could trip her mind into remembering that which he did not want her to remember.

He kicked the *chamaco*, who roused himself and spat a great jet of tobacco on to the ground, just missing the ringmaster's black patent shoes.

'Is he still alive?' asked Lorenzo.

'He is,' the man grunted.

'Here is the rest of your money.' Lorenzo threw the wad of pesetas on the ground next to the foul-smelling, filthy ruffian.

The man picked it up and greedily counted. 'This is not enough. You said you would pay more.'

'You have the horse. Sell that.' Lorenzo turned and walked away.

Inside the hut, Antonio was struggling with his ropes. He had found a piece of broken bottle in a corner, and he had spent every minute of the last few hours sawing away at his wrist ropes. He could hear the altercation outside and was relieved to hear that the horse was all right and still there. He pretended to be unconscious in case Lorenzo looked inside the hut, but the ringmaster did not want to soil his suit. He heard the *chamaco* roar with anger, and then there was a scuffle. He heard grunts and cries and the sound of bodies crashing into the door of the hut. The ruffian had drawn a knife on the ringmaster, forgetting that he was one of Mexico's best knife throwers. His adversary soon overcame the ruffian's feeble efforts at killing him. He stabbed him twice, in the neck and heart, and left him for dead.

Lorenzo looked around to make sure he had not been seen. Then he brushed himself down, cursing the man for ruining his suit, and hurried back to the procession of caravans that wound its way through the tracks and little fields that were close to the port.

* * *

128

Floradora rode her stallion, Thunderhead, and Isambard rode Jet. They both led the other mares which, though highly strung, were used to loud noises and sudden sounds, as were all circus animals. They rode behind the caravans, at the rear of the procession. The workers at the port looked on in amazement as the elephants were led on board the steam ship, up carefully reinforced ramps. The caravans were pushed and shoved and pulled by strong, wiry men, Arab seamen, most of them. The horses were blindfolded and led up the ramps. The lion cage was on wheels and the two strongest dray horses pulled it up safely, the lions meanwhile roaring their disapproval.

Olympia, dressed in a magnificent yellow feather boa over a tight, slit, red satin skirt, looking, she hoped, just like a sailor's whore, flaunted herself at the crew of the steamer. They, poor fools, thought she was beautiful, with her full red lips and her padded hips and buttocks. Her false breasts jutted from the satin dress and mesmerised the tars. She looked forward to the short voyage to Cadiz, even though she was still sore from the attentions she had received in Arrecife.

Salome's snakes were safely aboard in their closed jars, their live provisions, chirping piteously, in a separate perforated box.

Isambard saw to the lions' comfort while Floradora made sure her beloved horses were comfortable. The sea was calm; the sky clear blue. All was right with the world of the circus. These lost days of travel – *diaz perdidas* – which came in the life of a travelling circus were a time of relaxation and holiday for the performers. The daily toil and effort and danger were gone for a while, and they could enjoy themselves.

The Greek captain had met the stars of the circus and was aroused by the beauty of all the dancing girls and the pretty little equestrian. He also liked the looks of the snake charmer. But he particularly welcomed Olympia, who was his idea of what a woman should look like: big breasted, brash, vulgar, unambiguously and ultimately feminine – or so he thought.

He had already earmarked Olympia for his own. She, on the other hand, fancied the first mate – a chunky, youthful Greek with short, curly brown hair. He wore his uniform well, his bulge was promisingly huge, and he had almond-shaped, long-lashed, sleepy brown eyes. She would have him first, she promised herself. After that . . . well . . . she did not mind.

Antonio had freed himself at last and, hearing no sound outside, he plunged through the badly barricaded doorway to find the dead ruffian sprawled across his path, blood in a dark puddle seeping into the dry earth. He knelt to check for a pulse and saw the discarded knife, which he picked up. As he did so, half a dozen men in black sombreros appeared and, crying out, set upon him.

'Leave me, you fools, I did not do this. I was his prisoner,' he tried to explain.

'Tell that to the *guardia*,' said one, hauling him away.

'Unhand my son,' said the imperious Señora Octavia, who arrived just in time to see her son being half-carried by the angry men.

'Mother, what are you doing here?' said Antonio, amazed at the appearance of his mother and her manservant.

'I came to find you, my son,' she said. 'What has been happening here? Are you injured?'

'Oh, Mother, I have lost her, I have lost Floradora,' said Antonio.

The small crowd had parted to give way to the fine lady and her carriage, and for a moment it looked as if Antonio was saved. However, someone had called the *policia*, and three armed, uniformed men appeared and brandished batons at the crowd. Eventually, they took the still-objecting Antonio away, along with two witnesses who had seen him leaning over the dead man with a knife in his hand. His mother, Paco, and Jaime followed them to the police station in Arrecife, where the story was told.

Meanwhile, on board the steamship, the circus folk were settling into life on the ocean wave. The ship sailed close to the landmass of Morocco, and they could see the towering brown dunes and tiny white settlements of the borders of the Sahara.

Captain Papadopoulos invited all the stars and Lorenzo to share his table at dinner on the first evening. Olympia sat next to the first mate and played 'footsie' under the table. She also grabbed his crotch under cover of the tablecloth and made him moan with delight. The captain was sitting on the other side of Olympia, and Salome was on the other side of the captain. The captain had a busy evening trying to keep his dinner companions satisfied. He first gave his attention to the snake charmer, who had charmed her way into his trousers without trouble. Her long fingers drew out his snake from his smart white tropical uniform trews and played with it skilfully. Captain Papadopoulos was used to the ways of ladies on a sea voyage; he understood their needs. His sturdy snake rose and slithered in Salome's ardent fingers, and his own tanned hands were not lazy, either. He had negotiated the way up Salome's skirts to her bare thighs and was dipping fingers into her warm pool.

On his other side, he was having more trouble with Olympia's undergarments. She wore a tight-skirted sea-blue gown and he could not lift it high enough for his or her satisfaction. Instead he had to content himself with pressing on to her rather prominent pubic bulge. He felt something strain against his palm, and he wondered if there was another snake hidden under her skirt. He was right of course; Olympia's naughty cock was trying to escape its bonds of feminine attire to be closer to the masculine touch of the captain. Olympia squirmed happily, squeezing the first mate's organ faster. He gave a sudden yelp and excused himself from the dining table, holding his voluminous linen napkin over his crotch.

131

The captain was in similar ecstasies soon after, and had to repair to his cabin also.

Wine flowed and the circus troupe was cheerful and relaxed. Isambard sat opposite Floradora, gazing at her hungrily when he thought he was not seen. She was chatting to Alphonso on her left, while the stern figure of the ringmaster was to her right.

After dinner, when the captain and his mate had reappeared wearing their second-best uniform trews, there was an impromptu performance by the dancing girls.

La Roux, dressed in a tutu of red net, and showing off her red bush under a minuscule pair of transparent brief knickers, danced first, leaping on to her hands and giving everyone a fine view of her best attribute. Then Gina, the contortionist, folded herself into erotic knots which left her private parts tantalisingly spread before the mixed audience of sailors and circus folk. Her round face and almond eyes looked quite blank as she tied herself into impossible shapes. Anastasia danced a flamenco with Rosario, but Rosalita became jealous of the sparks of sexuality which flew between the dancers and furiously parted Anastasia from her brother and took her place, to the amusement of the audience. Alphonso played guitar, a sorrowful, sensual air, and the siblings flowed easily together, each staring hard into the other's eyes. The air was hot with sexuality.

Flamenco always had this effect on its audience and performers: the clicking heels of the dancers, the castanets, the ancient gypsy rhythm of the guitar, the deep song of the proud and masculine singers. These elements, brought together with the effect of heady wines, served to release the passions of the soul.

All eyes were on the two aerialists – the proud features of the lovely siblings, the narrow waist of Rosalita, the narrow hips of Rosario. There was loud applause when they came to the end of the dance. Much wine was drunk and many cigarillos were smoked. Hands stroked knees and thighs, kisses and promises were exchanged, secret assignations were made.

Floradora left the party to go to her horses. They were on the top deck in the bow, tied safely in a large, purpose-built horsebox. They whinnied at her approach. She stroked their noses and patted their sides. They were comfortable, she could see, and she went back to the cabin she was sharing with Salome. On the way down a small companionway, she found her path blocked by a sailor. He was obviously drunk and had followed her. She smiled at him and asked to go by, but he would not shift.

'Please let me pass, *señor*,' she said.

'If you give me a kiss, pretty one,' he said, but not in a friendly way.

'How dare you!' She tried to squeeze past him, but he grabbed her and began to move his rough hands all over her body, his evil-smelling breath on her face. She screamed and suddenly the sailor was on the deck, blood flowing from his nose.

'Oh, Isambard, thank you,' she cried, sobbing in relief. The black clown lifted her over the prone sailor and stood her on her feet, but he held her still.

'You saved me, Isambard, thank you,' she repeated and kissed his soft lips.

The erotic performance earlier had aroused the lion-tamer's daughter. She was easily aroused these days. It was as if a tap had turned inside her, and a constant drip of excitement filled her body. She yearned for the gaping void inside her to be filled. Her thighs, as they touched each other, felt like softest silk. Her internal muscles worked continuously, so she could make herself orgasm with no other help. She was hot with desire now for the black clown. He was very close to her, huge, muscled and handsome. She melted into his big arms. He lifted her and carried her like a doll to his cabin. The *chamacos* he shared with were still at the revels. They would not be disturbed.

'Are you still a virgin?' he whispered in her ear.

'A virgin? I think so, Isambard, unless you count sexual congress with a dildo.' She giggled and he frowned.

So, she had been led into lascivious habits, already. However, he felt less guilty about the act he was about to perpetrate. He would have this girl now, the girl he loved more than any other woman he had known.

Chapter Seventeen
Lost Love

*I*n the main saloon, crew and passengers continued enjoying themselves. The band played romantic melodies and there was dancing. Olympia's dance partner, the captain, stared at her corseted waist, her high, huge bosom. The captain whispered something into Olympia's ear and they disappeared, Olympia looking shy and demure. She winked at the first mate as she went past him and gave him a note. He looked at the scribbled message – 'Come to my cabin in half an hour'. He smiled and hastily hid the message in his pocket.

Captain Papadopoulos was short-sighted, making great use of his telescope when on duty on deck. His failing eyesight had not discerned the peculiarities of Olympia's physical attributes. He shut the cabin door behind him and turned to the wardrobe mistress. Olympia took a looking-glass out of her reticule and applied lip colour to her faded lips.

'Would you like a brandy, my dear lady?' he asked, unstopping the glass decanter.

'Oh, thank you, captain, that would be delightful.' Olympia's rich brown voice was music to the captain's ears. She was tall and strong, too; he liked that in a woman.

'But wouldn't you be more comfortable on the sofa?'

he asked, as Olympia perched herself on the edge of his mahogany fitted bed.

'Oh, I think we would both be more comfortable in bed,' Olympia giggled, and leant forward to kiss the captain.

He immediately began to undress her, pulling at her buttons and ribbons and ties.

'No, I am much too modest,' she said, 'to be seen by you. Please extinguish the light and I will undress myself.'

The captain blew out the lamp and undressed himself. He heard the sound of clothes dropping to the floor, the sigh of untethered flesh loosened from its corsets. He leapt into bed, into the arms of Olympia, and found, to his amazement, that he was in bed with a man.

Olympia hushed his exclamations of shock with caresses and kisses to his swollen organ, and the captain soon acclimatised to the situation. After all, he was a man who had sailed the seven seas and had seen many strange things and done not a few. What was a bit of buggery between shipmates?

The transvestite made love to him slowly.

'Captain, though I love your uniform, especially the tight pants, I think you would suit a skirt.'

'What?'

'Let me put this on you,' said Olympia, sliding her own skirt up the hairy legs and solid thighs of the Greek seaman.

Captain Papadopoulos felt the smooth satin enfold his legs, and Olympia moved her hands up inside the skirt to the captain's hairy balls. She folded the satin on top of his balls and stroked through the material.

It felt very good, thought the captain. His cock swelled and rose against the soft stuff. Olympia's other hand was on his cock, holding it firmly and squeezing it up and down the full length of the shaft.

Olympia still wore the lifelike falsies and stockings and suspenders. She wrapped her legs around the captain's waist and rubbed herself on the bulging satin skirt.

The captain was beside himself. Olympia turned over so her bottom was pressed on the captain's pelvis. The captain lifted his skirt and pressed his throbbing member between the wardrobe mistress's warm buttocks.

After the captain had had his way with the wardrobe mistress, she reclaimed her skirt and left him to keep her appointment with the first mate.

The young man in question was hot for Olympia, and pacing up and down the corridor outside the cabin. When Olympia arrived, looking rather dishevelled, the first mate explained that he had seen two circus hands enter the cabin ahead of them.

'Oh, never mind, you show me your cabin, then,' said Olympia, taking his hand.

'I can't do that, it is not allowed to take passengers to our cabins and, anyway, I share with another crew member.'

'Oh, very well, we'll forget it then,' said the huffy Olympia.

'Oh, no. Don't let's forget it,' said the randy tar, 'I want you!'

'Dear boy,' whispered Olympia and pressed a large hand to his crotch. The youth blushed and took her hand away.

'Come with me, I know of somewhere we can go,' he said.

A few minutes later, they were hidden from sight under a canvas canopy that covered the lifeboat.

'Oh, this is fun!' giggled Olympia. She lay down as best she could, lifting her skirt up to her thighs. She loosened her cock from its pouch and straps and let it hang out. The first mate had known all along that this was no ordinary female. Not as gullible as his captain, he took the stiff cock into his lips and sucked. After a few minutes, Olympia cried out. The youth let go his hold on her. She moved, bent over the thwart and lifted her bottom to his attention. He undid his flies and quickly mounted the wardrobe mistress from behind, first moistening the tight orifice with his own spit. He shoved into her and thrust again and again. Olympia welcomed the thick cock inside her; she pressed against it until he came noisily.

'Are you busy in the mornings?' she asked him, demurely.

'I'll meet you here at six a.m.,' he answered. 'Wear a looser skirt.'

Meanwhile, Floradora looked around the little cabin that Isambard shared with two of the circus hands. There were two bunks, one above the other, and a hammock strung from the beams.

'Oh, a hammock!' she said, laughing. 'Let's do it in the hammock.'

He took her in his embrace again and kissed her passionately. She felt very small in his huge arms.

'Come on, Isambard, let's climb into the hammock.'

The hammock sank under their combined weight until it nearly touched the deck. It swung gently, a not unpleasant motion, as they settled into a suitable position for love-making. Isambard lifted her on top of him and she snuggled into the shape of his bearlike body. Her white lace dress was tangled around her legs and he tried to shift it. He wore only a pair of suede breeches, having removed his boots and shirt. The breeches had a flap-fly opening, held with leather ribbons, which she soon had untied. She admired his half-flaccid prick, beautiful in its purple and brown hues, the shine of the fleshy rod, its interesting girth, as it flopped out and lay on his thigh. Floradora slipped her hands around it and felt it swell to twice its size. She slipped down the hammock, causing it to rock, and put her mouth over the head of his penis. He held her shiny blonde hair as she sucked him.

He begged her to stop.

'Why?' Her mouth was smeared with wet.

'Because I want to make love to you.'

138

She shifted again. 'Oh, Isambard, don't spoil things by being serious. It's only fucking, after all.'

'Floradora, how can you say that? It is the most sacred thing, to make love to someone you love. Floradora, I love you.'

She stopped playing with him. 'What did you say?'

'I said, I love you.'

'Oh God! Antonio! I love Antonio! Oh! Isambard! What have I done?' The girl hurriedly rearranged her clothes and averted her eyes from Isambard's erection. She crawled over him and out of the hammock, almost falling in the haste to get away.

'What? Not again!' The poor clown's prick shrivelled and he slowly dressed himself. Floradora was out of the cabin door before Isambard could stop her.

The ringmaster was waiting for her. 'Where have you been?' he asked.

She was wary. She had remembered everything, but did not want him to know that she remembered. She pretended ignorance and acquiescence.

'Oh, Lorenzo, I have been a naughty girl. I think you might have to punish me.' She smiled lasciviously.

'Come to my cabin. We have been waiting for you,' he said, and grabbed her hand.

In the sumptuous cabin, which had pink and yellow striped silk curtains hanging round the huge mahogany bed, and a bidet and washbasin in one corner, was Salome, tied to the bed posts, on her back, her legs splayed. She was blindfolded. Alphonso was there also, dressed in a leather loincloth which flapped over his huge genitals. He took Floradora from the ringmaster and tied her skirt up above her waist, so she was bare from the waist down. He held her arms while Lorenzo rubbed between her legs with rubber-gloved fingers. She squirmed, enjoying the sensual pressure, in spite of herself.

'You are a naughty girl, as you said,' said Lorenzo. He had taken off his clothes and wore only the rubber cloak over a rubber thong, which held his cock close to his belly. His balls also were clasped by the thong, which went up between his taut buttocks.

'Your punishment is to make love to Salome,' he said.

You call that punishment? she thought, and smiled.

'Master, I will do as you say,' she said, and she climbed on to the bed and slid between the snake charmer's legs.

Salome was awake but pretending to be asleep. She groaned slightly as Floradora bent over her and gently kissed her inner thighs.

Floradora suddenly felt the sting of a cane on her exposed bottom. She did not stop her caressing but lifted her buttocks higher. The cane came down on her white skin again and again. With each strike of the cane her tongue went further into the snake charmer's open sex-lips. She flicked her tongue on the erect bud that grew hard and full. Salome breathed heavily. Behind the two intimately entwined girls, Alphonso was milking the ringmaster. The massive tattooed man had loosened Lorenzo's bound prick and held it captive in his patterned hands, holding him from behind, so the ringmaster could still wield the cane.

'You naughty, naughty girl!' Lorenzo whispered, his prick growing as he watched Floradora's white skin grow pink and then a vivid scarlet. She rubbed herself on Salome's knee and thigh as she sucked. Her spasms came again and again, with each strike of the cane. Then she felt the spurt of Lorenzo's juices splash on her flesh.

Antonio was desolate. The circus had gone, and Floradora with it. He had seen the ship sail out of the harbour as he was taken to the *policia*.

The witnesses, who had seen him with a knife in his hands, blood on his clothes, leaning over the dead man, told their story to the *guardia*.

Antonio told how he had been beaten up in Teguise and then attacked in Arrecife and been held prisoner. He told of the ringmaster paying the ruffian for keeping him

140

there. The police said no money was found. Antonio said Lorenzo must have taken it after he killed the thug.

'Where is your proof? You were seen killing this man,' said the policeman.

'He nearly killed me. I did not attack him.' Antonio knew it was hopeless. The ignorant police could not grasp the complicated situation. Antonio was thrown into the cell for the night and his mother was not allowed to see him.

She made her own plans. She sent Paco and his son off to the *barrio viejo*, the old quarter, close to where they had found Antonio, to ask questions. She gave them plenty of pesetas to help jog people's memories. She went to the port on her recovered mare to ask questions there.

Eventually, after she had questioned many men, she found a fisherman who had seen a stranger in a bowler hat, and wearing a bloodstained jacket, coming from the direction of the scene of the crime. He had boarded a ship loaded with strange creatures and oddly dressed people, which had since sailed for mainland Spain – Cadiz, he thought. She paid him and thanked him and took his name, and the name of his boat. He would not come back with her to the police station, as he had to go fishing on that tide. He said he would be back in twenty-four hours.

Paco and his son had no luck at the village. Mouths were closed there, the people were unwilling to speak if they did know anything. They just shook their grey heads. Their wives, sisters and daughters stayed inside, behind the wooden shutters, in the gloom and cool.

Paco and Jaime went back to rendezvous with the *señora* and she told them what she had found out.

'*Señora*, you should have persuaded the fisherman to come back with you to tell what he had seen,' said Jaime.

'Tut, tut, my son, you must not talk like that to the *señora*,' his father chided him.

'No! He is right, Paco. I am tired and not thinking

straight. Let us go and find lodgings for the night and see him again tomorrow when he returns from his fishing trip.'

The *señora* and the unhappy trio went in search of stabling and a guesthouse in Arrecife.

Floradora was unhappy, too. She wearily made her way back to her own little bunk and tried to sleep, but her head was full of thoughts of Antonio. He had asked her to marry him. She had agreed. He had said he would be back to fetch her. Then everything had gone wrong. But why had he not come for her before the circus had left Arrecife? Had his mother stopped him from doing so? No, Floradora was certain the wise old woman liked her. Perhaps Lorenzo had found a way to stop Antonio taking her away from the circus. Yes, that was it, she was sure. She must be careful of Lorenzo in future. She must not let herself be mesmerised again. For that is what surely must have happened. She had heard of his mysterious powers but had not thought he would use them on her. Oh, how could he? The evil man! But then, she thought, I do enjoy the erotic punishment he metes out to me, and I am aroused beyond belief at the titillating displays of lewdness that he makes me indulge in.

If she was being honest with herself, she did enjoy every aspect of her new-found sexuality. She realised that a male member had not penetrated her. Salome had used the dildo and Anastasia and Floradora had impaled themselves on a banana, but no man had yet been allowed inside her secret valley. She blushed when she thought of her own behaviour towards Isambard. Had she really instigated the love-making that had so nearly occurred? She flushed bright red in the dark of her cabin.

She thought of the handsome Antonio. Where was he? Had he forsaken her? Her hands slipped down over her sleepy nipples and pinched them gently. Then she explored the contours of her waist and belly. She pretended they were the hands of a big strong man; it could have been Antonio, or Isambard, or even Lorenzo, whose hands were expert at tuning her nerves.

She licked her fingers and slipped them down to the ripe fruit of her sex, where she gripped them with youthful muscles. She explored herself, learning where to caress for the most intense pleasure. She pretended that it was Antonio making love to her for the first time. She imagined her fingers were Salome's. Her own body delighted Floradora. She forgot about her lover and loved herself.

Chapter Eighteen

The Contortionist

The gentle giant was frustrated beyond belief. He could not believe that Floradora had led him on and then let him down again. But he realised that she had suffered some sort of shock when he had said the words 'I love you'. Why was it a shock to her? She must have known he loved her and had done so for a long time. The day after she had so rudely refused to make love to him he went about his duties on the ship as usual, attending to the lions and the horses. He looked for her to ask her to talk to him at least, but she was staying out of his way. He was in the horsebox, feeding the Arab stallion, when Salome appeared.

'Oh, Isambard, are you here? I was looking for Floradora,' she said.

The man shook his head and grunted.

'Could you come and see the ringmaster when you've done? He wants to see you.'

'What does he want me for?' said Isambard, suspiciously.

'Don't be grumpy,' she whispered, and put a hand over his crotch.

His penis rose.

'You look better without your clown's make-up, quite handsome, in fact,' she said, rubbing her hands over his bulge.

He groaned and allowed her caresses to continue. She soon had his cock out of its tight parcel, and held it firmly between her red-nailed fingers.

'You are as big as my favourite python,' she hissed at him and, so saying, she knelt to take his thick rod in her mouth. She played with it, rolling her tongue around the dark head, and biting gently. He leant away from her, on the box side, between the stallion and the door. The horse whinnied and fidgeted.

Salome licked the length of his shaft and fondled his plumlike balls. His genitals were almost hairless, and his penis was indeed like a beautiful snake. She sucked and almost swallowed the snake, and he groaned his pleasure. Salome was dressed in soft-leather high boots, with a short leather skirt and waistcoat. He drew her up to him and lifted the hem of her skirt to find her naked underneath. Her large breasts fell out of the open waistcoat and he sucked them greedily. His hands were over her mons and between her legs. Her naked flesh was warm above the leather boots. He could feel that her sex-lips were ready, open and soft, moist and willing to be penetrated. He shoved into her without further foreplay. His sexual need was immediate. The horsebox shook with their efforts. The stallion whinnied again and turned his black head to look at the entwined lovers.

Isambard had lifted the woman and she had her legs round him, crossed over his back. The huge cock reached her depths and filled her. Her orgasms were earthquakes, her flood of love juice like a volcanic eruption of molten lava around his organ. He thrust hard into her again and again and came inside her with loud moans, hearing her cries somewhere beyond him, in another world.

Floradora found the two spent lovers on the straw-covered floor of the horsebox. She stepped back before they saw her, and went away. She had been alarmed at the noises coming from the horse's quarters, and was relieved that it was only Isambard. She was grateful to

Salome, too, for letting her off the hook of Isambard's love declaration. At least he wasn't pining away for her! She had seen the clown's erection dwindling, but still enormous, and she was impressed and aroused at the sight.

Perhaps I should not have been so hasty, she thought to herself. I could have explained my behaviour to Antonio by saying that I have been hypnotised, and could not help myself. He would have to forgive me.

She decided that perhaps she should be nicer to Isambard from now on. After all, he had been such a good friend and ally in the past. Perhaps he could help her in the future, when she tried to get away from Lorenzo. She had not thought how she would do this, but she was determined to try to make her way back to Lanzarote to be with Antonio. But what if Antonio was dead? How would she find out? Oh, there were so many problems to overcome. Yes, she would make Isambard, who said he loved her, help her to be happy. If he really loved her, surely he would help her fulfil her dream of marrying Antonio?

With this vague plan in her simple mind, she went to the lion's cage to check on their condition and feed them. Dead goats had been loaded on at Arrecife for the lions. She threw a carcass into the cage and the snarling beasts set to work tearing it apart. She was still watching them enjoy their feast when Isambard arrived.

'Oh, there you are, Isambard, I am sorry I left you so hurriedly last night. I felt suddenly ill. I apologise.' She smiled winningly at the besotted man, and did not guess his guilt that he had just left the arms of the lascivious Salome.

'Please do not apologise, Floradora. I thank you for feeding the lions, I have been busy with the horses.'

'Yes, I know,' she said, and he looked quickly at her face.

'I must go to see the ringmaster,' he said.

'I'll come with you. Gina says he wants to see me, too,'

she said, and took his arm and walked towards Lorenzo's cabin.

They knocked at the door and went in. On the large bed, Gina, the contortionist, was folded over backward like a rubber doll, seemingly boneless. She was naked except for a thong of rubber that went between her legs and buttocks and attached to a collar round her neck, dividing her small round breasts on the way. She was like a tied parcel of pink rubbery flesh, a large sexual organ, displayed and prepared with oils for others to enjoy.

Floradora gasped at the erotic sight, so unexpected in the morning light that came from a large porthole. Isambard flushed under his dark brown skin. His cock fluttered under his breeches. It had only just recovered from the battering it had received from Salome.

'There you are, both of you, come in and have a seat; make yourselves comfortable,' said the ringmaster. He wore his rubber cloak and nothing but boots underneath. 'I have some new clothes for you to wear, my dear.' He produced a pair of rubber chaps and gave them to Floradora. 'Put them on, my dear,' he ordered her.

She noticed the swinging pendant on the chain round his neck. He had it in his hand and swung it. She turned her gaze away from it with difficulty.

'Please help me put these on,' she said to Isambard.

'You must first remove all your clothes,' said Lorenzo.

'Of course,' she said demurely, and undid her old brown breeches and took off her blouse.

The men stood and watched silently. Gina was like a sculpture, unblinking, unmoving. Floradora slowly removed her breeches and stood naked before them. The men licked their lips.

'Help me tie the chaps, Isambard,' commanded Floradora. She knew what the ringmaster wanted.

Isambard tentatively took the rubber chaps, which were like crotchless, bottomless trousers with straps from the tops of the legs attached to a hip belt. He approached the naked girl and carefully helped her to

147

step into the chaps. He pulled them up over her thighs and tied the belt round her hips.

'Turn,' commanded Lorenzo.

She stood in the revealing garment and turned slowly so they could see her from all sides. Lorenzo's prick remained limp under his rubber cloak, though he fondled it casually. Isambard's rod, however, was thrusting against his breeches.

'Get out of your clothes, man,' said the ringmaster.

Isambard did as he was bid, removing his breeches and shirt as if in a dream.

'Now fetch me that riding crop,' came the voice of Lorenzo as if from a great distance.

Floradora expected Lorenzo to whip her, or for him to make Isambard whip her. Either way, she did not mind. Her naked sex and buttocks were hot with tension and expectation. She wanted to be touched, hurt even, if the end result was an orgasm. She strutted around the cabin, seeing herself in the tall mirrors; her fair skin, her blonde hair, her rounded hips and narrow waist, her little bubbly breasts bobbing up and down. Isambard watched her every move; she felt his eyes on her, feasting on her beauty. She looked at his erection. He was a fine-looking man. His cock rose towards his belly.

Lorenzo stroked himself under the cloak. 'Give the crop to the girl,' he ordered the black clown.

'Thank you, Isambard,' said Floradora.

'Now, bend over that and let her punish you,' said the ringmaster.

'Yes, sir,' said Isambard. He bent over the naked contortionist, being careful not to knock her over. His cock pushed against the girl's flesh.

Floradora drew the crop through her hand and took aim. Her breasts shook as she struck the crop on Isambard's taut bottom. The brown skin darkened as the crop marked it.

His cock leapt under him and found a soft orifice. He pressed into the contortionist. She did not murmur. The lion-tamer's daughter flicked the crop across his balls, and tickled his arsehole. She watched him thrust back and forth into the soft flesh of the dancing girl under him and she gave him the subtle kiss of the leather strap. It caressed and thrust him further into the fleshy opening. Floradora saw the black, fleshy rod, released by the contortionist and then sucked back. As he drew nearer his nemesis the ringmaster called a stop to his punishment.

Lorenzo's own erection had improved greatly since the start of the whipping. He rubbed himself to keep it erect, and told Floradora to place a rubber ring over the head of Isambard's penis and push it to the base. She did this slowly, enjoying the look in Isambard's eyes as her hands drew the ring over his juicy oily cock. His eyes rolled.

'Now, back to your passive position,' Lorenzo said, firmly.

Isambard looked to see where he was positioning himself this time. It was the contortionist's sex-pouch that his cock found, gaping and moist. The girl was covered in oil all over and he slid over her belly. Floradora saw Gina's fleshy tunnel fold over his cock and tug at it. Then the crop came down on his buttocks. The lion-tamer's daughter saw that he was close to an orgasm but knew he could not come with the ring holding his organ. Isambard groaned and went on with his thrusts. The slender girl's bare bottom flashed white as she struck with all her might at the black man's buttocks. Isambard was buried in the sexual parts of Gina.

Lorenzo grabbed Floradora's arm and made her touch his cock. She smiled and took the warm flesh into her palm.

'Come here,' he said, and sat down on the couch. He bent her over his bare lap and spat on his hand. She felt his hand come down hard on her buttocks. He spanked her firmly, and she felt fingers pressing under her and slip into her moistness. She moaned appreciatively. She watched her own image in the mirror: her erect nipples, her round bottom raised high to his erotic caress. She could see the other girl, the contortionist, practically buried under the massive shape of Isambard. She could see his big cock slide in and out of the gaping red flower, its petals plump and wide like an overblown rose. Were her sex-lips like that? she wondered. Was she as sexually attractive as Gina? She thrust her buttocks up higher and writhed on Lorenzo's lap, feeling his erection under her belly. Lorenzo spent his come over her as she came on to his fingers.

The poor clown was tricked into constant copulation and Gina came silently over and over again.

Chapter Nineteen
An Accident

The voyage was going smoothly. There were no
storms and the animals were surviving their
enforced inactivity. The horses were walked around the
deck each morning and evening by Isambard or Floradora but the elephants and lions had to remain in their
quarters.

Each night there was revelry and high jinx between
crew and passengers and Olympia guessed that she had
been intimately involved with at least half the crew. She
determined to make the close acquaintance of the other
half – except for those sailors whose inclinations veered
towards the real female performers – before they disembarked at Cadiz.

She continued her liaisons with the captain and the
first mate, yet managed to fit in several other tars during
her waking hours. She was wandering around the foredeck one early morning while the circus folk, exhausted
from the previous night's party, still slept, when she
came across a sleeping youth she did not recognise as
one of her conquests. He slept in pretty disarray, naked,
under a piece of sacking, on top of a pile of sacks. He
looked so innocent, so virginal, so unspoilt. Olympia
pulled back the sacking to reveal his beauty: olive skin,
unmarred by scars or life's experience, and fine curly

pubic hair around perfect genitals. He looked like a young Greek god. His olive-toned penis lay half-erect on his thigh, like a sleeping puppy.

Olympia, dressed in red silk negligée with stockings, corset and long blond wig, knelt to touch the vision. She took the sleepy prick in one hand and touched herself with the other. The lad stirred a little and about his soft full lips a smile was born. His prick rose and swelled under Olympia's unusually tender ministrations. He lay there, unaware, no doubt dreaming beautiful dreams, thought Olympia, while the wardrobe mistress massaged him and herself to ultimate satisfaction. In her throbbing throes of orgasm she did not notice the first mate, with whom she had a standing appointment at this hour, walk up and see the dastardly act as it reached its climax. The first mate yelled in fury as he saw Olympia frigging his nephew, the captain's cabin boy.

Olympia fled, as did the rudely awakened youth, as the first mate chased the wardrobe mistress around the deck, threatening her with a belaying pin. The rest of the crew was soon awake and became aware of the naughty wardrobe mistress's infidelity – each tar believing he was her only *amoroso*. They joined in the pursuit of Olympia and when they caught her – for she could not run fast in high heels – they stripped her of her negligée, but left her with her stockings, corset and wig, and each in turn had his way with her. The captain saw all from his high vantage point but let it happen.

Olympia was not cured of her lustful behaviour, but she was chastened and rather sore for the rest of the voyage, and determined never to make the same mistake. She decided there was only one thing to do – she would purchase a timepiece at the first opportunity, so she would not confuse her appointments again.

The ship stopped at Agadir to take on stores. Crew and passengers were allowed off for the day. The elephants were walked down the reinforced ramp and trumpeted loudly, glad to throw up their heels and find a muddy

152

puddle to wash in. Hannibal scrubbed their backs with a stiff broom and they threw water over each other and him. Children from the town heard the strange noise and came to gawk, gathering in a crowd around the giant beasts and bravely feeding them with almond-paste sweetmeats.

Floradora looked forward to taking the horses for a gallop. They were restless from so many days lacking exercise. She dressed in chamois breeches and a white, full-sleeved shirt and short riding boots and went to find Isambard.

However, Lorenzo had other plans for her. He did not want his favourite slave to be out of his sight in a strange country. She might decide not to return. Indeed, escape had crossed her mind, but she knew it would be difficult in a foreign country, with no friends, and how would she get back to Antonio? She had very little money. So, with only vague thoughts of freedom in her mind, she set off for the horses' quarters and found Lorenzo waiting for her. Isambard was there also, saddling up Thunderhead.

'There you are, my dear, and how charming you look,' said Lorenzo.

'Oh, good morning,' said Floradora.

Isambard was silent. The ringmaster was dressed in riding breeches and shirt with a hacking jacket and boots.

'I thought a little equestrian exercise would do me some good, my dear, so I have decided to come with you. Isambard can walk the lions around the deck while it's clear. They are terribly restless. All right, Isambard?'

'Yes, sir.' He nodded, sullenly. He too had looked forward to terra firma and some freedom from the restraints of shipboard life. Although the weather had remained calm, he still suffered nausea from the swell.

'Very well, my dear, let us make haste and enjoy the day,' said the ringmaster.

Floradora had to admit he looked very handsome in the tight-cut jacket and leather breeches. He had the figure for it. She helped with the horses' bridles and leading reins and they walked the beasts down the ramps and mounted. She rode Thunderhead, as no one else could control him, and Lorenzo had Jet, a misnomer for the almost-white Arab mare. Isambard watched Floradora and Lorenzo ride away, the other mares on leading reins, and turned back to the hated ship.

They rode through the white town, its minarets and towers gleaming in the early sunlight. Dogs chased at their heels and the horses whinnied and kicked at them. Soon they were out of the narrow streets and on to a dry brown plain, not unlike the landscape around Arrecife. Floradora thought with a pang of Antonio. She was careful not to show any sign of remembering him to Lorenzo, who still wore his gold pendant on the chain round his neck – his symbol of power over her mind.

The wind blew her hair from her hot neck, and they galloped over the sandy earth. The horses were exhilarated by the freedom, and Thunderhead called with a low thrill to his mares. Floradora had let them off the reins so they could go where they wished and avoid the small boulders and prickly bushes that littered the landscape. She held the reins low on his neck and leant forward over his black mane. The wind rushed through her hair and she felt free. Except that Lorenzo was there behind her, his moustache bristling over his red lips, his white teeth bared.

They came across a Bedouin camp with billowing white tents and camels tethered outside, kneeling on chained legs. They did not see the Bedouin people, though they watched the strangers pass by through chinks in their cotton tents.

They came to an oasis in the desert, with tall palms swaying in the slight breeze. They stopped to allow the horses to drink.

Suddenly Lorenzo took the girl in his arms and kissed her passionately. He had never done this before. Before, the sexuality was pure lust and a game he played. This

154

me she felt that there was more to the caress than he ared to explain. She felt her thighs grow hot under the ressure of his powerful legs, pressing on her. He placed cool hand on her breast and stroked firmly. Her nipple tiffened. He pressed her down on the grass that sur- ounded the water and caressed her. She received his isses with mixed feelings. He was evil in his intentions she must remember this. But his lips found her soft esh and drew out the sweetness of her juices. They lay ntwined, their clothes undone, the horses grazing earby. He pressed open her legs with his. She let him ub against her. She held his cock in her thighs and queezed tightly. He moaned and came suddenly on her gs and belly.

What a strange man he was, she thought, that he did ot seem to want to penetrate her. He only wanted the eaviness, the closeness of flesh, the near-coitus, and tensity of desire. He kissed her, though she was nsatisfied, left hot and silky with lust, sticky. They alked on slowly, drinking from their refilled water asks. Then she remounted Thunderhead and pressed er knees into his flanks. He began to canter, then gallop, nd she lay on the horse's neck, becoming part of the allion. Lorenzo whipped the mare to catch up with the peeding horse. He whipped her flank and Jet whinnied oudly, alarmed. Floradora turned to see the mare rear shock at the blows he gave her, and the ringmaster ll with a sickening thud on to the hard, boulder-littered round. She pulled in the stallion and turned him, otting back to the prone, still form of the ringmaster. he dismounted. The mares had run off and she sent hunderhead after them.

Was he dead? No. He breathed. She felt strangely elieved. She had an odd relationship with this man who ielded power over her. Part of her hated him, and part f her welcomed his subtle touch, his bizarre practices, nd the unfinished love-making he indulged in with her. he enjoyed the ongoing frustration of not being penetrated, yet kept in a state of intense sexual excitement by him.

She knelt and examined his bloody forehead. He was unconscious. She stripped a sleeve from her blouse and tore it in lengths to tie around his head. There were no buildings in sight where she might get help. It occurred to her that this was her moment of decision. Should she escape from him now? Leave him to survive or perish in the hot sun that now beat down on them? She could so easily disappear; leave the circus and all her friends, Salome, Anastasia behind for ever. She could leave the lions, and perhaps find her way back to Lanzarote and her fiancé. She knelt, undecided, the sun pounding down on her head. The man looked so helpless, so weak. Above them vultures wheeled.

She tried to lift him. He was heavier than he looked, long and solid in his comatose state. She called Thunderhead over to her, whistled to him. The horse knelt and she heaved the ringmaster up and pushed him over the saddle of her stallion. She made sure he was properly secured; she tied him on the saddle, so he would not slip off, and fetched the saddled mare, Jet, who was still skittish and nervous. She mounted the mare and led Thunderhead. The other mares followed. Wherever the stallion went they would follow. So, slowly, she retraced her tracks back to the port and the ship.

Meanwhile, on board the ship, other dramas were unfolding. Isambard had managed to walk three of the lionesses around the deck several times, giving the powerful animals some much-needed leg-stretching. However, when it came to the turn of the lion, Kwasi, he had trouble. The lion was nervous at the unexpected sounds of the port, the shouts of workers on the harbour, the strange sights. He pulled and tugged at the chain that held him to the black clown. He turned on Isambard and put out a huge paw to claw him.

Isambard, aware of the beast's nervousness, was ready for the attack. He cracked the whip at the lion, cutting his nose. The stung lion furiously leapt back and, in doing so, pulled the chain from Isambard's hand. Isambard grabbed at the chain but Kwasi was gone in a flash. The lion leapt over the side of the ship and half-fell, half-staggered, on to the dockside. Sounds of alarm came from the dockers and they fled before the yellow flash. Kwasi trotted, growling low, through the derricks and cranes and dockside buildings, free at last of his bondage. He called to his female pride – a loud yowling cry – but they were stalking their cage, roaring in frustration.

Isambard went back to the cage and opened it. The lionesses, not believing that they were free to go, stood stupidly, nudging the open cage door. Isambard flicked the whip at them. 'Go, go, you are free to follow your mate, go, you stupid creatures.' And the lionesses swaggered out of their prison and sniffed the warm air. They stood on the ship's side for a moment before leaping on to the pier and following the roar of their lord and master.

Isambard felt liberated by his action. He could not think why he had done it. It was like the time he had leapt from the hayrick on to the circus train and changed his life. It was a bid for freedom. He had always known in his heart that to keep the lions caged was wrong. The dockers hid in their huts while the lions roamed the docks. It did not take Kwasi long to find the way out of town into the desert, his harem of slender, yellow beasts trotting calmly behind him, their tails held high.

When Floradora arrived back at the port Isambard was waiting for her. He took the unconscious Lorenzo from the horse and carried him on to the ship. She told him what had happened and then she saw to her horses and left Isambard to deal with the ringmaster.

Salome appeared along with several of the *bastoneras*, back from the bazaar. They were carrying rolls of silk, baskets of limes, sweetmeats, honey, almonds, and bundles of rugs. She dropped her packages as she saw Lorenzo in Isambard's arms and ran up the gangplank.

'What has happened to him?' she cried.

Anastasia and Gina also ran to the ringmaster and exclaimed over his bloody head and his helplessness.

'Bring him to his cabin,' ordered Salome to the clown, and he followed her to the large cabin on the foredeck.

A little later, when she had finished grooming her horses, Floradora went to see how Lorenzo was getting on. She saw Isambard, looking shifty and guilty, outside the ringmaster's cabin.

'What is it, Isambard? You don't look well.'

'His lions – they have all gone.'

'What do you mean, "gone"? Gone where?'

'They escaped and jumped off the ship,' he mumbled.

'My God, Isambard, did you let them go?'

'I . . . the big one, he was too strong for me and he escaped.'

'And the others?'

'I released them.' He looked down at her pale face and smiled. 'I liberated them.'

'What? Deliberately?'

'Yes,' he said, proudly, his head held high now.

'But, Lorenzo will never forgive you. He will kill you. You must leave.' Floradora really believed that the ringmaster would vent his fury at the irreplaceable loss on the poor clown.

'No, I will not leave. This is my family, Floradora, as it is yours, and I cannot leave.'

'Pray that he does not recover then,' she said, her heart gone cold at what the clown said. He was right. The circus was her family, too, how could she ever hope to leave it and be free of the ringmaster? Her lover had not come for her. He had changed his mind and decided he did not want a mere circus girl as his wife. She knew now that she was worth nothing to him. She had been like a firefly in his night, a tiny spark of light that he saw for a moment, admired, and then it was gone.

She nearly gave way and cried. Her mother and father had died, her lover had disappeared, and she was alone. Only the ringmaster cared for her, and Isambard – a sad clown and a perverse sado-masochist. She was condemned to a life of tinsel and applause with no real love, no home, no comforting hearth. Only a perversion of love.

Salome came out of the cabin and saw Floradora standing, white-faced, the clown sullen.

'He is still unconscious,' said Salome.

The ship was ready to sail on to Cadiz. The elephants had re-embarked, a trail of admiring children cheering them from the dockside. The drunken *chamacos*, reeling from the strong *raki* they had found in a dockside bar, came back on board and slumped where they could in the shade. The lions were gone, to become a part of the yellow desert.

The dancing girls were quiet, nursing the ringmaster in turns. Olympia turned up wearing a parody of a nurse's uniform: stockings and corset, a short blue dress and white apron, and a lace cap tied over her blond wig. She said she had once been a nurse, in Liverpool, in England, and her mother had been a nurse, too. She said she knew how to care for a comatose patient and she bustled around the cabin, opening the porthole to let in fresh air, cooling his forehead with wet clothes, and changing his dressing. The girls drifted off, except for Salome, whose attachment to the ringmaster was stronger than the others.

The captain was unsure what to do. He took his orders from Lorenzo, or had done, so far. He had been the one who was going to pay for this voyage. He now worried that the man was not going to recover from the blow to his head. Who would pay him then? Also, he thought the ringmaster might demand to stay in Agadir until his lions were brought back. What sort of a circus would it be without lions?

Floradora was also in a quandary. She should have left Lorenzo in the desert. She should have made her escape while she had the chance. Instead of saving his life, she should have saved her own. Would Lorenzo want to continue with the circus now the lions had gone?

What would he do to Isambard? All these questions and more flew around her dizzy head. She had spent too long in the desert sun and had a terrible headache.

Olympia put a water-soaked flannel to the ringmaster's mouth and squeezed the liquid into his dry, chapped lips.

The captain came to the sick quarters to ask what he should do. No one knew what to say. There was no one who could make the decision, to stay or to go. The ringmaster's condition did not change.

Chapter Twenty
The Circus Disembarks

*I*n Arrecife prison Antonio paced his cell like a caged lion, back and forth, back and forth.

'Where is Floradora now?' he agonised. 'Has she given me up? Has the young trapeze artiste claimed her as his own?' He did not eat the gruel that was offered him. He could do nothing to hurry his fate. Only wait.

The *señora* was not idle. She went at first light to the docks to look for the fisherman who claimed he had seen the bloodstained man board the circus ship. She went with Paco's son this time. He insisted on accompanying her through the rough area, which was full of vulgar roustabouts and tough dockers. Paco remained at the lodgings with the other horses.

'There is his boat.' She pointed to a small fishing craft, which had just docked by the pier. 'Let us hurry to catch him before he takes his fish to market.'

The fisherman was not surprised to see the fine lady. He accepted the notion that he must go to the police with them and help clear her son's name. He would do this because he was an honourable man who would not shirk his duty.

'I must first sell my fish, *señora*,' he insisted. 'It is my livelihood. I too have a family to feed.'

So they had to wait an interminable time while he

unloaded his meagre catch and carried it in boxes to the fish market, which was close by on the dockside. There his wife waited to help gut and clean the fish. Señora Octavia would not let him out of her sight in case anything happened to change his mind about going to the police. After two hours he agreed to go with Jaime and Señora Octavia to the police station.

After several hours' waiting, during which time the fisherman nearly gave up and went back to his boat, the police commander called them into his office. The result of the interview with the fisherman was that Antonio was released, a free man, with an apology.

Now they must catch the real murderer – the ringmaster, Lorenzo. It was known that the ship had been headed for Cadiz, on mainland Spain, and should arrive there tomorrow or the next day. The plan was for the police to send two men to Spain to catch him. Antonio insisted on going, too.

'Be careful, son,' said the *señora*. 'They have tried to kill you already; do not trust anyone.'

'I must go and find Floradora, Mother.' He kissed his mother, shook hands with his manservant and Jaime, and left with the two armed policemen to catch the next boat across to Spain.

The fisherman was paid handsomely by the *señora* for his trouble and the time he had spent being a good citizen, and he went off happily to the dock.

In Agadir, the ship still waited for the captain to decide what to do: to continue to mainland Spain with the circus troupe, who had not yet paid for the trip and whose purse holder was unconscious, or to throw them all off here in Morocco and cut his losses.

Salome attended Lorenzo. He was pale and still. Olympia had tired of her role as nurse and had gone to change her clothes. Floradora had done her duty to the ringmaster by saving him from the vultures. What should she do now? She could not decide. Should she make a bid for freedom, as the lions had done? She could not abandon her horses. They would have to go wherever she went. She was sure in her mind that Antonio had abandoned her. She thought so little of herself that she believed she was not good enough for a great gentleman to consider making her his wife. She kept to her cabin and cried.

Later, there was a gathering of all the circus performers. They were worried about their future. Would the ringmaster survive? He was their employer, their security. They discussed alternatives.

'If he dies we could try to join the Cirque de Nuit that is presently in southern Spain,' said Rosalita to her brother.

'I could take the elephants there, too, perhaps,' said Hannibal.

'How can you think of leaving Lorenzo in his hour of need?' snarled Salome. She was genuinely concerned about the ringmaster. He was still unconscious.

'Oh, Salome, you know what he is like,' said Alphonso. 'We all owe him money and cannot ever become independent while he lives. It would be a blessing for us if he dies.'

The circus troupe muttered in agreement and looked at each other.

'We could all get other work if we were free of him,' Gina said, quietly.

The cumulative effect of the ringmaster's hypnotism was wearing off for some of his victims. Floradora was completely cured of her attachment and Gina and the other *bastoneras* were beginning to have their own thoughts and ideas for their future.

Salome now wore the ringmaster's gold chain and pendant, but she had not used it on anyone yet. 'I shall stay with him, anyhow,' she promised.

Isambard was troubled. He loved Floradora. He knew she loved the gentleman from Lanzarote. Perhaps he could help her find him again. If she would only allow him to serve her, he would be content. He pulled her to one side and begged to talk to her alone. They walked around the deck to where the horses were kept and he told her his plan.

'I am leaving the ship and the circus,' he told her. 'If I stay and Lorenzo lives I will have to pay all my life for the lions I set free.'

'What will you do?'

'I could go with you, wherever you wish?'

'What do you mean, Isambard?'

'I mean, I am ready to go where you go and serve you, Floradora. I have told you I love you . . .' At this the girl turned away from him. 'But do not fear, I do not need you to love me, only let me serve you, please.' The black clown's dark eyes pleaded, and she softened.

'Isambard, would you help me reach the other circus in Spain, the one that was in Cadiz recently?'

'Yes, my dearest, of course. But I thought you loved the gentleman with the Lippizaners.'

'I do, Isambard, but I think he has forgotten me and I will not chase him.'

'I see,' he said.

She sighed, and thought of the hardship that was to come. The journey had to be paid for if they were not going to be able to continue on the circus ship. Other transport would have to be found and it would cost. How would they do that?

'Isambard, do you have any money?'

'No, *señorita, nada*.'

'I too have nothing.'

'Can we join the other performers who want to join the Cirque de Nuit and work on the way to earn money, doing outdoor acts? If we travel overland, we can perform in every village we come across.'

'I do not think there are many people living in this desert, Isambard. It would take us for ever.'

'We could disembark with the others and perform here in Agadir until we have enough to charter another ship to the mainland.'

'That is an excellent idea, Isambard, let's go and

suggest it to the others.' She reached up to his big face and kissed his lips.

The clown's chest swelled in pride.

In the saloon the gathering was arguing still. Floradora clapped her hands and begged them to listen to the plan Isambard had suggested.

It was unanimously agreed that, if the captain threw them off the ship, or if the ringmaster died, the circus family would continue the performances without him, without the big top, but in the open, to the local population. Salome listened but left as soon as they had made a decision, to return to the sick bed.

She stroked the ringmaster's cool, alabaster brow, combed his dark moustache and kissed his blue lips.

The captain could not wait any longer. He decided to evict the circus from his ship. It was obvious he was not going to be paid for the voyage and he had already lost enough money. He announced his decision to the circus folk that night.

'I am sorry to have to do this, but I have to live. I have to pay my crew. I have fuel to buy. It is a sad shame but you will have to go,' he said, with a melancholy glance at Olympia.

'We'll at least have a goodbye party, won't we?' said Olympia, who already wore her best frock – red satin, low-cut, split to the thigh.

'Yes!' The circus folk, never gloomy for long, accepted their new fate, an uncertain future, with good heart.

Olympia ran off with the captain to his cabin. Gina, Anastasia and La Roux changed into revealing boleros that showed the curve of their breasts beneath, and tight-fitting briefs that showed the outline of their sex-lips, and left their buttocks bare. They began a display of the *equilibrista* act, Gina bending herself into an unlikely shape and Anastasia climbing on top of her, with La Roux on the very top. They fell and tumbled, rolled together in a ball of breasts and buttocks. The crew applauded the erotic sight. Gina was a special favourite; she seemed made of rubber, boneless.

The fire eater bared his tattooed body, swallowed a column of fire and blew it out again. He took a sword and put it down his throat, all twenty-four inches of it, to the amazement of the audience.

The sibling trapeze artistes displayed their slender bodies in spangled tights, threw each other into the air and tumbled and did amazing things with their supple limbs. It was not as thrilling as the high-wire act or the trapeze tricks, but they were entertaining and beautiful to look at. All the clowns dressed up and put on their make-up, tumbled about and threw buckets of white-wash at each other.

The crew drank *raki* and handed it to the circus folk. Soon they were in each other's arms, making the most of the short time they had left together. Three sailors penetrated Gina at one time. La Roux was coaxed to take off her panties and display her red hair, while two different sailors suckled Anastasia's magnificent breasts. The first mate, bereft of Olympia, who had not returned from the captain's cabin, made love to the well-endowed Alphonso.

The trapeze artistes caressed each other, watched avidly by half a dozen wide-eyed voyeurs, including the first mate's young nephew, who had been so recently introduced to erotic joy by Olympia.

In the captain's cabin Olympia's best dress was now on the captain's broad form, his hairy chest visible at the low neck, his hairy thigh bulging through the split skirt. Olympia was still wearing stockings and suspenders, high-heeled shoes and a red wig. The captain was on his knees on the bunk and Olympia mounted him from behind, groaning as she entered the dark puckered flesh.

In the ringmaster's cabin, Salome wore a very short rubber skirt and rubber waistcoat. Her breasts pressed forward out of the front opening. She was trying to revive her master in the way she knew he liked best. She knelt over him, her buttocks in his face, her face over his limp cock. He was clothed in a rubber sheet, above and beneath. She rubbed oil on to his thighs and scrotum, slowly massaging. She had already oiled her own bottom and sex. She took the flaccid prick in her hand and rubbed firmly. She sat on his face, churning her open flower into his nose and mouth. She leant forward, so her breasts rubbed his belly and cock, and took the member between her large globes. It had no obvious effect on the unconscious man, but the snake charmer was excited by her power over her master. She writhed on his face, pressing down on his nose so it penetrated her soft flesh. She sat down hard on it. She sucked the unwilling flesh that would not swell, bit and lapped at the sleeping balls. She drew the rubber sheet over them both and breathed in the warm scent of the rubber and her sweat. She was desperate for penetration, needed her spaces filled. The man slept on, unaware of the assault on his person.

Floradora, aroused by the lewdness and erotic performances around her, wandered off to find Salome. She was sorry they were going to have to part. She had become fond of the snake charmer and would miss the exquisite times they spent in each other's arms. She knocked on the door of the ringmaster's cabin and, getting no reply, she entered and came upon a lascivious scene. She gasped at the sight of Salome's full round buttocks, her open sex-lips, her thighs enclosed in high leather boots. The naked hindquarters of the snake charmer rose and fell, jerked and writhed, on the face of the ringmaster, while she sucked his poor, limp prick.

'Oh, Salome, is he awake?' Floradora could not help asking.

'Oh, it's you, darling! Come here, please, and help me.' Salome left off her hopeless task and welcomed the girl into the large bed. The smell of warm rubber and sex juices filled Floradora's nostrils. They fell into each other's arms. Salome's armpits gave off a sharp, strong scent, and her hair was plastered to her head, so furiously had she been writhing in her wild attempt at coitus with the unconscious ringmaster.

She tore at Floradora's white lace dress, pulling it up so she could see her bare thighs and belly.

'Oh, you are so beautiful, Floradora, stay with me for ever.' She pressed her fingers between the girl's thighs and touched her.

'I can't, Salome, I must earn my living. I have the horses to feed.'

'Oh, do not talk about the future. Only hold me now,' Salome whispered, kissing the white neck that was lifted to her, and the swell of the small neat breasts.

Floradora lifted the rubber skirt and pressed fingers into the hot moistness of the older woman's sex. She opened the rubber waistcoat and kissed the large nipples. Salome swooned. Salome took the girl's buttocks in each hand and churned herself against her belly. Floradora felt the rubber skirt dig into her slit. Its pressure on her was delightful. She rubbed herself on it.

'Is your dildo here?' whispered Floradora, shyly.

'Yes, darling, of course.' Salome reached under the bunk and brought up a carefully wrapped rubber truncheon. It had rubber balls attached and straps so she could wear the whole contraption. She carefully oiled the toy and caressed Floradora with it.

'Oh, Salome, it is a wonderful device. Do it harder. I love it so.' Floradora opened her legs to accept the caress of rubber.

The man next to them went unnoticed. His breathing was shallow and his eyes flickered. They kissed passionately and made each other happy for a while.

In the saloon the orgy developed. The dwarf clown, Jellico, tickled Gina. He had a long feather and was touching her upturned bottom with it, stroking her between her legs and drawing out the clitoris so it flowered like a budding rose. She had positioned herself so her face was next to her bottom and her belly was like a low table. Jellico smirked as the contortionist's mouth opened to receive his outlandish prick. He was exactly the right height to do this. He stood, his breeches down by his ankles, his huge cock thrusting in and out of the open petals. The feather continued its subtle caress.

People stood around and watched the lewd performance, kissing and caressing each other as they did so. *Raki* flowed. The dwarf finished and Rosario, who had been frustrated by his sister's refusal of complete coitus, threw himself on to the contortionist, caressing her roughly before penetrating her. The furious Rosalita, naked but for a ribbon of chamois that divided her buttocks and went between her legs, hurled herself on to the connected pair and pulled him off. She dragged him away from the rude girl and promised she would do whatever he wanted. He grinned and took her hand and ran off to their cabin, Rosalita sobbing.

Alphonso and the first mate had said goodbye and now Alphonso was swallowing someone else's blunt sword.

The saloon was filled with bare limbs, flashing pricks, wild eyes, and a mélange of sweat, sex juices, semen and *raki*.

Back in Lorenzo's cabin, the two women were locked in another embrace. Their faces were buried in each other's thighs, their lips sucked and lapped. Salome strapped the rubber prick on to her loins, so the prick stuck up between her legs and the balls dangled behind. Floradora giggled in delight at the rude sight.

'What do you want me to do?' she asked, wiggling her hips, opening her legs, and touching herself.

'Why don't you bend over that stool and let me spank you?'

'All right.' Floradora flicked her skirt over her head so she could see nothing and bent over the leather stool, her head low, her buttocks high. The next thing she felt was the thwack of Salome's hand on her bottom. The warmth spread through her flesh. Her thighs tingled and her sex-lips throbbed. She pressed against the hand that spanked her. Salome pressed the dildo between the girl's bottom-cheeks, briefly, giving her a taste of the hard rubber. The girl groaned and pressed up towards the truncheon which, however, had withdrawn. She felt the hand hard on her again and again. The heat had become something else. Her flesh had become all sex; her eyes closed, her mind closed, except to the hands and the rubber. Salome pressed again with the rubber. Floradora felt as if there was a man, a master, pushing his own flesh into her wetness.

Salome grabbed her round the hips and thrust hard into her so her belly was pressed against her. Floradora reached around behind her and felt for Salome's prick. Under it she felt the balls banging on her. Then she felt the open sex-lips, wet, large, begging for penetration. She put her fingers into the silky flower and felt Salome's strong muscles clasp and throb.

The ringmaster's eyelids flickered and he sighed softly.

Chapter Twenty-One
The Circus in Agadir

The following day the entire circus disembarked, except for Lorenzo and the snake charmer and her snakes. The big top stayed on board, too, as did the ropes and stays, wires and trapezes, which all belonged to the ringmaster. Salome knew where Lorenzo kept his gold and promised the captain he would be paid for their passage if he took them safely to mainland Spain. She hoped she could get specialist help for him there.

As she and the other performers were going down the gangplank, Olympia suddenly cried out and pushed through the crowd to get back on board. She ran to the captain and flung herself into his arms.

'I will stay with you, after all,' she said, sobbing and kissing the large Greek bear of a man. He was smiling and slapping Olympia's satin-encased buttocks with ill-concealed joy.

Salome said her sad goodbyes to all her friends as they unloaded their belongings on to the dock. The elephants went down the ramps again with their faithful Hannibal. The *chamacos* and *bastoneras* had only the clothes they stood in and perhaps some pots and pans. The caravans were hoisted off on to the dock. Floradora and Isambard hooded the horses to take them down the ramp again on to the pier. The entire troupe stood and waved at Salome and the crew as the ship sounded its horn and disappeared out of the harbour and into the open sea.

'At least we have the caravans to sleep in,' said Anastasia to Floradora.

'Yes, dear, we will be just fine,' she said, and she kicked her horse on and left Anastasia in the queue of gaily painted caravans that trailed out of the dock into the town.

People came to stare at the strange caravans full of daringly dressed people. The elephants trumpeted their joy at being off the ship at last. They did not care where they went as long as they were together and their loving Hannibal was there to scrub them and wash them and feed them if they could not find their own food.

The horses were skittish and wanted to gallop, but Floradora and Isambard kept them under control. The captain had advised the women to cover their faces while they were in Morocco, so as not to shock the local populace. They were supposed to wear long, concealing costumes, too, and Olympia had provided them all with diaphanous garments that almost hid their charms yet showed them. A caravan of circus costumes was unloaded and Olympia seemed quite happy to let it go with the performers. She still had her own chest of clothes.

The circus needed to set up and perform quickly if they were to make enough money to be able to eat and drink and save enough to pay their passage to Spain. They still had a few circus posters left over from Lanzarote and they plastered them around the town. They found a piece of unused ground on the outskirts of town – the usual location for a big top – but this time there was no tent. They drove the caravans into a circle and made a ring of bonfires on the inside. The band players, *chamacos* and *bastoneras* went out to proclaim the circus was in town and to drum up customers. The locals were bemused by the bizarrely dressed performers, but followed them back to the open-air circus.

The elephants had no drums to stand on; instead they

had boulders, carefully moved into place by the strong Alphonso. Everybody helped everyone out, and they pulled together as a real circus family.

Suddenly, there was a cry from the wardrobe caravan. Rosalita had been going through the rails of clothes when she had come across the cabin boy, the first mate's young nephew, Nico. He had hidden there before the caravan was unloaded from the ship and had run away to join the circus.

'How old are you?' she asked the curly haired youth who looked strong enough to be useful to them.

'I do not know – seventeen, eighteen?'

'Oh, you are old enough. I was younger than you are when I ran away to join the circus,' she said to him. 'Come, you can eat with us in our caravan and we will see what we can find for you to do.'

The happy youth followed the slender trapeze artiste, admiring her muscular bottom and strong legs.

'Oh, who have we here?' said Gina. 'The pretty boy!'

'Leave him alone,' said Rosalita, as if he belonged to her. 'I found him in the wardrobe caravan. He wants to join the circus.'

'What a time to choose!' said Gina. 'No ringmaster, no big top, no lions, no wardrobe mistress. What can you do?'

'Dunno,' he mumbled. 'Clean, cook, clean the captain's uniform.'

'Wonderful! You can look after our clothes and help cook for the troupe,' said Floradora, who had come on the scene and realised what the boy was doing there.

'Just what I was going to suggest,' said the trapeze artiste, coldly. 'He is to share with us, for the time being, but he can sleep in the wardrobe caravan.'

'Thanks!' said the cabin boy who was suddenly in charge of the exotic costumes and the cooking.

'You can sell tickets, too. Take over Olympia's tasks,' said Gina.

The boy was quickly assimilated into the troupe as all runaways were. There was always a place for a fit young man. He had dreams of becoming a clown or even a trapeze artiste. He could do anything he set his mind to. He was fairly disappointed when he realised that the transvestite wardrobe mistress had stayed behind on the ship to be with the captain. He had enjoyed the erotic game they had played. His one hope was that it would happen again to him, that he would be lying, slumbering, and someone would take his soft cock in his, or her, hand and milk it. He would have to do nothing at all, just lie there, pretending sleep, while his cock was cunningly massaged to spill its seed.

That evening, his first as wardrobe master, he handed out carefully ironed clothes, hung them back on hangers, caressed the silks and satins, sniffed at the crotches of the *bastoneras'* discarded costumes. He thought himself a very lucky lad.

There were many people at the circus performance that evening, and they were all men. They had come, not to see the spectacular feats of the elephants and horses, but to ogle the undressed girls. They were not used to such nudity. Their eyes were out on stalks at the contortionist. They pressed forward, offering more money to see her completely naked. She whispered to the other *bastoneras*, who nodded, surrounding her with a diaphanous silk curtain while she disrobed. The Arab audience clapped loudly at the emerging naked girl. She walked around on all fours, inside out, it seemed, and flaunted her sex at the audience. The men cheered and shouted at the erotic scene and threw gold coins into the temporary circus ring. The other performers were excited at the obvious possibilities that had opened up to them. Dressed in their circus costumes, their oiled muscles gleaming, they, in their turn, tumbled, threw themselves into the air and somersaulted, their breasts swelling under the stretched gauze, their buttocks flashing. The dissatisfied audience crowed and called for more nudity. The *equilibristas* threw off their clothes and Nico caught them. The nude girls pranced and hurled themselves

174

about, now on their hands, now on their heels, now doing the splits. Breasts shook and pink pussies flashed. The crowd roared and threw money and gold at the performers. Nico skipped between the girls, picking up the gold coins.

Floradora rode Thunderhead, the other horses following in a circle. She was dressed modestly in her Red Indian squaw costume, the little chamois skirt just reaching her thighs, the chamois waistcoat closed over her small bosom. She wore a feather in her headband.

She did all her usual trick riding; hiding under the horse's belly, then appearing on his side, pulling herself up to stand on his back. But the men were jeering and shouting for her to take off her clothes. She knew what they wanted, and she needed her share of the takings. Without losing pace, she rode on, leaping from one horse to the next, each time removing an item of clothing. The men threw gold coins as each item came off. First her headband, then her waistcoat, so her little breasts bobbed up and down as she rode. Then her boots and, last of all, her chamois skirt. She had nothing on underneath but a thin strap of chamois between her buttocks and legs and round her hips. It did not hide anything. The excited men rubbed themselves under their long voluminous garments at the sight of the fair-skinned, blonde equestrian. She lay back on the stallion's back, her legs each side of his neck, then stood on her head as the horse cantered around. She opened her legs wide and let go with her hands so that she was riding him balanced only on her head. She continued as long as they threw gold and then she left the arena, her mares following the stallion.

The audience was wild with excitement. They had never seen such a feast of young female flesh. The younger men stayed behind after the show and hung around trying to spy on the girls. It was decided that there should be two night guards, in case any of the randy youths decided to attack.

The girls went off to bed, tired but aroused by their

own erotic performances. The Greek runaway, Nico, could not believe his luck at having joined such a troupe, whose natural beauty was so readily displayed. He went to eat with the trapeze artistes before going to his new home, the wardrobe caravan, where he settled in a nest of satin and feathers, like a happy duckling.

Later, after frenzied masturbation, while thinking of all the girls in the circus naked, he slept, and as he slept a dark figure crept into the wardrobe caravan. Nico stirred as he heard heavy breathing. He lay, half-covered by a chiffon cloak, but naked underneath. He did not open his eyes. The chiffon was removed from his loins. His prick was taken into someone's hand. The hand was soft, the fingers slender. He lay still, not making any sign that he was aware of the caress. The fingers pressed the burgeoning flesh and it swelled under the delicate rubbing. He lay there, hearing the heavy breathing, smelling a strong lemony perfume. Was it a man or a woman? He did not care one way or the other. He lay still, only stirring slightly to ease his legs so the hands could reach under him and squeeze his scrotum. The intruder pressed his own flesh, pulling up the long gown he wore, stroking his own penis to a huge erection.

The man came all over the belly of the cabin boy, whereupon the boy ejaculated also. He then withdrew into the darkness once more, leaving the sighing cabin boy exhausted, still lying where he had found him.

'This must be heaven!' said the boy to himself. 'I am in heaven.'

In Floradora and Anastasia's caravan, the candle was blown out quickly and the two friends cuddled each other in the hard bed.

'You were very good tonight, Floradora,' said the admiring dancer. 'You were so pretty in your bare skin. I wish I had little breasts like yours.' She put her arms round the girl and pressed her two plump apples.

'Oh, no, mine are too small, yours are much prettier,' said the sleepy Floradora, allowing the bigger girl to caress her gently. She turned so they were belly to belly and they kissed each other's breasts, sucking at the erect nipples.

'You always smell so clean,' said Anastasia. 'You are perfect!' She slid down in the bed under the harsh blanket and paid homage to the perfect fruit between Floradora's soft thighs.

Floradora also had the joy of being caressed while she pretended sleep, and she soon reached bliss under the dextrous tongue of the voluptuous Russian, and slipped into real sleep.

Next day dawned pink and calm. The guards slept over the fire's embers. Yellow, skinny curs had appeared from nowhere to see what there was to eat. The circus awoke and realised that they had made lots of money from their first performance in Agadir. If they went on like this they would soon make enough to get a ship to Spain to join another circus.

Nico awoke and remembered the happenings of the night before. Had it all been a dream? He could not say for sure. He whistled a cheerful tune and went outside to see what he had to do today. *Chamacos* were lighting fires and brewing strong Arabic coffee. Pastries had appeared from somewhere. Small groups sat, wrapped in their *batas*, to eat and drink before they began the rituals of the circus.

True, there was no big top to mend or ropes to tighten after wind had loosened them; there was no trapeze to test and no net to adjust. But they had to clean the plates, fetch water, wash themselves, sort out costumes and make-up, organise the props – the buckets, the white-wash, the custard pies. Hannibal had to wash the ele-phants and find them food.

First, there was a general gathering of all the circus folk, to make decisions for the running of the circus. They had to have some overall design, now that the ringmaster had gone.

177

'I suggest we have a new ringmaster,' said Floradora, 'and I think I know the person to do it.'

'Who?'

'Isambard!' pronounced Floradora. 'He could wear his harlequin outfit and we have a whip. He would be good at it.'

It was unanimously agreed that the black clown should take on the mantle of ringmaster. Isambard could not believe it. He was proud to have been chosen – even if it was a ramshackle circus, with no tent, and no lions or snake charmer – it was a circus, and he was going to be ringmaster. No more being laughed at, no more sad face, white-painted to hide his black skin, no more buckets of whitewash over his head. He was to be ringmaster.

Chapter Twenty-Two
Antonio Searches in Vain

*A*ntonio and the two policemen were feeling seasick.
The ocean had grown angry since the circus ship
had made the voyage across the same waters. The waves
were high, dropping slowly into deep troughs, and the
swell was horrible to the landlubbers. Antonio kept to
his cabin and tried to sleep. He had not fully recovered
from the beating he had had at the hands of the ruffians
in the pay of the ringmaster. His head was still sore, and
now he wished he were dead. How could he ever have
wanted to be a fisherman? he thought wryly. Never
again would he go to sea – never – except to return to
Lanzarote with his beloved Floradora.

He stayed below in his cabin until the ship reached
Cadiz, where he left the police and went to find lodgings
on his own. They would liaise with him if they had any
information of the whereabouts of the Circo Lorenzo. He
found quiet sanctuary in a palm- and fern-filled courtyard, where a canary bird sang sweetly in its cage
hanging from the balcony of his room. Here he rested
and recovered from the awful voyage. That afternoon he
went back to the port to ask questions.

'Have you seen a circus ship unload, with elephants
and horses?' he asked. 'And pretty dancing girls?'

No one had seen the circus. He could not understand.

Then someone mentioned a snake charmer they had seen performing in a square in Cadiz that day.

'A snake charmer?'

'Yes, *señor*, a black-haired beauty, with big breasts and wide hips and a narrow waist, very daring in her costume, and she put the snakes in her mouth.' The old man laughed greedily. 'She can eat my snake any time she wants.'

'Tell me where she is,' Antonio begged, giving the man several pesetas.

'Over that way, near the church of Santa Maria,' said the old lecher.

'*Muchas gracias, señor*,' said Antonio and took off his sombrero to bow.

He made his way to the square of Santa Maria and found Salome and her snakes, as the man had said. She was writhing, half-naked, with a transparent veil over her mouth and nose; a veil also enclosing and drawing attention to her large jutting breasts and her erect nipples. Another two thin veils hid her pubis and bottom cleft. In her belly button glittered a ruby. A snake wound its way round her legs up to her thighs and thrust its head between her legs, shooting out its forked tongue towards her belly. She stroked its head as if it were a giant member growing between her legs. The men whispered to each other and chewed toothpicks between their gold-capped teeth, watching the snake and the snake charmer's hands. The snake slowly withdrew from her thighs and curled down her legs again to twist away into the pot.

He waited until her act was over and pushed through the crowd of men. She was bending down to pick up the thrown pesetas, and she did not immediately notice him.

'Is it Salome?' he asked her.

'It is Salome. Who asks?' said the snake charmer. She had not met the gentleman who had stolen her Floradora's heart, but he had seen her perform at the circus in Teguise.

'Excuse me, my name is Antonio Valera de Teguise. I

am looking for Floradora, the lion-tamer's daughter. Do you know where I can find her?'

'No, unfortunately, *señor*, I do not know. I am afraid the circus and I have parted company.'

'But where are the rest of the troupe?' he asked.

'Come with me to my room and I will tell you what I know. Perhaps you could help me carry my snakes,' she said, pointing to the ceramic jar.

'But of course, *señorita*, it will be my pleasure.' He lifted the jar, taking care not to shift the lid, and followed her to a room very similar to his own, but in a poorer part of town.

She broke a large piece of bread into two and gave him half. 'Have some wine. It is all I have,' she said.

He refused her rations but took a glass of wine. 'Now, tell me, where is Floradora? Where is the circus?'

'Alas, *señor*, I fear you are in the wrong country.' She smiled, looking at the interesting bulge in his trousers and playing with the pendant round her neck. She had put a transparent cloak over her exotic costume, but it did nothing to hide her curves.

He found he could not tear his eyes from the pendant, which swung as sickeningly as the boat he had just left. He held his head and shook it. He looked into her green eyes, which glinted and narrowed.

'Floradora has gone with Isambard and her horses to Morocco, *señor*. I fear she is already a slave or worse.'

He tried to lift himself from the chair, but found he could not. His legs were like lead.

'I don't understand,' he said.

'Never mind, *señor*, I will take care of you. Just relax and close your eyes. When you wake you will do as I say, do you understand?' The gold pendant swung higher and higher and he fell suddenly to the tiled floor.

Salome was jubilant. He was obviously a gentleman. She had caught herself a rich man. She vaguely remembered him from Teguise. He had sat in the front row next to a fine old lady in silks and lace. She had noticed his proud, sad face.

So he was Floradora's *amoroso*, was he? Well, he would not find her here. She was still stuck in Agadir, probably, with the raggle-taggle of the circus for company.

Salome had stayed with the ringmaster until he died, just as they docked at Cadiz. He had never regained consciousness. She had sobbed a while. Then she had paid the captain for their passage and taken the circus tent and paraphernalia off the ship and stored it in the dock. She was furious that Lorenzo had not as much gold as she had thought he had. When the funeral was paid for she had hardly anything left. She could not sell the big top, as no one would ever want such a huge tent, except for a circus. She was told that there had been another circus in town recently but it had moved north, inland. She had cursed her luck, and had sold all her snakes to the zoological garden, except for two, then had set up as street performer to earn her bread for a while, while she considered what to do next. She mourned the loss of her beautiful snakes more than she mourned Lorenzo. They had been everything to her. She had kept Lorenzo's pendant, however, and now found she could use her own power to mesmerise as he had done. She could, with her talents, earn much.

She dragged the man to her bed and undressed him. He had a smooth, hard body, a flat belly and taut buttocks. His cock, even in repose, was proud, slender, long. He was obviously a gentleman. She emptied his pockets and found gold in plenty. She covered him up and let him sleep, and she prepared her own body for him.

While Antonio slept, Salome shaved her pubic hair until her pubis was a smooth peach. Her underarms and her legs were depilated also. She washed her hair and dried it in the sun.

He slept.

She oiled her smooth skin all over, making it shine and gleam. She cleaned her teeth with ground-herb paste, bought from the morning market. She dressed in only a gauzy silk chiffon cloak, and wore the gold chain and pendant, just in case the hypnosis began to wear off. She sat by his side and played with his prick, flicking it up and down to feel the weight of it as it swelled.

He stirred.

She mounted the bed and sat astride him, so that when his eyes opened he found he was straddled by the voluptuous woman whose belly was close to his and whose large breasts swung in front of his eyes like the pendant she wore.

His cock was awake before him, stretching towards her shiny skin, caressing the soft inner thighs that gleamed and flashed above him. He was helpless beneath her. Her legs felt like molten glass, hot, liquid. She lowered her long nipples to his hungry mouth. He bit them, nibbled the areolae and sucked like a babe. The breasts swelled under his embrace. She sighed and held his stiff prick between her hands, rubbing hard, not letting go, pushing the cock over her naked sex, back and forth, feeling the force of it, its hardness and silkiness drawing out her moistness.

She forced herself down on his hardness and let it go deep into her, deeper than anything had gone before, deeper than Floradora's fingers, or Lorenzo's fingers, or the rubber prick, deeper even than the ringmaster's whip handle. It filled her with a completeness she had always known existed but had never experienced. This stranger's cock swelled inside her tunnel and made her full and happy, replete. She felt an explosion like a volcano erupting inside her body. She screamed as his throbbing flowed through her body. She felt the shooting of his come hit her womb. Her hands, arms, legs, feet, thighs, belly, breasts, neck, head – all of her – became sexually charged. She collapsed on to his fast-beating heart and lay there, sobbing from sheer bliss.

So that was what it should have been like with Lorenzo?

* * *

183

In Agadir, the troupe was weary. It was hard work keeping raiders and thieves away at night. The fires had to be kept going and food cooked. It was difficult finding enough water in this arid place. The elephants needed lots of water and there had been a drought. Nico was doing well, preparing couscous and vegetables and seeing to the wardrobe. Not that there was much call for costumes these days. The local men were willing to pay anything to see naked female flesh, and even naked male flesh, as they were to find out. But Nico was inventive with the costumes and adapted the original ones to show more flesh. He cut holes in the bodices and corsets so the dancing girls' breasts or just their nipples would be exposed. He cut out the crotches from their tights and one-piece costumes, so their pink pussies would be completely visible instead of simply indicated, as they had always been.

'I prefer to leave something to the imagination,' said Anastasia, disapprovingly, as she surveyed her rude costume.

'Perhaps the locals haven't got any imagination,' said Gina, wryly.

'You are right,' said the tight-lipped trapeze artiste. 'They are animals, all of them.'

'But animals with deep pockets,' said Alphonso, rubbing oil over his tattooed body. He wore nothing but a loincloth of leopardskin, which revealed his buttocks and loins and only just hid his bulging genitals.

'Hey, that's my costume,' said Rosario, grabbing at the skin.

'Have it, have it, it's too small for me,' said the giant, laughing and tearing off the offending article. His prick was half-erect and Rosario and the dancing girls leered as he took his time choosing another minuscule apron of cloth, this time in black rubber.

Nico was in his seventh heaven, helping the girls to dress, doing them up behind, sewing them into their naughty costumes.

Isambard strutted proudly in his harlequin outfit and practised aiming the whip.

Floradora kept her gold safely tied up in a cloth under her pillow. They had all collected gold coins thrown by the appreciative audience, and all were willing to show their bodies for more. At this rate they would soon have enough to move on. The horses and elephants had enough fodder, and life in the temporary circus went on, regardless of the hardships. They cooked over charcoal fires, ate what the locals ate, and performed in the late afternoons, as they had not enough lights to perform at night.

The trapeze artistes had set up a low tightrope – a wire stretched between two poles – and did various simple acrobatics on it. These tricks would have been less than exciting had it not been for the daring new costumes they wore. Rosalita's stretchy one-piece stockinet costume was cut to display her little breasts, which poked through the material and jutted prettily and, each time her legs splayed or she threw a leg in the air, her bare sex flashed like a ruby. Her brother, who wrapped himself round her like one of Salome's snakes, was scantily robed in an apron of chamois which rose and fell as he leapt, revealing his naked charms to all. From behind, he wore nothing but a strap round his hips. The audience applauded their almost coupling on the wire; their caressing; the youth's strong arms taking her weight as she stood on her head on his head, he balancing on the wire. She managed to show her bare privates many times and the crowd roared each time. In one exercise, she leapt into his arms and he held her between her legs and felt the moistness as she balanced on his hand. His cock rose and pushed the leather aside. The crowd yelled and threw coins.

Floradora, watching from the side, grew hot and wet, too, as she saw the prick stiffen. Every eye was on the erotic aerial dance. Floradora drew her gaze from them to watch the audience, all men, all groping under their long, concealing cloaks, caressing themselves.

Alphonso, his muscles twitching as he lifted heavy stones and breathed out pillars of flame, was not such a success with the audience. They booed and threw bad eggs at him. In dismay, he lifted his loincloth and showed off his tattooed prick. That was more like it. The audience preferred the sight of his snake-eyed prick writhing lewdly. La Roux joined in, instinctively, and so did the other *bastoneras*, dancing and leaping just out of his reach, their seven veils hiding nothing but their mouths, bells dancing on their flashing feet, tassels bobbing on their nipples. Anastasia blindfolded Alphonso and the girls danced around the erect snake of the tattooed man as he tried unsuccessfully to catch them. They grabbed at his cock and toyed with it, to the loud joy of the crowd. He sank to his knees as La Roux put the snake in her mouth as she had seen Salome do. The redhead toyed with the decorated prick, letting it escape from her wide mouth, until more gold was thrown, then she set to and sucked him hard until he and the crowd were satisfied.

Chapter Twenty-Three
Nights in the Desert

The third night in Morocco, Alphonso was on guard with two of the *chamacos*. They had banked up the fires and settled down with cigarillos and a bottle of *raki* for the night, remembering to walk round the circumference of the circus every half-hour to check for prowlers.

It was about two o'clock in the morning and Alphonso was reeling from one caravan to the next. When he came to the wardrobe caravan, he looked around him furtively, quietly opened the door and crept inside. As he expected, Nico was asleep on a pile of animal skins and covered only by a light filmy sheet. He gazed at the beautiful boy, admiring his white flanks, his taut buttocks, the curve of his back, and his dark curls. Most of all he admired the slender erection. How could the boy be erect so often? Alphonso had forgotten what it was to be young. He knelt quietly and drew back the sheet from the sleeping youth. The boy lay on his side, his cock stretched out on one thigh. Alphonso touched the fleshy rod and stroked it to its full length. He touched himself as he caressed the youth, and then leant forward to stroke the boy's cock with his own. This was an exquisite torture. He would have liked the youth to suck him, but he was frightened of rebuttal.

He continued the delicate caressing and made do with

187

fondling the boy while caressing himself. The boy stirred and moved on to his back, so releasing his balls from between his legs. Alphonso stroked under the boy's cock at the root and consequently fondled his balls, too. The boy's cock grew very stiff and solid, as if a bone grew inside it. Alphonso recognised the signs. He stroked faster, his own cock was also given a more thorough rubbing and, as had happened the previous two nights, he and the happy youth came simultaneously.

Alphonso crept out of the caravan. The youth opened his eyes and sighed contentedly. Did the old fool really think he had been asleep? He smirked and turned over, drawing the sheet over him, and slept.

In another caravan, Anastasia and her *chamaco* lover, Yulias, were entwined in an erotic embrace. However, Floradora was lying next to them, trying not to hear the love cries. In the end she gave up and turned towards them.

'Look here, Anastasia, I cannot stand this any longer. I am too excited. Can't I join in, please?'

'Oh, yes, dearest, of course you may,' the Russian girl laughed. She turned away from her masculine lover towards the lion-tamer's daughter and caressed her little breasts.

Floradora was moist from the sounds and scents of the lovers' actions. She was exhausted by her earlier performance but too aroused to sleep. She encouraged Anastasia to caress her while Yulias sucked his lover's nipples. The bear of a man grunted and shifted his weight and slid over Anastasia so he was between the two girls. He put a tentative hand across Floradora's belly and stroked her. She welcomed the big, rough hand, with its huge thumb, which soon found her little bud and caused it to harden. She came almost immediately but his caresses continued. After the first spasms had faded, more arrived and developed inside her, and she came again. Then he ceased his caressing and moved on top of Anastasia, penetrating her without further ado.

He thrust in and out of her, his bulk causing the bed to rattle and shake. Floradora knelt so she could watch the love act. She saw his thick, pale cock come nearly out of the girl's sex, then penetrate her to the hilt. Anastasia shuddered as his cock filled her. His balls, Floradora noted, banged hard on her companion's buttocks. With no invitation, Floradora began to caress the man's balls, slipping her hands under his buttocks as he rose and fell. Her fingers could not help but touch Anastasia's moistness also. Anastasia showed her appreciation with loud moans. The large Hungarian groaned also at the extra pressure that was placed on his genitals. They came together as Floradora stroked fast and firmly, and she even felt the moment of orgasm thrill through the entwined pair.

Yulias withdrew and fell back on to the far side of the bed, and Floradora found herself next to her female companion again. Anastasia smiled sleepily at her and said, 'Thank-you, sweetest girl, that was wonderful, was it not, Yulias?' But the *chamaco* was asleep. 'Typical!' she said, and began to thank Floradora properly.

Anastasia slid down the bed to caress Floradora with her eloquent tongue. The *chamaco* remained asleep. Floradora turned on to her belly and lifted her bottom high.

'Spank me, Anastasia, please,' she begged.

'With pleasure, my naughty girl,' said Anastasia.

Floradora missed her punishment sessions with Lorenzo. She also missed the rubber sheets and cloaks that Lorenzo had provided. They had remained on the ship with Lorenzo and Salome. Anastasia slapped the upturned rosy flesh, and stroked between Floradora's open thighs with the palm of her hand. She spanked hard so the flesh became red and fiery. She slapped occasionally at the pouting flesh between Floradora's legs, and Floradora groaned and thrust out her bottom to meet the stern caresses.

Anastasia found a purple-skinned long vegetable that they had bought in the local market. She did not know its name but it was good to eat stewed with peppers and tomatoes and fresh herbs and spices, the way the locals prepared it. It was an interesting shape, ideal for certain practices. After removing the prickly stalk with a knife, Anastasia inserted the thin end of the bulbous vegetable into her vagina and rubbed the other end between Floradora's buttocks. She continued spanking but thrust the slender aubergine into her friend's buttock-cleft, too.

Floradora lifted her bottom higher still, so that her sex-lips were assaulted by the ripe vegetable. It hammered her inflamed flesh and Anastasia's fingers found her erect bud. The sensations were so intense for both girls that they soon swooned and cried out and fell apart, hot and finished.

In another caravan there was yet more illicit carnal delight. Rosalita was massaging her younger brother with fragrant oils. He was stretched out on their bed, naked, belly up, his arms and legs splayed out, his cock erect and pointing to his belly. She concentrated on his thighs, rubbing them hard. She was almost naked, too, wearing only a pair of transparent loose-legged split-crotch drawers. She straddled one of his legs, rubbing herself on his hard thigh as she massaged him. His cock jumped with each stroke of her strong little hands on his legs. She carefully neglected his genitals, preferring to keep him aroused for longer. He put out a hand and grabbed her swinging breasts, caressing them with no finesse but causing the nipples to stiffen hard, anyway. She was aching to have his cock inside her, but they were always careful not to transgress the unwritten law of incest.

Their practised caresses came close to penetration but always they drew back before it was too late. It was an awful strain to have to stop just as they were at their moment of greatest need but, so far, they had always done so. Instead of full intercourse, the siblings had developed a different intimacy. They used their fingers and mouths, of course, but they also had found the rubber dildo that had been used by Salome and Floradora. Salome had carelessly left it lying around and Rosalita had picked it up and failed to return it to its rightful owner. Now she made Rosario strap it on above his own erection and rub his own prick over the entrance to her sex while inserting the false prick, oiled, inside her.

This way she had the best of both worlds, and it felt as if two men were interfering with her simultaneously. She closed her eyes and let him rub the device over her perineum, or was it his cock he waved? She was in a swoon of delight. She heard his breathing get faster. She held his cock and squeezed it hard, stopping his impending ejaculation. He breathed more quietly. She loosened her grip slightly and felt the blood pump into her brother's prick. The dildo was deep inside her and she squirmed and gyrated her hips, feeling his balls bang on her, enjoying the warmth of his rod on her buttocks. Her legs were round his neck and he held her by the buttocks, slamming the dildo hard inside her. She retained her firm grip on his prick until he reached the height of his excitement, and they managed to come together, as they usually did.

Gina and the dwarf were having fun in another caravan, with two *chamacos* watching, as the contortionist arranged her body so the dwarf could reach her while she stood on her head. He stood on a bucket and was held by the wide-eyed voyeurs. She held her legs wide open and balanced on her elbows. The unusual view of her open flower was like a magnet to the men. They could not take their eyes from her pink petals, the darker red softness within like a tongue. The randy dwarf was in heaven, dipping his prick in and out of her. She was happy enough, especially when the other *chamacos* decided to join in, taking out their stiff cocks and rubbing them over her thighs and buttocks. She was adept at taking more than one penis into her at once and she encouraged the *chamacos* to push into her. Unfortunately, Jellico lost his balance without the *chamacos'* helping hands and fell out of her with a cry. The other two took advantage of this unexpected vacuum and plunged together into her ripe fruit. She satisfied them both between her own orgasms.

'That's enough, boys,' she ordered them, 'I am tired. I'll see you tomorrow. If you like we can try that act in public. The Arabs will love it.'

'But what about me?' said Jellico, jumping up and down.

'Yes, you too, of course, big boy.' She smiled and wound her body down and sat in an orthodox position. She looked so different the right way up; they almost did not recognise her.

Isambard slept alone, only a fragment of chamois leather keeping him company. It had been wrapped between Floradora's legs at one time, and still he could discern her musk in the folds. He sniffed it and wrapped it round his penis and rubbed, imagining her taut thigh muscles gripping him, her soft lips on his. He loved her truly, but he was content now to be her slave if she wished it; he wanted only to serve her. He rubbed his balls hard with the strip of chamois and closed his eyes. His imagination was good enough to give him beautiful images of a naked Floradora. He remembered her showing herself to the male crowd, the flash of her white thighs, her sex visible as she scissored her bare legs.

He had no hope of ever making love with her now. He had had his chance, twice, and the act had not been consummated. It was meant never to be. He was content with her fragment of leather, her fragrant scent on his cock. He came with a rush, his sperm wasted on his belly.

Chapter Twenty-Four
Antonio and Salome

*A*ntonio awoke to sun leaking through the wooden shutters. His head was aching and he felt exhausted, although he had slept for twelve hours. He heard a gentle hissing coming from the tall ceramic jar in the corner of the cool-tiled room. He remembered the snake charmer, and his loins ached from the memory of the night before. He tried moving but found he was shackled to the iron bedstead by his wrists. He grinned to himself. Had she not finished with him yet? Where was she? He was alone, apart from the snakes. He wore a rubber loincloth, he realised, to his embarrassment. He did not remember a rubber loincloth as being part of the previous night's wardrobe. Perhaps he did not know what she had done with him. He was thirsty and needed to empty his bladder. Anger grew as he waited in vain. Where was the snake charmer?

Salome had left him tied to the bed with chains in case the hypnosis wore off and he tried to escape. She was scouring the market for suitable fresh food for her two snakes. They had not eaten for a week and were probably getting hungry.

Antonio writhed and twisted until his legs were on the floor, though he was still attached to the bedhead by his wrists. The chains were fairly loose, though, and allowed him adequate movement to walk two paces from the bed. He tried to free himself, yanking on the chains. He searched for a tool with which to break the links. He found a large, rectangular brass tray, highly decorated and rather beautiful, and he could just reach it with one hand. He clasped the corner and tried to edge it closer so he could grab it properly but it slipped from his fingers and fell on to the ceramic jar, shifting the lid. It dropped to the floor with a loud clang and the snakes hissed angrily and nudged their heads out of the now open jar. He stood absolutely still as the snakes slowly slithered up and out of their cool dark home and made for the tiled floor, where they searched the tiles for something to eat. He could not look as one of the creatures, its skin dry and scaly, moved across his feet. He had never liked snakes, not since he was a small child and had come across a nest of them copulating. It had been like a vision of Dante's inferno: the writhing dark things, their alien eyes and devil's tongues, the females trying to slide away but the males slithering after them.

He shuddered involuntarily and, when Salome unlocked the heavy, studded door and entered, he was grateful and relieved to see her.

'What are you doing with my snakes?' Her green eyes glinted in the shadowy room.

'What are your snakes doing with me?' he snorted, bravely. 'I wanted to relieve myself.'

'In their jar?' She put her hand down to her snakes and they climbed her arm and curled round her neck and breasts. 'There, there, my beauties, be calm, be calm, I have brought you some breakfast. Delicious mice.' And she emptied a bagful of rodents into the jar. The two snakes slithered down her limbs and made for their jar.

Antonio felt rather stupid standing there in the minuscule rubber garment with his hands still attached to the bedhead.

'Salome, unshackle me,' he said.

194

'But you begged me to leave you like that,' she lied, smiling.

'Did I?' His head ached so and he really could not be sure what was dream and what was reality.

Waving the gold pendant before his face for a moment, and seeing that he was not himself, Salome undid his chains and, laughing, rubbed his wrists to remove the marks. She had brought bread and coffee with her from the market and she made breakfast for them both, heating the bread and spreading it with honey. The coffee and food revived him, but he felt confused.

'How did I get here?' he asked her, aware of her near-nudity under a garment so sheer her nipples almost pierced the cloth. Her body was perfumed with sandal-wood and myrrh and she was suddenly irresistible. They lounged on the silk-tasselled day bed, languorously eating grapes from a large bunch she had bought with his money.

'An angel brought you to me.' She smiled and put her tongue to his lips.

'Ah, well, then, I had better be nice to you, in case you feed me to your snakes.'

'Yes, you had better.' She flicked her tongue into his mouth and stole the grape he was just about to swallow. His hands went out to her jutting breasts and he caressed them, pulling them close together and putting his tongue in the cleavage. She pulled him towards her by the rubber loincloth and he felt her sharp fingernails scraping his tender flesh.

His cock rose, and he felt desire flood his body. What was it about this woman that made her so irresistible? Was it her voluptuous body, the way she moved, like her snakes, writhing and sly in her sinuosity? Was it her fragrant skin, the mélange of body scents and artificial perfumes she used? Or was it her long, thick, dark ringlets, like Medusa's savage curls? No, it was her hypnotic green eyes, he decided, slanting, long-lashed, evil and sensual, and cold as her snakes'. Hypnotic! Hypnotic! That was it! He was being hypnotised! He realised with a shock that she had been waving the gold pendant at him again, a silly affectation he had thought it, but now he realised its significance. He had been mesmerised by this woman. What had he done? He could not remember. Why was he here?

He had to keep his wits about him so that she did not realise he knew he was being duped. He must pretend to be completely in her thrall.

'Salome, what would you like me to do to you?'

'What would *I* like to do to *you*, you mean,' she said, smiling.

'Very well, do what you will, I am yours to command, you exquisite creature.' He kissed her passionately, pressing her breasts to his chest.

'Well, let me see now. Sit down on that chair,' she ordered him.

He could see no harm in doing as she asked, and he smilingly complied with her wishes.

She raised his loincloth and released his erection – a thick, heavy swelling. He groaned and took her weight as she sat on his lap and writhed a little to get comfortable. His prick was between her open thighs, sticking up as if it grew from her loins. She rubbed herself over his throbbing organ and he had to allow her to do it if he was to keep up the pretence of being her slave. It was not too high a price to pay, he thought, as the sensuous rubbing continued. She lifted her buttocks slightly and sat down hard on him, directing his prick into her. She sighed as the cock filled her. Her eyes narrowed and her breasts and neck became inflamed with a warm blushing. She sat on his lap, on his prick, rising and falling on it. His warmth and silky hardness filled her, hit her, and pummelled her clitoris and the outer walls of her swollen sex-lips. He saw her as sex incarnate, a snake consuming her prey. He was helpless under her attack, the constant rise and fall of her voluptuous body on his lap. He held her breasts and sucked them, seeing the nipples harden and stretch like apple stalks. She was writhing around on his stem. He felt as if his cock hit her brain, touched her heart and lungs. Her whole body became as one sex organ. She heaved and breathed heavily and he felt her juices spurt around him. Antonio, in spite of his awareness that he was in effect her prisoner, and should beware, was too sexually aroused to control himself. He let himself enjoy the pure physical lust she aroused in him. He thrust hard into her moistness and had his own satisfaction.

Later, they showered together in a large ceramic basin, not unlike the snakes' jar, and he thought again that he was like one of her snakes, trapped, in her thrall, for her use only. It was a liberating feeling for a man who had always been in charge, all of his life, once of a stud farm, and now in charge of the *finca* and the servants. His mother had turned to him after the death of his father and he had had to make all her decisions for her. It was a lonely existence. He remembered Floradora's slight ballet dancer's figure, her little breasts in the dark velvet jacket, her red petticoat rustling under the long, dark-blue skirt. He nuzzled the large breasts of the woman who held him prisoner and enjoyed her, yet all the while he planned how to get away and find his love. What was it the snake charmer had said? The circus folk were in Morocco? And where was the ringmaster, the murderer? He could not ask her any questions until he had her chained and helpless. He made passionate love to her, to keep her occupied, and she, foolish woman, thought he was enthralled by her.

She was lax with the pendant, failed to hypnotise him again, assuming he was already too far gone in his need for her body.

Late in the afternoon, when the sun's rays came through another window and hit the tiled floor, she lay asleep, exhausted by his wonderful love-making.

He lay still for a while, until he was quite sure she slept, then he took the rubber loincloth and tied her hands to the bedstead. He dare not use the noisy chains in case she woke. She stirred slightly as he removed himself from the bed and dressed. He tried the door, but she had locked it. Damnation, where was the key? He opened the window that was in shade, and looked out. They were on the second floor. He vaulted over the little ironwork balcony and climbed down the thick vine that clung to the building, sliding down as quietly as he could into the empty courtyard. People were still at their siesta and he left undetected.

It was not until he reached the harbour that he realised his money had gone. It had been taken from his breeches pocket, presumably by the snake charmer. He would have to return and get it, or he would not be able to get to Morocco or home again. Then he remembered the police. He had agreed to liaise with them if he had any news of the circus or the ringmaster.

He found the police department of Cadiz quite easily and asked to see the Lanzarote police. They were having a siesta, he was informed, and could not be disturbed.

'Damn their eyes! They will see me!' he fumed, and the duty police officer went to wake the two men.

He told them about the snake charmer being in Cadiz, and said that she had told him that the circus and she had parted company, and the rest of the troupe was in Morocco. He also explained that she had stolen his money. However, the police had no pity for his predicament, assuming he had willingly compromised himself and allowed her to get the better of him. He went with the police officers to the harbour to find the ship which had carried the circus performers. It was still there, loading up for a return journey to the Canary Islands.

Olympia was on deck, dressed in a becoming striped sailor dress, a beribboned hat on her head. The captain was overseeing the loading of crates of oranges and bales of cloth. He greeted the police with suspicion. 'What do you want? I have all my papers,' he said.

'Relax, *capitan*, it is not you we are interested in. What happened to the circus you carried from Lanzarote? We need to know the whereabouts of the ringmaster.'

'Lorenzo? He died on board ship as we docked. I told

the authorities, and he was buried in the cemetery here. It had nothing to do with me.'

'How did he die?'

'He fell off a horse, I believe.'

'He was riding a horse on board ship?'

'No, they had all disembarked at Agadir for some exercise while we took on more stores. There were lots of people and we needed more food and water, for the beasts, too. He went riding with the horsewoman.'

'Floradora went with him?' asked Antonio.

'Yes, that was her name, Floradora.'

Olympia, pulled to the captain's side by her love of gossip and her love of a handsome man in uniform – and the policemen were both young and handsome – heard the equestrian's name mentioned. She stared at the fine gentleman and realised who he must be: Floradora's famous lover – the horse breeder.

'Excuse me, *señor*, are you Floradora's friend?'

'Yes, I have that honour.' Antonio bowed low to the bizarre-looking woman, whose muscular legs showed under the striped skirt and whose large feet were crammed into high-heeled shoes.

'Continue the story of the ringmaster and how he came about his injury,' said one of the policemen.

'She brought him back to the ship, carried over one of the horses. He was in a bad way. Had fallen, by all accounts, and banged his head. He never recovered.'

'And why did the other performers leave the ship in Morocco?' said Antonio.

'I could not continue to pay for their food and drink and carriage while the ringmaster was unable to pay.'

'So you abandoned them in a heathen land?' said the outraged Antonio.

'Yes!' The captain smiled a broad smile. 'But the snake charmer stayed with the sick man and paid her passage and his.'

'I bet she did,' said Antonio. 'So, will you take me to where the rest of the circus has encamped, *capitan*?'

'Do you have the money to pay for your voyage, *señor*?' asked the Greek seaman.

'I . . . I will have it. When do you sail?'

'At four in the morning, *señor*.'

'Right, I will be here.' Antonio turned on his heel and went back into the town the way he had come.

Now that their suspect had died it meant that the case was closed and the police could return home. They insisted that this ship carry them back to the Canaries, free of charge, and the captain had to agree.

Antonio climbed back up the vine and into the open window of Salome's room. She was still tied to the bed, and her eyes looked daggers at him. He removed her gag and asked her to tell him where his money was hidden.

'Money? I have spent it,' she hissed, and spat at him.

'All of it? That is not possible.' He began to search the room but could not find the money. He did not think to look – and indeed he could not have retrieved it if he had – in the snake jar. It was the safest place for it, of course. Only Salome could get at it.

He gave up eventually, but snatched the gold chain and pendant from her neck. She snarled at him.

'Leave me that. It is all I have of Lorenzo,' she said.

'Did he die of injuries to his head?' he asked.

'Yes, that is so.' She bowed her head.

'Then, what are you going to do?'

'Me? I fail to see what business it is of yours.'

'You could run the circus without Lorenzo, couldn't you?'

'I . . . I had not thought of it.'

'Did he have relations who would inherit his wealth?'

'He never mentioned any family,' she said.

He could not help noticing her tears. His tender heart gave way and he untied the thief of his money. 'There, I will not press charges if you return my gold,' he said, quietly.

She wrapped a chiffon wrap round her shoulders and

smiled. She went to handle her pendant, forgetting that he had it.

'Ah well, you win, *señor*, here is your money.' She took off the lid, picked up her flute, and began to play a haunting air. The snakes hissed and lifted themselves, hypnotised, out of the jar.

'You do not need a pendant to mesmerise your snakes,' Antonio said.

The snakes wrapped round her legs and waist and hissed at him.

'It is safe now, you can reach in for the money,' she said.

He reached a long arm into the jar, felt the money pouch, and caught it in his fingers.

'Come to Morocco with me and find the rest of the performers. You can start again.'

She thought about it. There was the tent and the trapeze and other paraphernalia, safely in storage. Yes, it was not beyond her stretch of imagination to start up the circus without Lorenzo if the performers were still together.

She smiled and stroked his unshaven cheek. '*Si, señor*. I will come with you.'

Chapter Twenty-Five
The Voyage to Agadir

*B*y four in the morning of the next day, the big top and other gear had been retrieved and loaded on to the ship. Antonio had got the policemen to carry the snake jar on board. He kept the hypnotist's pendant round his own neck, not trusting the snake charmer to have it back just yet.

She was still rather amazed at herself for agreeing to go with this man whom she had recently kept prisoner and had used sexually. He was indeed a gentleman to free her and he had shown a great kindness by offering his services to her and suggesting that she run the circus without the ringmaster. It would never have occurred to her to do such a thing. It was Antonio's money that had paid for the big top's storage. They had to pay for a month's storage, even though the stock had been stored only for a week.

The ship sailed with the tide, as planned, with Antonio, the two young policemen from Lanzarote, Salome and two snakes. They had not been able to find the zoo keeper in order to buy back her other snakes. The captain had insisted on seeing the colour of their money before all embarked.

Olympia showed them to their cabins and stayed for an hour chatting to the policemen. They had two bottles of light-coloured Jerez, which they had bought in Cadiz.

'Share a drink before you retire,' said one officer, offering the bottle of sherry to the bizarrely dressed woman. She had on a long exotic gown of swans' down and lace, with a slit up to her thigh.

'*Muchas gracias, señores,*' she simpered, and fanned herself, sitting between them on the lower bunk.

They had soon reached the bottom of the first bottle and had started on the second. Olympia had one hand on one policeman's crotch, and the other hand on the second policeman's thigh. They had their free hands inside her gown. She giggled and wriggled and enjoyed the rough caresses. They had discovered their mistake, but were too drunk and aroused by her erotic handling of their privates to stop. She pulled out one short, stubby cock, and sucked it to its full size. The other man had a more promising weapon and it soon became engorged. Olympia crowed over its wide girth. They tried to remove their uniform trousers, but Olympia begged them to keep them on.

'You are so handsome,' she said, 'with them on. Who knows, I might not fancy you without them.'

So they kept their trousers on and let her play with their exposed cocks. The swans' down tickled them delightfully. They lifted her dress up to her waist and discovered her cock above the tightness of her silk stockings. The three intoxicated lovers enjoyed each other's hard bodies, and harder cocks. Olympia had the pleasure of both cocks pressing inside her at once.

Her joy was great and she went back to the captain's cabin just in time for the end of his watch on deck. She was flushed and prettily dishevelled and he jumped on her straight away, leaving his uniform on, of course.

He was disposed to forgive Olympia her peccadilloes as he loved her very much, especially her silk stockings. He would have to give her up when his wife met him in Athens in two months' time but, until then, he would enjoy his happiness. He was worried about what his sister would say when he told her her son had run away to join the circus. He would be blamed for it – that was sure. He wondered fleetingly how the lad was faring.

Nico was having the time of his life. Life at sea had never been like this! He was satisfied every night, sometimes several times, by the stealthy guards, and he was learning how to be a clown and an acrobat. Isambard had taken it upon himself to teach the boy some tricks of the trade. He said he wanted to be a trapeze artiste one day, but for now he would have to be satisfied with starting on the circus floor, tumbling and playing the fool. He learnt to look doleful, by careful make-up. He learnt the art of timing, very important when making people laugh. He had to do lots of menial, dirty tasks, but everyone had to do that when they started. No one could be a star straightaway.

'The lad has good looks,' remarked Isambard to Floradora while they were mucking out the horses together.

'Which lad?' she said.

'Nico, of course, and he is coming along nicely,' said Isambard. The mare turned her slender nose and nuzzled his hand.

'Oh, yes, he is rather sweet, isn't he,' said Floradora. 'Would he like to learn to ride, do you think?'

'I'll ask him. He needs to learn everything he can at his age. It would be good for him to ride, in case he does not prove to be any good on the high wire.'

'Little hope of getting on a high wire with this circus for a while,' said Floradora.

'But we are earning plenty of money with the nude performances,' said Isambard. 'We shall soon be able to sail to Spain and find work in another circus.'

'Yes, if we can find another circus.'

Isambard and Floradora finished grooming the horses and left them to their fodder.

'Isambard, could you please massage my back after I have bathed?' said Floradora. 'I am rather sore. I think I overdid the last performance.'

She had been a great hit with her acrobatic equestrian performance. Floradora had started off wearing only her chamois leather G-string, long, soft boots to her thighs, and a headband with a white feather in it. As her stallion cantered round the imaginary ring, she had stood on his back and removed the G-string, and then had lain flat on his back, her legs open in a wide V. She had stood again and removed the feather from her chamois headband. She had begun to caress herself with the feather between the legs, and moaned and gyrated on it, to the utmost delight of the gathered Arabs. The circus family watched, impressed with the virgin's lithe charm. Her little breasts bobbed up and down; her muscled thighs and flat belly shone with oil. The feather was where the entire audience wanted their fingers to be. The crowd murmured low. She did several circuits of the dirt ring, so all could get a good look at her bare sex with the feather tickling her pink petals and causing her bud to pout. Isambard had had to close his eyes; it had all been too much for the poor man.

'Yes, of course I will ease your pain for you, Floradora,' he said eagerly.

After both had bathed in the oasis pool, the big man, bare to the waist, rubbed perfumed oil over his rough hands and then began to transfer the oil on to the naked back of his heart's desire. She lay on the couch in her caravan, the windows and door open to catch the breeze. He slowly caressed her shoulders, firmly circling his hands. He squeezed the aching muscles, pinching her flesh and pressing into the tired tendons. The pinched nerves of her slender back were released by his tender ministrations. She sighed and sank her blonde head on to her arms. He moved slowly down her back and lowered the cotton sheet that covered her bottom and legs. He rubbed oil over her lower back and thighs and then massaged it over her pert buttocks. She drifted into a light sleep. It felt so wonderful, the big hands doing their magic on her. She felt them caressing her thighs, moving to the inner soft part, and the oil turned her skin to satin. The rough fingers scratched her soft flesh. She felt something move in between her thighs: his wet tongue, a satiny sinuous weapon which insinuated itself between her buttocks. Her wetness surged. She felt his thumbs prise open her legs and she allowed him this freedom. He moved quietly, softly singing a lullaby.

She sighed and relaxed completely, letting him do whatever he wanted. She felt a nudging of something hard between her throbbing thighs. It entered her. A hard softness like nothing else she had ever felt. It was like the rubber dildo in its girth and length, but harder, more pliant, pressing her inside, pushing up, up, filling her. She sighed and shifted slightly and it went even further. She had not imagined anything that size could find room inside her. It slid out slowly, gently, and he sang the lullaby in her ear. His breath was on her neck. He kissed her nape, licking her with his tongue that had been inside her. His rod was moving slowly in and out of her, hitting her everywhere in the most tender, exciting manner. She still lay quiet, pretending sleep. She noticed how his excitement became almost unbearable as the fleshy rod nearly withdrew completely, then pushed in again hard. She instinctively thrust against it, but gently, so he did not know she was awake. It was bliss to lie still and be used by this huge man, with no effort on her part to please him, yet she felt that she was pleasing him profoundly.

Her soft young flesh felt like heaven on his rough palms. He had tasted her virgin flesh on his tongue. He had his heart's desire. At the very thought of the little body under him he began to orgasm. He quickly withdrew and spent his seed over his own belly, but still pressed into her flesh with fingers and thumb. Now he did not care what happened to him for the rest of his life. He had made love to Floradora, the lion-keeper's daughter.

* * *

Next day, Floradora decided to see what Nico was made of. She imperiously commanded Isambard to fetch the lad to her. He willingly did as she asked.

Nico had been trying to repair the torn and tattered garments of the dancing girls. The local audience had become rather exuberant lately and had actually joined the dancing girls and helped them remove their garments, except that they had been rather too enthusiastic. The one-piece and two-piece flimsy garments were torn to shreds.

'It hardly matters, they don't want us to wear them, anyway,' said La Roux. But the careful Nico was thinking of the future, when they had found another real circus, and would need their clothes again.

'You are quite right,' said La Roux to the youth, stroking his black curls, 'you are a sensible boy. Come and see me later and I will reward you.'

Isambard took Nico away from his needle and thread and accompanied him to the area of the ground where Floradora exercised her horses and put them through their paces, trying out old and new tricks.

'There you are,' she said, and Nico and Isambard smiled back. She looked so sweet in her fringed suede chaps and her cowboy hat and waistcoat.

'Now, Nico, you want to learn to ride my horses, do you not?'

'Yes, please, Floradora. I do know how to ride. I used to have a pony when I was a child in Thessalonika.'

'Good, that is a start, anyway. Now, mount this mare and let us see what you can do.' Isambard steadied the little mare and Nico mounted. He sat well, she thought, and looked right. He did as she asked and trotted, cantered and walked the animal round the ring drawn in the dust.

'Good,' she said. 'Now let me see you ride her with no hands, just your knees.'

He did this well, his legs nudging the flanks, his thighs tightening to keep her moving in the right direction, his feet talking to the mare. Jet moved beautifully, easily, smoothly.

'Can you get up on her back?'

'I'll try,' he said, and stood on the bare back of the steady mare.

'Yes, you have good balance, Nico. You will do well,' said the lion-tamer's daughter. She admired the boy's shoulders, his strong muscular legs, his taut buttocks. She sighed and thought of love. She had not forgotten Antonio. On the contrary, she thought of him daily, and nightly. She yearned for his touch, his kiss, but she had given up hope of seeing him again. Life had to continue and bread had to be earnt.

The circus folk gathered every morning, before the sun became too high, to discuss performances and any problems any of them might have. It was at one of these regular meetings that Floradora spoke of the idea she had had for some time.

'I suggest we give our travelling circus a new name,' she said. 'We cannot carry on calling it Circo Lorenzo any longer. He is no longer here.'

'Thank goodness,' said a voice.

'So, what shall we call ourselves?' said Rosalita.

'I suggest we call ourselves Circo Erotica,' said Floradora.

'Hands up, all those who agree,' said Isambard, and he stood and counted the hands that were raised.

Everyone thought it was an excellent idea. New posters would bring in more audiences. Only the men came to see them anyway, so such a suggestive name would pull in more people, and from further away.

The *chamaco* who created the posters started straight away with the new images. He drew vivid portraits of La Roux with her flaming red hair, and the attractive sibling trapeze artistes intertwined on the tightrope. He drew a naked white-skinned Floradora on her black stallion. The clowns were caricatured with huge penises. The posters were wonderful and the *chamacos* rode across the desert and stuck them to stucco walls in small villages and hamlets where the women tore them down and the men put them up again in their coffee shops and meeting houses.

The advertisement worked. That night, more men than ever flocked to see Circo Erotica, to catch of glimpse of naked flesh.

The circus ring had become more sophisticated since the first performances in Agadir. They had built a wooden ring with wooden, stepped seats and a proper ticket office. They had bought canvas from the Bedouin tribes and sewn it into a billowing tent, which they held up with tall bamboo poles. This worked well and kept off the hot sun and made the performances more private, so people had to pay to get inside. They paid well, in rubies, diamonds, amethysts and silver. Nico collected the takings in cloth bags and hid them in the wardrobe caravan. Everyone liked Nico: he was a smiling, good-natured lad and he knew he was lucky to have fallen in with these circus folk, who were generous with their time and their affections.

This evening's performance was to be his first with the horses. He was not going to ride but he would help Floradora. Isambard was busy at other things now he was the ringmaster. He had to make sure the performers were ready on time, that the band knew what to play and when, and that the *chamacos* did their duty, carrying props and clearing the ring when necessary. He enjoyed his new role, though he missed his daily homage to Floradora.

Floradora was pleased with Nico's involvement with her horses. He was a natural rider and very gentle with the steeds. He was also physically attractive and she desired him, even if he was very young.

This first evening as her assistant, he dressed as a Red Indian brave in a chamois loincloth which showed off his delectable buttocks, firm loins and strong thighs. He wore war paint and feathers and looked rather magnificent, she thought. She wore a costume he had devised for her. It was an apron made of long feathers which hung down between her legs, suspended from a strip of chamois round her hips. Her buttocks were bare apart from a strip of leather that divided her white globes. Her breasts were covered in a little curtain of glass beads, which rose and fell heavily on her upper breasts. She wore a long black wig of straight hair. She knew she looked delectable and very, very desirable.

Chapter Twenty-Six
Circo Erotica

*T*he crowd was huge. Hundreds of dark eyes stared from white cotton hoods; thin hands clutched each other, trembling with anticipation. There was a hush of expectation as the band began the triumphant opening music. The tent smelt of men's bodies and Turkish delight. The black ringmaster entered, cracking his long whip, and La Roux danced in after him dressed in a revealing costume. Only spangles and three tassels covered her nudity. She stood on a platform against a painted target.

Two *chamacos* dressed in leather straps, chained her to the target with her legs wide and her arms above her head. The *chamacos* moved out of the way quickly as the ringmaster – who wore only a long white cloak and a G-string of white goat hide – flicked the whip-end at the girl. She flinched and the crowd hissed. A red mark appeared on her flank. He flicked the whip again and this time one of the nipple tassels was whisked off. The crowd whistled in delight. Isambard had been practising with the long leather whip. He nearly always got it on target. The second tassel was removed in this fashion and the girl's red rouged nipples were stung into erection. The crowd roared. Isambard took careful aim and flicked off the final tassel, exposing her red pubic hair, which was trimmed into a neat diamond.

211

She was still tied to the target and the crowd roared for her to be punished further by the erotic dancing of the whip. Isambard pretended to roar furiously, and cracked the whip aggressively at her but, in fact, he was too far away to do her any harm. Instead, he moved in very close to her and put the other end of the whip, the thick plaited handle, between her stretched legs. She cried out in mock ecstasy as he drew it in and out between her thighs, and the crowd was happy. In fact, La Roux did enjoy the caress of leather on her flesh and wanted it to continue. She whispered to Isambard to carry on with his rough fondling and he opened his satin cloak to show the audience his oiled torso before putting his hand between her legs. She threw back her head and moaned aloud. Many of the young men in the audience fainted at this point, unused as they were to the sight of female flesh being handled thus. Their fathers threw water over them or ignored them, only laughing at their unfortunate sons.

Next came the elephants, which were greeted with boos until Gina, the contortionist, was lifted on to the matriarch's back and began to display her charms as only she could. The crowd was amazed. Was she human – this upside-down, inside-out creature with female parts? She had a round, unsmiling face, but her bottom was painted with eyes and nose, and her sex was decorated like a painted mouth. She had another sex painted between her little round breasts, and it looked so real that the crowd assumed she was well endowed indeed. A perfect woman! The elephant was a slow-moving, tall platform for her interesting display. The baby elephant followed its mother, clutching her tail in its trunk. Gina was a great success with the crowd.

The clowns were a welcome relief for the overheated audience. They impressed with their tumbling, leaping and somersaults. They wore hilariously huge mock pen-ises and balls on the outside of their costumes. Before, they had worn them inside and had revealed their red balloon bottoms upon their exit from the ring. But now they displayed them immediately and made lewd movements at the crowd and each other, in mock buggery. But Jellico did not need to wear a false prick. His own was so huge, especially in relation to his small frame, that it looked false. He waved it at the crowd and shoved it at the buttocks of the other clowns. Only Isambard had as impressive a prick. He kept it covered for now, in his new, important role as ringmaster. He whipped the clowns through their routine, and the crowd was amused.

Next came the lion-tamer's daughter, delectable as a rosebud in a pink tutu with nothing underneath but thigh-high white stockings, held up with elastic ribbons. Her little nipples poked out over the bodice and the frilly, net tutu bounced as she rode bareback, so her bottom and sex-cleft were exposed and then hidden. The Arabs admired a good mount. This one was perfect. Her haunches were high and proud, her legs sturdy. Her face was masked, as was the local custom for females. She rode and leapt from horse to horse and hid under their bellies and jumped and stood on her head with her legs apart. The crowd loved her. The men had their hands under their voluminous garments and their faces were red with breathlessness and desire. Some were fondling the youths in the audience, and their enjoyment was obvious.

Isambard watched Floradora from the side of the ring, saw the flashing rosiness of her bud, the red-rouged nipples staring like eyes at him. He devoured her with his eyes. Nico also watched. He wore ballet dancer's tights, torn in all the right places, so the boy-loving members of the audience could see his sturdy charms. Floradora could not help but notice them, too, as he helped her dismount at the end of her rousing performance. His cock was full and heavy on his plump balls, and was visible right through the transparent, stockinet tights.

'My goodness, is that all yours?' she asked jokingly. 'Or have you borrowed a clown's dildo?'

213

'It is mine, Floradora, but it is yours if you just say the word,' said the forward youth. He was half in love with her, and yearned for her approval.

She laughed, handed him Thunderhead's reins and ran off to change.

Next came the finale: the stars – the trapeze artistes – chained to the earth for now, with no high wire. But they did have a wire fixed up on two poles, a few feet above the ring. It was the best they could do under the circumstances. They were dressed in torn, weblike, stockinet, one-piece costumes. Their private parts were exposed through the holed garments. Rosalita's perfect jutting breasts proudly pushed through the holes. The stockinet cut into her around her breasts, making the tiny peaches look more plump and ripe. Her tights were shredded and torn very charmingly, her buttocks stuck out of the holes, and her shaved sex was displayed like a split, ripe fig. Rosario was dressed in a similarly torn garment. His G-string was only good for dividing his taut buttocks. It was torn apart where his cock jutted, so the member swung and flapped on his thigh.

The men's eyes were on the couple's private parts. They did not notice the expertise of their act, only the flash of sex and the bounce of breast, the balls lifting and falling and the cock filling and swaying. They were quiet as they gazed at the siblings. Rosalita had her face covered, as was proper in this region, but the rest of her was theirs to consume with hungry eyes. Brother and sister held each other close and kissed and caressed each other, to the delight of the crowd. Rosalita lay back across the taut wire. Her brother lay over her and licked through the holed costume. She writhed on the wire, her legs high and wide. He lapped at her, his buttocks in the air. The audience was wild with joy and they jumped up and down and wailed loudly. The act climaxed with a tantalising view of Rosario's proud young cock aimed at his sister's crotch. He stroked her to orgasm and she, still balancing on the wire on her back, reached down to his erection and rubbed it hard until he came all over her cobweb garment.

The takings were up each day and Circo Erotica was a resounding success. The circus folk decided to raise the ticket price. News of their prowess and naked beauty had spread to the surrounding countryside. Travelling tribes came like flocks of white swans to settle in the area and visit the circus. Their tents surrounded the circus tents. They brought silver goblets and jewels to barter for a ringside seat. They did not mind the primitive big top; they were only interested in seeing the lovely young flesh.

A powerful Spanish *bandito* had arrived with his retinue of white-cloaked henchmen. His tents were magnificent, like billowing palaces, red and white striped, with tassels and flags decorating the central poles like a medieval castle. He had come to northern Africa many years ago on a raiding party from Andalucia and had stayed. He enjoyed the climate, the easy takings, the exotic life. His face has grown darker in the harsh sun and his moustache and beard had whitened. He looked like an old man, but he was vigorous and cruel. The local Moroccans were afraid of him and his reputation. It was said he had fought many chiefs for their horses and was the richest bandit in Morocco. His men had torn the Circo Erotica posters from the palm trees and taken them to him. They were like children, wanting to see the horsewoman, the trapeze artistes, and the clowns.

He bought all the tickets for the next six performances.

'We shall all be rich,' said Rosalita, her dark eyes glinting with greed. 'We shall go to Europe to be a great success with royalty.'

Floradora was sitting in her caravan, resting, when Nico came to the door.

'May I come in?' he asked.

'Of course, Nico, come in and talk to me. I am lonely,' she said.

'Lonely? You? But you are the most beautiful creature in the world. You cannot be lonely,' he said, and she laughed.

'Well, thank you, Nico, but I am.' She was tempted to tell him about her lost love, but decided against it. It might put him off if he thought she belonged to another.

'You are getting on well with the horses,' she said. 'How would you like to join me in the act?'

'Could I? Oh yes, that would be marvellous!'

'We must practise first, of course. But I think the two of us would be a hit with the crowd.' Floradora was rather jealous of all the attention that Rosalita got with her brother and sister act, and thought she might do something similar.

'Now, Nico, I can see you are shy, but you must relax with me,' she said, stroking his cheek.

He blushed. Her close proximity always caused this embarrassing reddening of his face, she had noticed. She opened her kimono a little and revealed her little belly and a flash of her Mount of Venus, freshly depilated and oiled. She shifted on the couch and patted the seat next to her. 'Sit next to me,' she commanded him.

He cleared his throat and found he could not speak.

She touched his crotch and he hardened. 'There, that's better,' she said. 'If we are to work together it must look real, as if we are lovers.'

She lowered her kimono so her shoulders and breasts were revealed to him. He leant forward and kissed her nipples, as if she were a religious icon.

'Harder,' she urged him. 'Kiss harder, yes, like that.'

She kissed his generous mouth and breathed in his clean sweat. She leant back on the couch and let her kimono open further, so her belly and her white thighs were displayed to him. He breathed heavily. She took his hands and placed them on her thighs. 'Do not be afraid, I won't bite you,' she said, smiling. 'You are old enough, Nico, to be taught how to please a woman.'

The young Greek boy's cock was tumescent and throbbing. It strained against his tight breeches. She opened

216

the flies with deft fingers. The solid flesh reared out of its prison, seemingly eager to be closer to her delectable nakedness. She smiled happily. He had a good, big cock which would fill her nicely. He tore off his other clothes and stood over her, naked and muscular as a statue.

She leant back with her hands above her head and told him, 'Do what you want. Let me see what you can do.'

This was a mistake! His cock withered at the challenge.

'Oh, Nico, poor darling, I should not have said that. I expect you to do nothing. Let me show you what to do,' she said, understanding his nervousness. She had forgotten he was so young. 'Lie down here and let me teach you.'

He lay down, still nervous and limp, but she took his boy's soft cock into her knowing hands and rubbed gently but firmly. She kissed his eyes and mouth and licked his face like a mother cat cleaning her kitten. He closed his eyes. The boy was beautiful, she thought. She weighed his balls in her hand – good solid plums and hairless, too; she liked that. His chest swelled naturally, and his belly was as flat as her stallion's back. His cock grew and thickened in her hands.

'I want to kiss you between the legs,' he said.

'Do you, darling?' she said.

She allowed him to slide down and push his curly head between her closed legs. She lifted her buttocks but kept her thighs together, enjoying the sensation of his tongue licking the little slit and trying to gain access to her cunt. She lifted herself to his caress and closed her eyes. He had moved around so his buttocks were close to her face. She slid a hand between his buttocks and caressed his balls and the root of his cock, which felt as hard as a rock. She rubbed and stroked and he lapped her silky sex-lips. She gradually opened her legs so he could get further in with his searching tongue. She held his cock at the base to keep him from coming too soon. He was a gentle lover, and lapped with enthusiasm. Then, when she was ready, she urged the inexperienced youth to turn around and she got on top of him. His

217

eager prick rose to meet her. She sat on it, carefully, pressing it into her.

She rose and fell, sitting up straight on his hard cock. He lay still, his arms behind him, his face and neck flushed. She held his arms down and fucked him. He was moaning and turning his head from side to side. She eased herself off and then dropped like a bird on to him. Her flesh was melting. She felt like hot wax. He pierced her. His flesh filled hers. She felt her spasms overcome her and, as she came, he came also, and filled her with his seed.

Chapter Twenty-Seven
The Bandit Chief

Nico had hidden the gold that the bandit, El Toro Blanco, had paid for the tickets in the usual place – the wardrobe caravan. Nico was in love with Floradora, he had decided. He would do anything for her. He dressed with care that afternoon for this, his first equestrian performance with her. They had practised all day for several days on the horses, and he was sure he would not let her down. The new act was certain to be a big draw. The poster artist had produced an erotic rendering of their part of the act. In the picture, Nico stood on one of the white mares wearing nothing but a pair of brown suede cowboy chaps, which drew the eye to his naked groin. He held Floradora close to him, her lithe form half-hidden by a very short cowgirl dress, torn so one breast was exposed, and her bare bottom visible under his big hand. The posters were very popular with the local populace and most were stolen from the walls and used as aids to lonely masturbators, or even as marital aids to heighten couples' excitement.

But not all the circus folk approved of this new development. Rosalita especially did not like the way Floradora was taking over as the new star of the circus. She felt that she and her brother had been handicapped since they had left Lorenzo because they no longer had a

219

high wire or their trapeze to perform on. They could only do meagre acts on the low tightrope. She had a plan and she told her brother what they were going to do. As usual, the lazy lad shrugged his muscular shoulders and agreed with her.

El Toro Blanco and his large band of white-cloaked men took all the seats at the ringside. The circus performers did the initial parade round the ring all together, and wearing clothes, or at least their *batas*. Then Isambard whipped the clowns into their first act, with their mock phalluses flying. Jellico, as usual, waved his own huge prick at the laughing crowd. On this occasion, Isambard also displayed his magnificent weapon. His white satin cloak lifted and his prick was rampant. The dancing girls were all agog at the black rod, which glistened with oil and was held close to his belly by leather straps. His body was powerful, his face was intelligent and stern, and he looked like a prince. Gina and La Roux drooled at the sight. Gina did her naked contortions with the elephant's broad back as her stage. La Roux and the other girls leapt and leant over the audience, masks hiding their faces but with their erogenous zones exposed between pale diaphanous veils.

The *bandito* sat quietly, his hawklike face still and emotionless, no smile on his thin lips. He was not a handsome man; rather, he was imperious and compelling, and his face had hidden depths, as if he had seen many horrors. He was the most terrifying man Floradora had ever seen. She shuddered as she looked at him from the corner of her eye.

The performance continued and the Spaniard showed no sign of enjoyment or interest. He smoked a long cigarillo and his men kept him provided with alcohol in a silver goblet. He seemed bored rather than anything else.

However, when it was Floradora's act, he sat up straight in his seat and leant forward to see better. First, Floradora circled the ring on her black stallion. Her revealing costume rose and fell, showing her bare pudenda and her pert buttocks as she stood, then lay prone on his back. She did a double somersault and the crowd roared. Then Nico, in his revealing chaps, his thick cock proudly bobbing on his oiled balls, ran into the ring with a lasso, bringing the mares with him. He wielded the plaited leather and aimed the loop at the girl on the cantering horse. He missed her, and ran after her, his genitals lifting and falling on the soft suede. He wore a penis ring at the base of his rod to help keep him stiff. She had insisted her assistant wear this device, as she knew he was very nervous and he needed to keep his erection for the duration of the performance.

Nico's sturdy frame was good-looking and the sight of his swollen cock pleased the lustful crowd. Floradora leapt from her stallion to the following mare in a pretend attempt to escape the cowboy. Nico's next lasso throw caught the girl round the shoulders and tied her arms to her sides. She sat across the lively mare, holding on with her knees. Nico leapt up behind her and held her tight in an erotic embrace. She was still tied, helpless to stop his attack. Then he moved from behind her to in front of her, facing her. His cock was prodding her bare flesh and the crowd roared. He moved in and out in mock intercourse.

She thrust against him, her slit nudging at his cock. She almost preferred this incessant foreplay to the real thing, she thought. It reminded her of the Great Lorenzo and his erotic torture.

The *bandito* was very impressed with the fair-skinned equestrian. Her blonde hair had been high on her head in a tight knot, but now it fell out of its pins and swept her breasts and back in a gold wave of silk. He sighed and clenched his teeth.

The whole audience and the circus family watched the veiled girl and the golden youth as they rocked and strained against each other on the mare. She was tied with the leather lasso, and his cock was still stiff as they rode out of the ring to wild applause.

Isambard had been concentrating on Floradora, as usual, and now, looking around for the next performance – the trapeze artistes – he was confused to see they were not there.

He sent on the clowns instead, and Jellico was turned upside down and milked by the others while Isambard searched for the missing siblings.

But they had gone. Rosalita and Rosario were on a pair of camels heading for the docks and the first ship out of Agadir.

Their absence was noticed only by the circus folk. The audience was happy with what they had seen. The aroused Spanish bandits were in a frenzy of mutual masturbation. They leapt upon each other and indulged in all sorts of homosexual practices.

The band played the finale and the Circo Erotica was over for another night.

'Nico was excellent, wasn't he, Isambard?' said Floradora proudly. She handed the mare to the new ringmaster as if he was still her assistant.

'Shall you need a massage later?' he beseeched her.

'Well, yes, I probably shall need one,' she sighed happily. 'Come in an hour, when I have bathed.'

'Yes, Floradora, I will be there. Floradora – Rosario and Rosalita have gone.'

'Gone, where?'

'Who knows, they seem to have disappeared. That is all I know.'

'Poof! Who cares? I certainly don't.' She ran off to her caravan and changed into her *bata*, then she bathed in the oasis pool. When she went back to her travelling abode, she collapsed in a pretty heap on the bed, and fell into a light slumber. There was a knock at her door.

'Mm,' she murmured, hardly conscious.

The door opened quietly, and a figure crept in and picked up the scented oils that were arranged by the bed.

'Oh, yes, just there, that's so good,' she said, as hands soothed her aching muscles.

222

She was naked and the hands were firmly stroking her buttocks and inner thighs, just touching the delicate flesh between sex and anus. She sighed and allowed the hands access to her secret flesh. There came another knock at the door and she said nothing, but the hands stopped fondling briefly then returned to their duty.

She felt another pair of hands, larger, firmer, stronger on her body. Hands held her firmly round her tiny waist, meeting and clasping each other. Fingers stroked her feet and ankles, drawing lines to her knees. Kisses behind her knees brought shudders from her. Her calves were pummelled, her buttocks slapped. She felt as if there were six men fondling her, punishing her erotically. She lay still and acquiescent, safe in the knowledge that these two men adored her. They were slaves to her beauty and would do anything in their power to please her. She opened her legs and felt a tongue slide up her thigh. Her breasts were held from behind, clasped and squeezed, the nipples held between hard fingers. Her neck was caressed. Her thighs melted. Her feet tingled. She wanted something hard between her legs. She waited for a fleshy rod to touch her. But there were only tongues and fingers, and hot fumbling caresses.

Rosalita and her brother were dressed in Arab garments bought from the tribe who had also sold them the camels. Rosalita looked like a delicious boy with her dark, gypsy eyes, abundant curls and her slender figure. They looked like twins, the trapeze artistes, or so El Toro Blanco thought as he surveyed the prizes that his men had brought. The siblings had not got far when the bandit's men captured them. They were always on the lookout for unusual sex slaves for their demanding master.

'So, are you male or female?' he asked her.

'Why should you care?' she said defiantly. She was furious that her plan to steal the money and leave the circus had been thwarted. However, the bags of gold and jewels were still in the pannier that her camel wore.

The two beasts were drinking water with the tribe's animals. She had watched and not seen anyone look inside the bags, yet. No doubt the *bandito* was already so rich he did not need mere gold and silver and gemstones.

'How dare you speak to me like that! Remove his clothes,' the *bandito* ordered two of his armed men.

Rosario attempted to escape the clutches of his captors to aid his sister, but he was restrained.

'So, it is a girl,' said the *bandito*, smiling. 'And now that one.' He pointed to Rosario.

The siblings stood holding each other protectively, naked and afraid.

'Charming, charming. Take them to be bathed and return them to me. I missed your performance earlier. We all missed you, you know, but we will see your performance later, Mm?' The *bandito*, whose eyes had witnessed many evils, and whose cruelty showed in his lips, smiled thinly, and waved them away.

On the ship that was headed for Agadir, Salome was playing with her snakes. She allowed them to slither all over her and she welcomed the cool, scaly embrace. She thought about the man who had paid for her to be on this ship, and who was ensuring that her future was safe. He was a handsome man. She was a little envious of Floradora to have so distinguished a suitor. Would he come to her in her cabin, she wondered, now she had not the mesmeric power over him that she had had in Cadiz? He still carried Lorenzo's hypnotic pendant. She put the snakes back in their pot and placed the lid on top. She lay in her bunk and touched herself. Why had she left the rubber dildo behind? That was stupid. She had to make do with her own long fingers and sharp nails. She looked in the snakeskin bag that held her belongings to see what other implements of erotic possibilities she could make use of. There was a belt; yes, that would do.

She placed the wide leather belt between her legs and pulled it tight to her pudenda. She felt the cool leather caress her flesh. She drew the strap up and down so it rubbed and stroked her and she lay back and thought of Lorenzo and his erotic torture. Ah, the way he would spank her and caress her and not let her orgasm! He was so greedy for her flesh, but always withheld the final payment. His rod would pound her but he would not penetrate her. She had learnt to love the everlasting frustration of withheld fulfilment. Her flesh now demanded to always be sensitive to another's touch, and she felt desire run through her like a flame across dry grassland.

Salome drew the leather belt hard into her soft flesh, open to the rough caress. Her bud was swollen and almost sore from the self-inflicted bondage. She bit her lip as she came, almost silently, breathing fast as if she gave birth.

Antonio, alone in his cabin, thought of the lion-tamer's daughter in her midnight-blue velvet costume, the full skirt lifted to expose the frivolous scarlet froth of net beneath, and her legs in the silk stockings, shining. He imagined his hand sliding up inside the petticoat, up those silken stockings to the bare white thigh. He held his erect cock and rubbed it unconsciously. Then he remembered the snake charmer and her jutting breasts with the large nipples so erect and suckable. He put his erection away in his breeches and went to her cabin and knocked quietly. If she slept he would go away.

'Come in.'

'*Señorita*, I beg your pardon, I am in need of help.'

'*Señor?*' Salome was draped in a coloured shawl but had nothing on underneath it. She sat on the edge of her bed, her legs apart, and the shawl's fringed end hung down between her thighs. Her toenails were painted red, he noticed, like her lips.

'How may I help you?' She smiled.

'I am wondering if you can tell me anything about my fiancée? Do you know if she was being . . . comforted by anyone since I did not keep my promise to her?'

'Comforted?' Salome moved slightly so the silk shawl shifted and slid up to her thigh. She did not need a pendant to mesmerise a man. 'Well, I tried to comfort the poor girl,' she said.

'Oh, thank you, Salome, that was kind of you. He sat next to her on the dishevelled bed, aware of her scent and the bare thigh next to his.

'She is a sweet little thing,' Salome said, smiling gently. 'A very sweet creature, who has much affection to give.'

'Yes,' said Antonio, sliding a hand inside her shawl. He was shocked at her wetness.

She turned towards him and kissed him. Then she leant back on her elbows so her belly was thrust forward and her legs opened wide. He churned his palms on her belly and pressed fingers in her and, leaning over her, kissed her neck passionately as her head was flung back in total abandon.

'Use your belt on me,' she said.

He removed his leather belt from his breeches and slapped her tender flesh with its tail. Her flesh reddened. Her flower opened and he watched the bud ripen as the strap came closer. He had his cock in his free hand, but now he pressed it on her flesh. She stayed leaning away in a swoon of delight as Antonio pressed his thick rod into her. He knelt over her and penetrated her to the hilt. She closed her eyes. Antonio sucked and bit the jutting breasts and pounded her with his full prick. She came again and again and the vibrations that caressed his cock made him give up his seed in a rush.

Chapter Twenty-Eight
Rosalita and Rosario's Private Performance

*E*l Toro Blanco had killed many enemies in his life and would not care if he killed more. He was the most powerful and rich bandit in this part of the desert. His needs and desires were met immediately by his henchmen or they died. He was not a man used to being thwarted or frustrated. He had wanted the blonde circus performer – the equestrian. But there was time to get her later. Now, he would enjoy the private performance that the unexpected capture of the truant trapeze artistes would give him.

They were naked except for plaited ropes of gold silk that encircled their oiled bodies as if they were parcelled up, separately. The female's parts were painted with a scarlet aphrodisiac dye, as were the young man's genitals. Rosario had had a gold ring placed over his cock so he could not lose the fullness of his erection. In the gloom of the large tent, with only candles to throw shadows, their perfect young figures swayed together on the trapeze the rich *bandito* had had erected. They gave a display of shocking erotic intensity. They were joined at the groin; Rosalita hung from her brother, holding on with her internal muscles as they swung above the masturbating *bandito*.

She swung there, hanging on to her brother for her life, for there was no net and, if she fell, she could break her neck.

The *bandito*, once he was sexually satiated, had his servants lower the pair and they were freed of their bonds. They lay exhausted, breathing deeply, trying to come to terms with what they had been made to do. It had not been their choice, of course, they had had to do what the *bandito* had commanded or, they had been given to understand, their fate would have been a long lingering death.

Rosalita sobbed and her brother held her face in his hands and kissed her tears. 'Do not worry, my sister,' he said. 'It cannot be wrong if we were forced to do it. We did not choose to do this thing.'

'But we did it, we did it, and we will surely rot in hell.'

They were carried away to be kept prisoner until the next time the *bandito* required a private viewing of their high-wire expertise.

Early next day, as the red sun rose in the haze of desert dust, Nico was in the wardrobe caravan, sewing. He was looking forward to the next circus performance with the delectable equestrian. He had never been so happy. Alphonso visited him nightly and helped relieve the passion Nico felt for Floradora. Daily, Nico had close contact with her desirable body. The massage sessions he shared with Isambard would continue, he supposed, as long as Floradora wished. He admired the black ringmaster for his strength and serenity. He never looked anything but calm, and Nico wanted to be like him.

At that moment, Gina came into the caravan, and asked for a blond wig and a yellow veil. She wore nothing but wigs over her buttocks in her circus performances and had her sex painted to look like a face, over which she wore a veil to compound the confusion.

228

Nico greeted her and asked if she would like to help him count the money they had made so far.

'Oh, all right, if you need help,' she said.

He lifted the trunk lid and put his hand inside for the bag of jewels, silver and gold. It was not there. 'I must have put it somewhere else,' he said, and began rummaging around to find the treasure.

'It's not here, Gina. Oh, my goodness, it has been stolen!'

'It's that bitch Rosalita! They've gone with our money!' Gina spat, and her usually calm Oriental features twisted in anger and hatred.

'Oh, what can we do? We must tell the others.' Nico ran from the caravan and knocked on the other caravan doors, shouting as he went and not waiting for anyone to open them. 'Help, help, our money has gone.'

Heads poked out of the doors, and sleepy eyes stared in disbelief. *Batas* were thrown over shoulders and tired, aching limbs stretched and stepped down into the pink sand.

'What are you saying, Nico?' shouted Floradora as she watched him fly from one caravan to the next.

He came back to her and the others gathered around.

'Our takings have gone. Disappeared with the trapeze artistes, most likely,' said Gina.

The circus folk were stunned. What could they do now? Most of them had hoped they had earnt enough money by now to get them to Spain, or anywhere other than this desert where they had to bare their bodies each day in order to eat.

'We'll just have to carry on and make more money,' said Floradora, determinedly. She did not care where she worked. She had no one who cared for her anywhere but here in the circus, and so it did not matter to her if they stayed here.

Ilia, one of the clowns, said, 'I have heard news of the aerialists.'

'What have you heard?' said La Roux.

'One of the tribesmen told me that the *bandito* has

them. He is a powerful man in these parts and does what he likes, apparently.'

Floradora shuddered as she remembered the cruel face leering at her. She shivered, and said, 'The poor things do not deserve whatever it is he is doing to them.'

'They deserve everything they get,' said La Roux. 'Circus folk do not steal from each other. It is like stealing from your mother.'

There was a murmur of agreement and the disconsolate troupe drifted off and made their morning victuals, washed, and performed their usual duties.

'Do not worry, Nico,' said Floradora. 'We will soon make lots of money again. We will put up the entrance price. The *bandito* can afford anything we charge.' But, all the same, she was concerned that this powerful man could seemingly abduct anyone he chose and keep them as prisoners. What if he chose to capture her? She shuddered again.

That evening, the band played the opening chords that introduced the first act – the clowns. Nico still sat in the ticket booth, taking money. The usual crowd pushed and shoved to get in. No *bandito* tonight, Nico noticed. He usually bought all the tickets so only he and his retinue could sit in the circus tent. The other, less fortunate, tribesmen would stand outside trying to see through the chinks of canvas.

The *bandito* was having his own private circus act performed for him. An old crone painted the aphrodisiac dye on Rosalita and Rosario. She pawed at the young flesh and squawked with delight and wickedness as they squirmed under her harsh caresses.

Rosalita spat at the hag and tore away from her, but saw that her unfortunate brother's cock grew at the old woman's touch.

'What is this stuff you paint on me, old woman?' he asked, covering himself with his hands.

She laughed loudly and spoke words they could not understand. She removed his hands from his groin with gnarled fingers and put the penis ring over his cock. He groaned. The siblings were dressed by the crone, who reminded Rosalita of an old crow, in their spangled tights and vests torn into delicate, revealing webs.

Rosario was left with his cock and balls wrapped in a tight cobweb of thin-strapped netting, and his cock looked swollen and trapped, but enticingly half-revealed. Rosalita was similarly exposed. Her pointed breasts rudely pressed through too-narrow holes so they were distorted and squeezed, and her swollen and itching sex-lips throbbed under the stretched netting between her legs, and poked out of the holes. She wanted to scratch and push something hard inside her. She gazed longingly at her brother's desirable genitals and tried not to remember what they had done together the night before.

The *bandito* was ready for them. He had been bathed and oiled by his favourite servant boy and was ready for some entertainment. He lay on a low leather couch with lion skins under him and silk cushions around him. He smoked an aromatic tobacco in a long cigarette holder and there was a gold goblet of whisky balanced on the skull of an old and revered enemy by his side. He clapped his hands lazily.

The trapeze artistes were swinging from one trapeze to the other high above him. He watched with narrowed eyes and saw the female try to reach the crotch of her brother and release the swollen member from its spider-web of silk threads. Every time they swung close, Rosalita would reach for her brother's groin and tear at the flimsy costume so eventually it came apart and his cock was free. She grabbed it and pressed herself on him in the air. He in turn tore at her breasts and freed them of their bondage and kissed her nipples as they met and passed on their trapezes. She was desperate for release from the dreadful itch between her thighs. She could not concentrate on the balancing and swinging. Should she jump now and reach for his hands or feet? She suddenly could not remember and flung herself too late from the trapeze into thin air. He tried to grab her as she fell, but his hands only brushed her head and he watched in horror as she fell with a sickening thud at the feet of El Toro Blanco.

Chapter Twenty-Nine
Floradora and El Bandito

*R*osario was heartbroken. He was still the prisoner of the evil bandit but he did not care what happened to him now that Rosalita was dead. That night the *bandito*'s men disposed of her body. Her brother did not know how – probably it was left on the mountainside for the vultures to destroy, he thought, tearing at his long curly hair in his extremity of grief. But the *bandito* was not interested in having just the boy; he needed to watch a pair of young lovers.

He remembered the blonde equestrian. He called his henchmen and gave instructions. They galloped off on Arab mounts from El Toro Blanco's encampment in the mountains to Agadir. The *bandito* then decided that he would like to see Floradora perform on her horses one more time before he took her away from them and held her captive to perform lascivious acts with the gypsy boy. It was a shame the gypsy girl had been killed, he thought. Such a close relationship was particularly titillating to an old man. But he had coveted the blonde equestrian ever since he had first seen her, and he particularly liked the fact that she was obviously frightened of him.

* * *

Antonio and Salome were discussing the future of the circus. At least, that is what Salome said she wanted to discuss with him when she knocked on his cabin door. They sat close on the small leather couch and she showed him some designs she had made for new costumes for the snake-charming act. They were rather good illustrations of a naked woman with long black ringlets, not unlike herself, tied to a pole with leather straps and chains, the snakes depicted as hissing, terrifying creatures about to strike their venomous fangs into her. Antonio looked a bit hot and bothered. She stood and unwound the silk kimono she wore and revealed her clean-shaven naked flesh. Wrapped round her hips and buttocks and breasts were long, plaited leather straps.

'This is the sort of thing I had in mind. What do you think?' she said, twisting so he could admire her firm round buttocks with the leather strap dividing them.

Antonio gulped. She held him in the palm of her hand and she knew it. He grabbed at the straps that split her jutting breasts. He pulled her to him and kissed her hard and she yielded to his passion, grateful for his rough handling and the way he used her. She needed this passionate greed for her body. She wanted to be wanted. He tore at her bondage straps and pushed his tumescent rod into her, hurting her with deep violent thrusts. She stood, pinned by his powerful body against the wood-panelled cabin wall, breathless with desire.

He took his pleasure from her generous body and threw her to one side. She knew that she was making him into another man – someone who knew no love nor tenderness, only lust. He looked frightened of the man he was becoming under the influence of Salome's exotic beauty, with her need to be violated and hurt. It was she who made him pull the straps tight and mark her flesh. She it was who wanted the pain and frustration. He only did it because she wanted it, she knew. She slumped now, still beautiful in her disarray, her hair wet and matted and hiding her full lips and narrow eyes.

He dressed himself and left the cabin.

'Señor Antonio, I want to speak with you, please.' It was the transvestite, Olympia.

'Of course, *señorita*,' said the embarrassed Antonio. 'What can I do for you?'

'Ooh, don't ask, I might tell you,' she giggled, but then looked serious. 'No, really, I do need your help,' she said. 'I want to come with you and join the circus again.'

'I do not know if we will find the circus. We can only look for them,' said Antonio. He had thought about the difficulties of finding the travelling circus in the desert, and was concerned that they might have driven very far north by now, and might even be in Casablanca. The ship was not scheduled to dock anywhere except Agadir, so he would have to travel by land if they had left that town.

'Oh, I am sure everyone will know where they are,' said Olympia.

'Why do you want to leave the captain?' asked Antonio, noticing for the first time the tear-streaked make-up on Olympia's face.

'He has told me he is married,' Olympia sobbed. 'I refuse to be the reason for some poor woman's unhappiness. He is an animal – all men are – begging your pardon, *señor*.' She blew her nose loudly. 'No, I will bow out of this nautical naughtiness and go back to the life I know best. I miss all my costumes, anyway,' she sniffed. 'There's only so much you can do with a sailor's uniform.' She nudged him, confidingly.

'Well, of course, *señorita*, you may come with the snake charmer and myself to search for your circus. I cannot stop you.' Antonio shrugged and smiled, and a happier Olympia left him, dabbing at her mascara which had streaked her cheeks with black.

Their ship docked at Agadir the following day, and they unloaded the circus paraphernalia that Salome had acquired from Lorenzo's death. The ship was stopping for half a day, so the policemen disembarked and went to a local bar for refreshment.

Antonio paid several sailors to help with sorting out the big-top tent, the high wires, and the other circus equipment that Salome had 'inherited'. They hired three camels and a handler and loaded the canvas on to their backs. It was while Salome was looking through a large wooden chest of Lorenzo's belongings – things she had not thought of as valuable such as old circus bills, posters, his papers – that she came across a locked metal box. Tied to it was a bundle of papers describing each gambling debt of every *chamaco* and circus performer who had gambled so unsuccessfully. Every time he had lent money he had made a note. There was the history of Floradora's father's debts, Horatio's debts and many others. They searched for the key and could not find it so Antonio used a knife to prise open the chest. Inside, there was the money that the *chamacos* had lost to the usurer.

'It is a fortune!' said Salome.

'Will you return it to the circus folk?' asked Antonio.

'I . . . but of course!' said Salome.

As they were finishing loading the various equipment, the policemen returned, excited and agitated.

'We will come with you,' they announced. 'We have heard that the notorious bandit, El Toro Blanco, is here in Agadir somewhere. If we can catch him, it will mean a reward, medals and promotion for us. He has been seen on many occasions in these parts and apparently has grown lazy and will not expect attack.'

The other policeman added, 'We have seen a poster for a circus and we know where it is being held.'

They arranged for more camels to carry them all, and in an hour they were ready to go.

Olympia gave a tearful farewell to the sailors, and the captain waved his cap at the small group on the dock: Antonio, Salome and her jar of snakes, Olympia and her little suitcase, the policemen, the camel handler and the three camels.

On their way out of the docks they saw the circus poster. It proclaimed Circo Erotica and mentioned the venue. On the poster was a luridly painted image of a totally naked Floradora, her sex a red slash of paint, her eyes a brilliant blue, her hair yellow and her nipples scarlet. She lay on the back of her black stallion, her legs open wide, an inviting smile on her red lips.

'Take us to the Circo Erotica,' said Antonio, pointing at the poster he had torn from the wall. His eyes were dark with anger and love.

The evening performance was about to start. The circus folk had done their initial parade, as was traditional. The clowns were leaping about, phalluses – mock and real – waving, and they squirted water at each other. The audience was small and exclusive: just the *bandito* and his courtiers. They laughed and drank and smoked, not paying much attention to the clowns. They were waiting for the naked women. They had paid highly for the pleasures of the flesh and they were impatient for the real show to begin.

Isambard, magnificent in a white leather G-string and white leather cloak, cracked his long plaited whip and a drum rolled. The elephant lumbered on with her little one tagging on to her tail. On the matriarch's broad grey back were the *bastoneras* – La Roux and Anastasia. They stood, one behind the other, naked and tied to each other by gold ropes. Hannibal, the elephant trainer, pretended to whip the girls as he came in behind the elephants. They screamed in the appropriate places. The whip reached nowhere near them but the audience loved the idea of it. The girls' breasts bobbed up and down and they writhed in a pretence of fear. They were, of course, veiled over their faces, but nowhere else.

The bandit chief looked bored and clapped his hands. Isambard sent the elephants off and then in came two of the *chamacos* carrying a small chest. They put it down and lifted the lid. Inside, curled up like a snake, was the contortionist, naked of course. To a tune, played on a pipe by Isambard, in the role of snake charmer, she uncoiled her seemingly boneless body. She was painted to look like a snake, zigzagged in green and yellow, with a snake mask on her head. Very realistically did she move, easing her lissom form over the top of the chest and sliding to the floor. She slithered convincingly and coiled herself around Isambard's legs and waist. He stood still, playing the instrument as she hissed and slithered and then she slid down again and moved slowly back to her box. When she had coiled herself up into a ball again the lid was closed and the *chamacos* carried her off to loud applause.

'Where is the horse rider?' boomed the imperious voice of the *bandito*. 'Bring on the horse rider.'

Isambard had recovered himself after the close proximity of the naked contortionist, and picked up his ringmaster's whip and announced the equestrian's entrance.

'Floradora, the lion-tamer's daughter!' he shouted, 'and her handsome assistant, Nico!'

The stallion cantered round the ring, seemingly riderless, and then the lithe and fair form of Floradora appeared from under his belly. She pulled herself up and sat on his back. She wore a flimsy garment of chamois, torn and tattered and fringed to look like a Red Indian squaw's dress, but revealing one white breast and split up to her crotch, which was obviously bare and shaved. The audience stared. The *bandito*'s mouth literally watered as he watched the white female bounce on the horse's back. She stood on her hands on the neck of Thunderhead, and everyone cheered as the tiny leather skirt fell and revealed her bottom and sex parts. She quickly sat again and cantered Thunderhead in a circle. Then a white mare appeared with a whooping cowboy in the saddle. He had a wild-west-style saddle with a hard pommel in front to hang on to. He wore a dashing cowboy outfit of tan chamois; his chaps came up to his solid, tanned thighs and firm buttocks. He stood in the stirrups and whirled his lasso over his head. It was to show the audience that he too had no covering on his genitals. His penis was ringed, as usual, to keep him erect for the performance. Nico did not really need this device, he thought, because he always felt so full of desire when he watched the naked equestrian perform. But Floradora insisted he wore it and, whatever Floradora desired, she could have, as far as Nico was concerned.

They cantered around in pretence of flight and chase for a while, each performer showing bits of him or herself to the audience and getting much applause. Then Nico caught her in the lasso and held her arms tight to her sides. He leapt from his mare to her stallion's back and rode behind her, throbbing cock up close to her buttocks. The crowd loved it. The pair looked so good together – the blonde girl and the golden Greek boy with his dark curls.

El Toro Blanco was quiet – not smiling but enjoying the feast of flesh before his eyes. He knew Floradora would be his very soon. He saw the look in her eyes as they rode past him. She loathed him, he could tell. All the better for him. He did not ask for love, only the satisfaction of his tired flesh and his decadent mind.

The act was over and the horses went off. The bandit chief did not wait for any of the other inferior acts. He stood, and his retinue moved off with him. The circus ring was empty and the audience had gone. Isambard stopped the band playing and told everyone the show was over and they could go to bed.

Nico was desperate to satisfy his desire in the usual way. He and Isambard would meet up at Floradora's caravan as soon as they had finished their other duties – seeing to the horses and cleaning up. He kept his penis ring on and was proud of his rampant state. The excitement he had felt when he rode with Floradora was still there. Isambard and the boy worked silently and companionably together, rubbing down the horses and making sure their hooves were clean.

Meanwhile, Floradora had donned her *bata* to hide her nakedness, and had headed back to her caravan. It was dark now, and the shadows hid danger, but she was not ready for it. Suddenly a knife was at her throat and two pairs of arms grabbed her. A hand clasped her mouth to silence the scream. A dog barked somewhere close. She smelt sour breath and sweat that was like old goat's milk. She tried to fight her abductors but she was hit hard, blindfolded, gagged, bundled into a sack, and thrown over a horse's back. After that there was merciful blackness.

Chapter Thirty

Rescue

*B*y the time that Antonio, Olympia and Salome had reached the circus ground it was too late; Floradora had gone and her disappearance had been discovered. They arrived just as the confused Nico and the alarmed Isambard came rushing out of the equestrian's caravan calling her name into the darkness.

'Salome! Olympia, what are you doing here?' said Isambard.

'Where is Floradora?' said Antonio, interrupting his question.

'We do not know. She wanted us to . . . to assist her and told us to be here, but she is not here,' said the ringmaster.

Anastasia arrived with several other circus folk to see what all the noise was about. Salome and Olympia were greeted enthusiastically by the *bastoneras* and *chamacos*.

'Where is Lorenzo?' asked Gina. 'Has he recovered?'

'No, he died as we arrived at Cadiz,' said Salome.

'I pray you, tell me where Floradora is,' beseeched Antonio.

The circus folk searched the caravans and came to the conclusion that she had been taken by the *bandito*.

'But why would he take her?' said the distraught Antonio. 'And where?'

They told him the entire story as far as they understood it: the disappearance of the aerialists with all their money, the birth of Circo Erotica in order to make more money quickly, the rumour that the powerful El Toro Blanco had captured the siblings and held them prisoner.

'He was here tonight,' said Anastasia, 'and he watched Floradora closely, as if he wanted to eat her.'

'Oh, God!' Antonio cried aloud, imagining the worst. 'Who will come with me to save her?'

'We will come,' was the wholehearted cry from the crowd of circus folk who had gathered.

Isambard saddled Floradora's horses and he, Antonio, Nico and Alphonso mounted them. The knives from the knife-throwing act were found – no one had used them since Lorenzo's accident – and the whips. The *chamacos* always carried fearsome-looking stilettos for their own protection and they willingly offered these as weapons.

Some of them had their own horses and they soon had them ready. One of the circus hands had a good idea where the bandits were camped.

'Wait for me,' came a cry. It was Hannibal. Not one to miss the action, he had mounted his elephant. The little one was tagging along as usual. 'She is a weapon in her own right.' He patted his elephant on her head and she trumpeted loudly.

'I want to come, too, and bring my snakes,' said Salome. She was lifted on to the elephant's back with her two remaining snakes wrapped round her like scarves. She had not had time to milk the poison from their fangs, but they would never hurt her.

'Good luck!' The few remaining circus folk waved and cheered as the motley posse galloped off into the desert darkness. The moon was just rising and brought a blue haze to the surroundings. What a strange caravan they made: an elephant and her baby, a dozen horses and their mounts, and a snake charmer complete with snakes.

Antonio led on Thunderhead. The other horsemen followed and the elephants came last. They made a strange silhouette on the ridge of the dune.

* * *

At the bandits' encampment, where a canopy of canvas replaced plaster ceilings, and candles lit the gloom of the huge billowing tent, a party was in progress. The *bandito* had just returned from the circus and had bathed and been prepared for the rest of the night's entertainment. The crone had dressed the remaining aerialist, who was swinging in a lonely arc high above rich red carpets, on which were tasselled silk cushions and low tables laden with fruit and sweets and goblets of gold. Poor Rosario swung on the trapeze upside down, a sad, incomplete figure, helpless and useless without his sister. Tears muddied his make-up.

Floradora was untied, bathed by two dark-skinned leathery old women, who exclaimed over her the whiteness of her soft skin, and dressed in flimsy transparent veils of palest blue from head to foot. Only her blue eyes, outlined in black, showed.

She was furious and defiant. She realised immediately what had happened and she was determined to escape if she could from the evil old man.

She was dragged into his presence. He lounged on a pile of lion skins, surrounded by silk cushions and silk carpets. A black concubine, naked but for a chain round her hips, fed him with grapes, which she peeled first.

Floradora stood, hatred seeping from her every pore as she stared at the aged, hooked-nosed Andalucian. He looked even more loathsome in his own surroundings than he had in the circus tent, she thought. Suddenly she noticed the swaying wires above them. She looked up and saw the semi-naked form of Rosario, hanging from a trapeze.

'Rosario! It is you! Where is your sister? Why did you steal our money?' she shouted, ignoring the *bandito's* thunderous glare.

'I ... Floradora!' The youth pulled himself together and stared down at her. He could not get down until and unless El Toro Blanco ordered him lowered, so he was stuck up there in the roof of the tent, helpless.

'It is our floor show,' said the bandit. 'Or rather, it is

our roof show. You will be the floor show, my dear,' he said, and lunged at her. She drew away from him.

'I will die first,' she said.

'That can be arranged.' He did not smile.

At that moment there was a shout from outside, then several men shouting and a prolonged scream. The canvas was torn open and horses flew through. The bandit chief stood up with a long, cruelly curved scimitar in his hand. He flashed the weapon at the first horseman and a *chamaco* fell at his feet. Floradora screamed. She ran to get out of the way of the hooves. She grabbed the little concubine and led her to safety. Outside the tent, all hell had broken loose. The *bandito*'s men had been taken by surprise, and they were terrified of the lumbering elephant which trampled through their tents as if they were mere paper bags. The *chamacos*, tattooed man and Isambard yelled and flung knives at the fleeing bandits. Salome pressed her snakes to slither down from her limbs and slide into the main tent. Antonio rode fearlessly into the palace tent to find his beloved.

'Floradora!'

'Antonio?' She could not believe her eyes. And suddenly the *bandito* had her in his grasp and held the sharp-edged scimitar at her white throat.

Antonio stopped Thunderhead in his tracks. The horse reared and backed off. Behind the bandit, unseen and silent, slid one of Salome's 'husbands'. He licked at the bandit's ankles with his forked tongue, stared fixedly up at him and, without the bandit knowing where the blow had come from, the snake struck. El Toro Blanco screamed and stared with unseeing eyes. He dropped the scimitar and let go his hold on the lion-tamer's daughter. Thunderhead neighed and Antonio stretched down and lifted Floradora on to the stallion's back with one arm.

'Don't forget me!' It was the trapeze artiste. They let him down and he sobbed and said he was sorry about the money and knew where it was – it was still there. He begged to be allowed back into the family of circus folk.

He told the sad story of his sister's death and Floradora was sorry for him.

'What do you think, Isambard?'

'Let the lad come back,' he declared.

Salome and Floradora kissed briefly and the snakes were gathered back to the snake charmer's bosom.

'Lorenzo is dead, you know,' she told Floradora.

'I'm sorry,' said the girl. She was so glad to have her lover back she could be sorry for the rest of the world.

The surviving ruffians had fled. Nico helped Rosario find the camel that carried their money bags. They took the camel, too, and rode back, triumphant, to the circus. It was nearly dawn when they arrived, tired, dusty, sand in their ears and noses and in every orifice. But Floradora did not care. She was deliriously happy. She had Antonio.

The circus folk were still awake, waiting for the safe return of the others. The band played, the clowns tumbled, the *bastoneras* ran out to greet the *chamacos* and kiss Floradora. Olympia took the trapeze artiste to the wardrobe caravan and Nico kindly offered to share with them both. Olympia was very happy with that arrangement – two pretty young men to look after!

Next day, after a long rest, Floradora and her horses were ready to leave with Antonio. The circus folk stood in a large group to say goodbye. They were going to reorganise themselves, pick up the big top from the docks, and take themselves to mainland Spain to be a proper circus again. Salome would buy back her other snakes. She looked forward to that.

Floradora kissed Isambard goodbye. 'If you ever consider leaving the circus, Isambard, would you come and work for us, breeding horses on Lanzarote?' she asked him.

'Thank you, Floradora, I will remember your kind offer. But at the moment I am content to be ringmaster of the circus.'

'I am sure you will continue to be a wonderful ringmaster.' She kissed him again.

Nico and Isambard stood together watching as the handsome horse breeder and the lovely lion-tamer's daughter rode off together.

'Would you like a massage, Salome?' said Isambard.

'That is a very good idea, Isambard, and bring your little friend along, too,' she said.

BLACK LACE NEW BOOKS

Published in May

SAVAGE SURRENDER
Deanna Ashford
£5.99

In the kingdom of Harn, a marriage is arranged between the beautiful Rianna and Lord Sarin, ruler of the rival kingdom of Percheron, who is noted for his voracious sexual appetite. On her way to Percheron, Rianna meets a young nobleman who has been captured by Sarin's brutal guards. Their desire for each other is instant but can Rianna find a way to save her young lover without causing unrest between the kingdoms?

ISBN 0 352 33253 0

THE SEVEN-YEAR LIST
Zoe le Verdier
£5.99

Julia – an ambitious young photographer – is invited to a college reunion just before she is due to be married. She cannot resist a final fling but finds herself playing a dangerous erotic game with a man who still harbours desires for her. She tries to escape a circle of betrayal and lust but her old flame will not let her go. Not until he has completed the final goal on his seven-year list.

ISBN 0 352 33254 9

MASQUE OF PASSION
Tesni Morgan
£5.99

Lisa is a spirited fine-arts graduate who is due to marry her wealthy fiancé in a matter of weeks. As the day draws closer, though, she's having second thoughts, though, especially as her husband-to-be is dismissive of both her growing antiques business and her sexual needs. The rural English village where Lisa lives is home to some intriguing bohemian characters, including the gorgeous David Maccabene. When David introduces Lisa to kinky ways of loving, her life is set to change in more ways than she can imagine.

ISBN 0 352 33259 X

CIRCO EROTICA
Mercedes Kelly
£5.99

Flora is a beautiful lion-tamer in a Mexican circus. She inhabits a curious and colourful world of trapeze artists, snake charmers and hypnotists. But when her father dies, owing a large sum of money to the dastardly Lorenzo, the circus owner, Flora's routine is set to change. Lorenzo and his perverse female accomplice, Salome, share a powerful sexual hunger and a taste for bizarre adult fun. They lure Flora into their games of decadence. Can she escape? Will she even want to?

ISBN 0 352 33257 3

COOKING UP A STORM
Emma Holly
£7.99

Abby owns a restaurant in Cape Cod but business is not booming. Then, suddenly, someone new comes into her life: a handsome chef with a recipe for success. He puts together an aphrodisiac menu that the patrons won't be able to resist. But can this playboy-chef really save the day when Abby's body means more to him than her heart? He's charming the pants off her and she's behaving like a wild woman. Can Abby tear herself away from her object of desire long enough to see what's going on?

ISBN 0 352 33258 1

Special announcement!

WOMEN, SEX & ASTROLOGY
Sarah Bartlett
£5.99

Here's a first from Black Lace: an astrology book which is exclusively about sex and desire. You can draw up your own, unique erotic chart, check your compatibility with other signs, and find out what turns you and your partner on. Sarah Bartlett uses a potent mixture of astrology, mythology and psychology to create an easy-to-use workbook which will reveal your deepest desires. If you have ever wanted to know how the planets affect your sexual psyche, look no further than this book.

ISBN 0 352 33262 X

To be published in July

THE BARBARIAN GEISHA
Charlotte Royal
£5.99

It's the 17th century and Annabel Smith is shipwrecked and washed up on the shores of feudal Japan. However, she is taken into the hands of the brutal warlord, Lord Nakano, who is enchanted by her beauty. He takes her to his fortress home where the Mamma San is to teach Annabel the art of giving pleasure. Will she ever be accepted as a barbarian geisha?

ISBN 0 352 33267 0

DRAWN TOGETHER
Robyn Russell
£5.99

When Tanya Trevino, graphic artist, creates a sexy alter-ego in the form of Katrina Cortez, private investigator, she begins to wish her life were more like that of her comic-strip characters. Tanya's bank-manager boyfriend expects her to play the part of the executive girlfriend but she's not so keen. Especially as the gorgeous Stephen Sinclair with whom she works is giving her the green light. If only Tanya could be more like Katrina – a voluptuous wild woman!

ISBN 0 352 33269 7

If you would like a complete list of plot summaries of Black Lace titles, please fill out the questionnaire overleaf or send a stamped addressed envelope to:-

Black Lace, 332 Ladbroke Grove, London W10 5AH

BLACK LACE BOOKLIST

All books are priced £4.99 unless another price is given.

Black Lace books with a contemporary setting

ODALISQUE	Fleur Reynolds ISBN 0 352 32887 8	☐
VIRTUOSO	Katrina Vincenzi ISBN 0 352 32907 6	☐
THE SILKEN CAGE	Sophie Danson ISBN 0 352 32928 9	☐
RIVER OF SECRETS	Saskia Hope & Georgia Angelis ISBN 0 352 32925 4	☐
SUMMER OF ENLIGHTENMENT	Cheryl Mildenhall ISBN 0 352 32937 8	☐
MOON OF DESIRE	Sophie Danson ISBN 0 352 32911 4	☐
A BOUQUET OF BLACK ORCHIDS	Roxanne Carr ISBN 0 352 32939 4	☐
THE TUTOR	Portia Da Costa ISBN 0 352 32946 7	☐
THE HOUSE IN NEW ORLEANS	Fleur Reynolds ISBN 0 352 32951 3	☐
WICKED WORK	Pamela Kyle ISBN 0 352 32958 0	☐
DREAM LOVER	Katrina Vincenzi ISBN 0 352 32956 4	☐
UNFINISHED BUSINESS	Sarah Hope-Walker ISBN 0 352 32983 1	☐
THE DEVIL INSIDE	Portia Da Costa ISBN 0 352 32993 9	☐
HEALING PASSION	Sylvie Ouellette ISBN 0 352 32998 X	☐
THE STALLION	Georgina Brown ISBN 0 352 33005 8	☐

RUDE AWAKENING	Pamela Kyle ISBN 0 352 33036 8	☐
EYE OF THE STORM	Georgina Brown ISBN 0 352 33044 9	☐
GEMINI HEAT	Portia Da Costa ISBN 0 352 32912 2	☐
ODYSSEY	Katrina Vincenzi-Thyne ISBN 0 352 33111 9	☐
PULLING POWER	Cheryl Mildenhall ISBN 0 352 33139 9	☐
PALAZZO	Jan Smith ISBN 0 352 33156 9	☐
THE GALLERY	Fredrica Alleyn ISBN 0 352 33148 8	☐
AVENGING ANGELS	Roxanne Carr ISBN 0 352 33147 X	☐
COUNTRY MATTERS	Tesni Morgan ISBN 0 352 33174 7	☐
GINGER ROOT	Robyn Russell ISBN 0 352 33152 6	☐
DANGEROUS CONSEQUENCES	Pamela Rochford ISBN 0 352 33185 2	☐
THE NAME OF AN ANGEL £6.99	Laura Thornton ISBN 0 352 33205 0	☐
SILENT SEDUCTION	Tanya Bishop ISBN 0 352 33193 3	☐
BONDED	Fleur Reynolds ISBN 0 352 33192 5	☐
THE STRANGER	Portia Da Costa ISBN 0 352 33211 5	☐
CONTEST OF WILLS £5.99	Louisa Francis ISBN 0 352 33223 9	☐
BY ANY MEANS £5.99	Cheryl Mildenhall ISBN 0 352 33221 2	☐
MÉNAGE £5.99	Emma Holly ISBN 0 352 33231 X	☐
THE SUCCUBUS £5.99	Zoe le Verdier ISBN 0 352 33230 1	☐
FEMININE WILES £7.99	Karina Moore ISBN 0 352 33235 2	☐

Black Lace books with an historical setting

THE CAPTIVE FLESH — Cleo Cordell
ISBN 0 352 32872 X ☐

THE SENSES BEJEWELLED — Cleo Cordell
ISBN 0 352 32904 1 ☐

HANDMAIDEN OF PALMYRA — Fleur Reynolds
ISBN 0 352 32919 X ☐

JULIET RISING — Cleo Cordell
ISBN 0 352 32938 6 ☐

ELENA'S CONQUEST — Lisette Allen
ISBN 0 352 32950 5 ☐

PATH OF THE TIGER — Cleo Cordell
ISBN 0 352 32959 9 ☐

BELLA'S BLADE — Georgia Angelis
ISBN 0 352 32965 3 ☐

WESTERN STAR — Roxanne Carr
ISBN 0 352 32969 6 ☐

CRIMSON BUCCANEER — Cleo Cordell
ISBN 0 352 32987 4 ☐

LA BASQUIASE — Angel Strand
ISBN 0 352 32988 2 ☐

THE LURE OF SATYRIA — Cheryl Mildenhall
ISBN 0 352 32994 7 ☐

THE INTIMATE EYE — Georgia Angelis
ISBN 0 352 33004 X ☐

THE AMULET — Lisette Allen
ISBN 0 352 33019 8 ☐

CONQUERED — Fleur Reynolds
ISBN 0 352 33025 2 ☐

JEWEL OF XANADU — Roxanne Carr
ISBN 0 352 33037 6 ☐

THE MISTRESS — Vivienne LaFay
ISBN 0 352 33057 0 ☐

LORD WRAXALL'S FANCY — Anna Lieff Saxby
ISBN 0 352 33080 5 ☐

FORBIDDEN CRUSADE — Juliet Hastings
ISBN 0 352 33079 1 ☐

TO TAKE A QUEEN — Jan Smith
ISBN 0 352 33098 8 ☐

ILE DE PARADIS — Mercedes Kelly
ISBN 0 352 33121 6 ☐

NADYA'S QUEST	Lisette Allen ISBN 0 352 33135 6	☐
DESIRE UNDER CAPRICORN	Louisa Francis ISBN 0 352 33136 4	☐
THE HAND OF AMUN	Juliet Hastings ISBN 0 352 33144 5	☐
THE LION LOVER	Mercedes Kelly ISBN 0 352 33162 3	☐
A VOLCANIC AFFAIR	Xanthia Rhodes ISBN 0 352 33184 4	☐
FRENCH MANNERS	Olivia Christie ISBN 0 352 33214 X	☐
ARTISTIC LICENCE	Vivienne LaFay ISBN 0 352 33210 7	☐
INVITATION TO SIN £6.99	Charlotte Royal ISBN 0 352 33217 4	☐
ELENA'S DESTINY	Lisette Allen ISBN 0 352 33218 2	☐
LAKE OF LOST LOVE £5.99	Mercedes Kelly ISBN 0 352 33220 4	☐
UNHALLOWED RITES £5.99	Martine Marquand ISBN 0 352 33222 0	☐
THE CAPTIVATION £5.99	Natasha Rostova ISBN 0 352 33234 4	☐
A DANGEROUS LADY £5.99	Lucinda Carrington ISBN 0 352 33236 0	☐

Black Lace anthologies

PAST PASSIONS £6.99	ISBN 0 352 33159 3	☐
PANDORA'S BOX 2 £4.99	ISBN 0 352 33151 8	☐
SUGAR AND SPICE £7.99	ISBN 0 352 33227 1	☐

------------✂------------------------

Please send me the books I have ticked above.

Name   ....

Address   ....

              ....

              ....

              .... Post Code ....

Send to: **Cash Sales, Black Lace Books, 332 Ladbroke Grove, London W10 5AH, UK.**

US customers: for prices and details of how to order books for delivery by mail, call 1-800-805-1083.

Please enclose a cheque or postal order, made payable to **Virgin Publishing Ltd**, to the value of the books you have ordered plus postage and packing costs as follows:

UK and BFPO – £1.00 for the first book, 50p for each subsequent book.

Overseas (including Republic of Ireland) – £2.00 for the first book, £1.00 each subsequent book.

If you would prefer to pay by VISA or ACCESS/MASTERCARD, please write your card number and expiry date here:

....

Please allow up to 28 days for delivery.

Signature   ....

------------✂------------------------

BLACK
lace

WE NEED YOUR HELP . . .
to plan the future of women's erotic fiction –

– and no stamp required!

Yours are the only opinions that matter.

Black Lace is the first series of books devoted to erotic fiction by women for women.

We intend to keep providing the best-written, sexiest books you can buy. And we'd appreciate your help and valued opinion of the books so far. Tell us what you want to read.

THE BLACK LACE QUESTIONNAIRE

SECTION ONE: ABOUT YOU

1.1 Sex (*we presume you are female, but so as not to discriminate*)
    Are you?
        Male   ☐
        Female   ☐

1.2 Age
        under 21   ☐   21–30   ☐
        31–40   ☐   41–50   ☐
        51–60   ☐   over 60   ☐

1.3 At what age did you leave full-time education?
        still in education ☐   16 or younger ☐
        17–19   ☐   20 or older   ☐

1.4 Occupation _____

1.5 Annual household income _____

1.6 We are perfectly happy for you to remain anonymous;
but if you would like to receive information on other
publications available, please insert your name and
address

_____

_____

_____

_____

SECTION TWO: ABOUT BUYING BLACK LACE BOOKS

2.1 Where did you get this copy of *Circo Erotica*?
    Bought at chain book shop □
    Bought at independent book shop □
    Bought at supermarket □
    Bought at book exchange or used book shop □
    I borrowed it/found it □
    My partner bought it □

2.2 How did you find out about Black Lace books?
    I saw them in a shop □
    I saw them advertised in a magazine □
    I read about them in _____
    Other _____

2.3 Please tick the following statements you agree with:
    I would be less embarrassed about buying Black
    Lace books if the cover pictures were less explicit □
    I think that in general the pictures on Black
    Lace books are about right □
    I think Black Lace cover pictures should be as
    explicit as possible □

2.4 Would you read a Black Lace book in a public place – on
a train for instance?
    Yes □   No □

SECTION THREE: ABOUT THIS BLACK LACE BOOK

3.1   Do you think the sex content in this book is:
        Too much   ☐   About right   ☐
        Not enough   ☐

3.2   Do you think the writing style in this book is:
        Too unreal/escapist   ☐   About right   ☐
        Too down to earth   ☐

3.3   Do you think the story in this book is:
        Too complicated   ☐   About right   ☐
        Too boring/simple   ☐

3.4   Do you think the cover of this book is:
        Too explicit   ☐   About right   ☐
        Not explicit enough ☐

Here's a space for any other comments:

SECTION FOUR: ABOUT OTHER BLACK LACE BOOKS

4.1   How many Black Lace books have you read?   ☐

4.2   If more than one, which one did you prefer?

4.3   Why?

SECTION FIVE: ABOUT YOUR IDEAL EROTIC NOVEL

We want to publish the books you want to read – so this is your chance to tell us exactly what your ideal erotic novel would be like.

5.1 Using a scale of 1 to 5 (1 = no interest at all, 5 = your ideal), please rate the following possible settings for an erotic novel:

Medieval/barbarian/sword 'n' sorcery ☐
Renaissance/Elizabethan/Restoration ☐
Victorian/Edwardian ☐
1920s & 1930s – the Jazz Age ☐
Present day ☐
Future/Science Fiction ☐

5.2 Using the same scale of 1 to 5, please rate the following themes you may find in an erotic novel:

Submissive male/dominant female ☐
Submissive female/dominant male ☐
Lesbianism ☐
Bondage/fetishism ☐
Romantic love ☐
Experimental sex e.g. anal/watersports/sex toys ☐
Gay male sex ☐
Group sex ☐

5.3 Using the same scale of 1 to 5, please rate the following styles in which an erotic novel could be written:

Realistic, down to earth, set in real life ☐
Escapist fantasy, but just about believable ☐
Completely unreal, impressionistic, dreamlike ☐

5.4 Would you prefer your ideal erotic novel to be written from the viewpoint of the main male characters or the main female characters?

Male ☐ Female ☐
Both ☐

5.5 What would your ideal Black Lace heroine be like? Tick as many as you like:

Dominant	☐	Glamorous	☐
Extroverted	☐	Contemporary	☐
Independent	☐	Bisexual	☐
Adventurous	☐	Naïve	☐
Intellectual	☐	Introverted	☐
Professional	☐	Kinky	☐
Submissive	☐	Anything else?	☐
Ordinary	☐	_____	

5.6 What would your ideal male lead character be like? Again, tick as many as you like:

Rugged	☐		
Athletic	☐	Caring	☐
Sophisticated	☐	Cruel	☐
Retiring	☐	Debonair	☐
Outdoor-type	☐	Naïve	☐
Executive-type	☐	Intellectual	☐
Ordinary	☐	Professional	☐
Kinky	☐	Romantic	☐
Hunky	☐		
Sexually dominant	☐	Anything else?	☐
Sexually submissive	☐	_____	

5.7 Is there one particular setting or subject matter that your ideal erotic novel would contain?

_____

SECTION SIX: LAST WORDS

6.1 What do you like best about Black Lace books?

_____

6.2 What do you most dislike about Black Lace books?

_____

6.3 In what way, if any, would you like to change Black Lace covers?

_____

6.4   Here's a space for any other comments:

_____
_____
_____
_____
_____

Thank you for completing this questionnaire. Now tear it out of the book – carefully! – put it in an envelope and send it to:

   Black Lace
   FREEPOST
   London
   W10 5BR

No stamp is required if you are resident in the U.K.